# NRA CET - Matriculation Pass

## General Awareness

**Latest Edition Practice Kit**

**16 Tests**

16 Topic-Wise Test

Topic Wise Chapters with Questions

✓ Thoroughly Revised and Updated

✓ Detailed Analysis of all MCQs

| **Title** | : NRA CET - Matriculation Pass General Awareness |
| **Author Name** | : Mr. Rohit Manglik |
| **Published By** | : EduGorilla Community Pvt. Ltd. |
| **Publishers Address** | : 12/651, First Floor Opp. Arvindo Park, Near Jama Masjid, Indira Nagar, Lucknow, Uttar Pradesh-226016, India |


## Copyright EduGorilla

ISBN : 978-93-55560-90-2

First Edition



## Disclaimer EduGorilla



**Compiled and created by EduGorilla Community Pvt. Ltd**

**Printed By EduGorilla Community Pvt. Ltd.**

**ROHIT** MANGLIK
**CEO,** EduGorilla

### Dear Applicants,

People say *"Success comes to those who work hard."* But I've seen people working hard for their exams day in and day out for marginal success. While others succeed in their examinations by putting in just half the work. So are they God Gifted? No! I believe that it's because they work *smart* and not just *hard*. Similarly, for your exams, you should strategize your preparation so as to increase the likelihood of success. Well with EduGorilla get ready to increase your *chances of selection* in your exam by *16x*.

EduGorilla helps you in not only working *hard* but also working in a *smart and strategic* manner. With EduGorilla's preparation package, you get a chance to make your exam preparation easy, and a fun learning path towards selection. Finding the right path to your preparations can be difficult if you don't know in which direction to head. Don't worry, we have you covered! EduGorilla will be your guide to success in your journey. With our Preparation Package, you can prepare strategically and beat the exam in just one attempt.

EduGorilla's Preparation Package includes-

- **Test Series**
- **Books**

Our preparation package is handcrafted as per the latest changes, expert opinions, and students' discretion. Thus, enabling you to get through each stage of the selection process for your exam.

Our Books are designed by the teachers and experts of the respective exam with a combined 150+ years of experience; to provide you with easy, efficient, and effective learning. Our books are smart, in the sense that not only do they give you the answers to the questions but also provide similar questions for practice.

EduGorilla's competent Test Series gives you real-time experience and confidence through which you can clear your offline or online exam in just one attempt. We currently host 83,000+ mock tests for 1,440+ competitive and academic exams.

Thus, EduGorilla misses no chance to assist you in your preparation and covers all stages of the exam, so that you don't have to look anywhere else.

We provide complete preparation packages for defense, banking, teaching, and other National & State-Level exams. Hence, it doesn't matter which exam you aspire to because you will reach your success.

### ALL THE BEST !

Let EduGorilla be your Guide to Success.

*Rohit Manglik,*
*Founder and CEO, EduGorilla*

# INTRODUCTION

EduGorilla focuses on guiding students to succeed in their examinations. With that in mind, our book, titled "NRA CET - Matriculation Pass : General Awareness", has been drafted through the collective efforts of our distinguished experts with 150+ years of combined experience. This book consists of questions that are created following the latest changes in the syllabus and exam pattern. We compiled the book on the basis of questions that are most likely to appear in the . Through EduGorilla's "NRA CET - Matriculation Pass : General Awareness" your chances of success will increase 16x.

EduGorilla does this through our Complete Preparation Package. This package consists of well-conceptualized and structured content in the form of questions that are tailor-made according to your needs and will help you practice for exams in a smart way by pinpointing all the necessary information. It also provides hints and solutions, along with a smart answer sheet for your self-evaluation. You can assess your shortcomings and work accordingly on areas that may require more of your attention.

EduGorilla promises to help you succeed in your examination and accomplish your dream goals. We believe in our aspirants and see them at the top of the merit list. And the first step towards the top is to start preparing with us. EduGorilla's "NRA CET - Matriculation Pass : General Awareness" includes the following attributes.

➤ Well-Researched Content

➤ Top-Notch Quality

➤ Detailed Answers and Analysis

➤ Smart Answer Sheet

➤ Exam Relevant Questions

Therefore, EduGorilla fortifies your preparation and makes it durable enough to help you stand tall and beat the examination.

# TABLE OF CONTENTS

**Q.1** 'Matki' is a popular folk dance of which of the following?
A. Assam
B. Madhya Pradesh
C. Bihar
D. Rajasthan

**Q.2** Where is Pushkar Fair held?
A. Udaipur
B. Jaisalmer
C. Jodhpur
D. Ajmer

**Q.3** Which of the painting is mixture of Rajasthani and Mughal?
A. Kangra painting
B. Pahari painting
C. Madhubani painting
D. Basohli painting

**Q.4** Kathakali dance style belongs to:
A. Karnataka
B. Kerala
C. Tamil Nadu
D. Andhra Pradesh

**Q.5** Charkula is famous folk dance of:
A. Bundelkhand
B. Brij bhumi
C. Avadh
D. None of the above

**Q.6** Which among the following is the musical instrument of Uttarakhand?
A. Veena
B. Sitar
C. Hudka
D. Tanpura

**Q.7** To which state of India do the 'Khuded' folk songs belong?
A. Chhattisgarh
B. Odisha
C. Jharkhand
D. Uttarakhand

**Q.8** "Thulo Dhuska" (Thulo Khela) in Uttarakhand culture is:
A. Revolution
B. Marriage
C. Wrestling
D. Pahadi Ramayana

**Q.9** Which one of the following is a major tribal group of Uttarakhand?
A. Jaunsari tribe
B. Tharu tribe
C. Raji tribe
D. All of the above

**Q.10** Jhora folk dance belongs to which state?
A. Uttarakhand
B. Karnataka
C. Assam
D. Assam

**Q.11** Ujali or Aneri Holi is associated with:
A. Jaunsari Tribe
B. Bhotia Tribe
C. Tharu Tribe
D. Raaji Tribe

**Q.12** With which form of performing art is Teejan Bai associated?
A. Burra Katha
B. Pandavani
C. Lavani
D. Nautanki

**Q.13** Which of the following pairs is correctly matched?
A. Ellora Caves - Shakas
B. Meenakshi Temple - Pallavas
C. Khajuraho temple - Chandelas
D. Mahabalipuram Temple - Rashtrakutas

**Q.14** Katputli, the string puppetry belongs to -
A. Rajasthan
B. Karnataka
C. Madhya Pradesh
D. Uttrakhand

**Q.15** Which of the following pairs is INCORRECT with reference to paintings in india?

*[SSC Sub Inspector (CPO), 2020]*

A. Saura Paintings – Odisha
B. Bagh Paintings – Madhya Pradesh
C. Phad Paintings – Rajasthan
D. Guler Paintings – Karnataka

**Q.16** The 'Gandhara' School of Art was influenced by the art from which of the following European countries?

*[SSC Sub Inspector (CPO), 2020]*

A. Italy
B. Belgium
C. Hungary
D. Greece

**Q.17** Bhand Pather theatre is a tradition primarily of which of the following States/UTs of India?

*[SSC Sub Inspector (CPO), 2020]*

A. Dadra and Nagar Heveli
B. Goa
C. Jammu and Kashmir
D. Kerala

**Q.18** 'Aloo Posto' is a traditional delicacy of which state of India?

*[SSC Sub Inspector (CPO), 2020]*

A. Haryana
B. Uttarakhand
C. Gujarat
D. West Bengal

**Q.19** Who among the following was associated with Vaisheshika School of Philosophy?

*[SSC Sub Inspector (CPO), 2020]*

A. Kanada
B. Patanjali
C. Gautama
D. Jaimini

**Q.20** What do Madhubani paintings depict?
A. Life of Bhagwan Buddha
B. Western Culture
C. Nature and Hindu religious figure
D. Life of Birsa Munda

**Q.21** Mohini Attam form of dance developed in:
A. Odisha
B. Karnataka
C. Tamil Nadu
D. Kerala

**Q.22** The famous Brihadeshwara Temple is located in _______.
A. Madurai
B. Thanjavur
C. Kanchipuram
D. Rameshwaram

**Q.23** 'Ghoomar' is a folk-dance form from the state of _____.
A. Jharkhand
B. Bihar
C. Tripura
D. Rajasthan

**Q.24** In which among the following states, Kamakhya Temple is situated?

**A.** Karnataka  
**B.** Kerala  
**C.** Assam  
**D.** Meghalaya

**Q.25** The paintings of Ajanta belongs to which religion?

**A.** Jain  
**B.** Sanatan  
**C.** Buddhism  
**D.** Christian

**Q.26** In which state Surajkund festival is celebrated?

**A.** Rajasthan  
**B.** Madhya Pradesh  
**C.** Haryana  
**D.** Gujarat

**Q.27** Which of the following is a harvest festival celebrated in South India?

**A.** Pongal, Onam and Bihu  
**B.** Pongal and Bihu  
**C.** Pongal and Onam  
**D.** Onam and Bihu

**Q.28** Shanti Devi, Phulwa Filma are related to which of the following dance forms of Rajasthan?

**A.** Chakri Dance  
**B.** Gawari Dance  
**C.** Shankariya Dance  
**D.** Bam Dance

**Q.29** Dhol Folk Dance belongs to which area?

**A.** Banswara  
**B.** Jhalawar  
**C.** Jalore  
**D.** Udaipur

**Q.30** Which dance form of Rajasthan is performed by Bhambi communities?

**A.** Chari  
**B.** Ghoomar  
**C.** Kalbelia  
**D.** Kachi ghodi

# // Smart Answer Sheet //

**Correct** — Indicates percentage of students who answered questions correctly.

**Skipped** — Indicates percentage of students who skipped questions.

| Q. | Ans. | Correct / Skipped |
|---|---|---|
| 1 | B | 84.88 % / 13.13 % |
| 2 | D | 77.99 % / 18.59 % |
| 3 | A | 77.67 % / 10.49 % |
| 4 | B | 78.43 % / 19.14 % |
| 5 | B | 80.49 % / 13.04 % |
| 6 | C | 80.46 % / 11.12 % |

| Q. | Ans. | Correct / Skipped |
|---|---|---|
| 7 | D | 83.35 % / 11.74 % |
| 8 | D | 82.9 % / 15.31 % |
| 9 | D | 80.83 % / 11.88 % |
| 10 | A | 69.87 % / 30.01 % |
| 11 | C | 79.38 % / 10.37 % |
| 12 | B | 80.84 % / 14.7 % |

| Q. | Ans. | Correct / Skipped |
|---|---|---|
| 13 | C | 87.28 % / 11.03 % |
| 14 | A | 77.82 % / 10.85 % |
| 15 | D | 86.99 % / 11.36 % |
| 16 | D | 84.83 % / 11.3 % |
| 17 | C | 77.87 % / 19.16 % |
| 18 | D | 87.34 % / 12.35 % |

| Q. | Ans. | Correct / Skipped |
|---|---|---|
| 19 | A | 77.57 % / 22.05 % |
| 20 | C | 88.1 % / 11.43 % |
| 21 | D | 77.16 % / 10.39 % |
| 22 | B | 77.34 % / 20.53 % |
| 23 | D | 84.73 % / 14.19 % |
| 24 | C | 86.37 % / 10.21 % |

| Q. | Ans. | Correct / Skipped |
|---|---|---|
| 25 | C | 77.61 % / 21.92 % |
| 26 | C | 84.16 % / 11.35 % |
| 27 | C | 85.7 % / 13.06 % |
| 28 | A | 80.97 % / 10.67 % |
| 29 | C | 82.88 % / 10.5 % |
| 30 | D | 87.36 % / 12.51 % |

## Performance Analysis

| | |
|---|---|
| Avg. Score (%) | 46.67% |
| Toppers Score (%) | 60.0% |
| Your Score | |

# //Hints and Solutions//

**1.** 'Matki' is a popular folk dance of Madhya Pradesh.

- Matki dance form has been developed by nomadic tribes in Madhya Pradesh.

- Performed using a small pitcher is a folk dance originating from central India known as the "Matki Dance".

- This "pitcher dance" belongs to the state of Madhya Pradesh, and is mainly performed in the Malwa region.

Hence, the correct option is (B).

**2.** The Pushkar Fair held at Pushkar in the Ajmer district of Rajasthan is well-known worldwide in India. Pushkar fair is also called Pushkar Camel Fair. this is one of the largest fairs in India. It is a unique animal fair, which other Fair's are not identical. This important fair is celebrated in Pushkar, the small but beautiful city of Rajasthan.

Hence, the correct option is (D).

**3.** Kangra painting is a mixture of Rajasthan and Mughal. The pictorial art of Kangra is one of the finest gifts of India to the art world. It originated in a small hill state 'Guler' in lower Himalayas in 18th century when a family of Kashmiri painters trained in Mughal Style of painting sought shelter at the court of Raja Dalip Singh of Guler.

Hence, the correct option is (A).

**4.** Kathakali is a major form of classical Indian dance. It is a "story play" genre of art, but one distinguished by the elaborately colorful make-up, costumes and face masks that the traditionally male actor-dancers wear. Kathakali is a Hindu performance art in the Malayalam-speaking southwestern region of Kerala.

Hence, the correct option is (B).

**5.** Charkula is a dance performed in the Braj region of Uttar Pradesh. In this dance, veiled women balancing large multi-tiered circular wooden pyramids on their heads dance to songs about Krishna.

Hence, the correct option is (B).

**6.** Traditional Musical Instruments of Uttarakhand reflect the values of Uttarakhand people. Damama, Hudka, Turturi or Turhi, Binaee, Mushak Been or Bagpipe, and Flute are the most famous musical instruments in Uttarakhand. Uttarakhand's traditional musical instruments are quite simple but unique in the emotions they evoke.

Hence, the correct option is (C).

**7.** "Khuded" is one of the famous folk songs of Uttarakhand. The song describes the misery and pain of a lady who has been living apart from her husband. This song is very painful and emotional. It echoes the suffering of the woman who is left alone after her husband leaves her and goes to another place in search of a job. This song depicts the life of a low-income family where the husband has to move out in search of a better job so that he can run his family. Each and every word of this folk song has a very deep meaning attached to it.

Hence, the correct option is (D).

**8.** "Thulo Dhuska" (Thulo Khela) in Uttarakhand culture is Pahadi Ramayana. Thulo Dhuska is folklore in the Eastern Kumaon, Uttarakhand. It means play of Rama. In this play, the story of Rama is depicted.

There are 2 different versions of Thulo Khela. It has divided version 1 into 15 episodes and version 2 into 11 episodes. These two versions are preserved in manuscripts by the families of principal singers called Bakhani.

The Thulo Khela is sung mainly in three tunes, the principal one is termed Dhuska. Dhuska is based on classical music. The other main tunes are termed Khela and Chalali. The accompanying musical instruments in the Thulo Khela are hudka and mijara (pair of cymbals).

Hence, the correct option is (D).

**9.** Tribes of Uttarakhand mainly comprise five major groups namely Jaunsari tribe, Tharu tribe, Raji tribe, Buksa tribe, and Bhotiyas.

- In terms of population, the Jaunsari tribe is the largest tribal group in the state.

- Tribes of Uttarakhand represent the ethnic groups residing in the state.

- Every district of Uttarakhand has more or less a moderate percentage of the tribal population.

- In the state of Uttarakhand, the main concentration of the tribal population is in rural areas.

- As per records, around 94.50 per cent of the total tribal population resides in rural areas and the remaining percentage of the tribal population lives in urban centres.

- These tribes of Uttarakhand have been scheduled in the Constitution of India.

Hence, the correct option is (D).

**10.** Jhora dance originated in the Kumaon region of Uttarakhand. This is a magical folk dance form that binds people of all castes. Jhora dance is generally performed in the spring season. Jhora dance is usually seen in the evening at weddings or fairs. The men and women join hands and move in the circular formation. They bend their bodies smoothly.

Hence, the correct option is (A).

**11.** Ujali or Aneri Holi festivals are associated with Tharu Tribe. The community belongs to the Terai lowlands, amid the Shivaliks of the lower Himalayas. Most of them are forest dwellers and some practiced agriculture. The word Tharu is believed to be derived from Sthavir, meaning followers of Theravada Buddhism. The Tharus live in both India and Nepal.

Hence, the correct option is (C).

**12.** Pandavani is a lyrical folk form of narration of scenes/events from Mahabharata without the use of props. It usually has a lead singer/narrator and two accompanying musicians with instruments. It is popular in tribes in Chattisgarh especially the

Pardhi community. Traditionally, it was practiced only by men, but since the 1980s women have also been performing.

There are two styles of Pandavani: Vedamati and Kapalik.

In Vedamati, the artist sits on the floor and performs in a simple manner. In Kapalik, the performance is lively, where the artist enacts the scenes/characters and there is a lot of improvisation. Jhaduram Dewangan (Vedamanti style) and Teejan Bai (Kapalik style) are the most renowned performers of Pandavani. Some of the contemporary artists are Ritu Verma, Shantibai Chelak and Usha Barle.

Hence, the correct option is (B).

**13.** Ellora caves are located 25 km away from Aurangabad (Maharashtra) in west northern direction It is famous for rock-cut cave temples Here, total 34 rock-cut caves are found These caves are constructed in various periods but not associated with Shakas Meenakshi Temple was constructed by Pandyas and Mahabalipuram Temple was built by Pallavas Khajuraho temples were built by Chandelas Therefore, option (C) is correctly matched.

Hence, the correct option is (C).

**14.** Katputli, string puppet belongs to Rajasthan.

Puppets are one of the oldest entertainment programs played at the oldest theater in the world. Puppets are made as different types of dolls, clowns etc. Its name is Puppet because the former was also made of wood ie wood. The puppet made of the type wood was named Puppet. World Puppet Day is also celebrated every year on 21 March.

Hence, the correct option is (A).

**15.** Guler Painting is associated with Himachal Pradesh.

- It is a kind of Pahari painting.
- Guler is said to be the birthplace of Kangra paintings.
- The term Guler was derived from Gwala which means cowherd.

Hence, the correct option is (D).

**16.** The 'Gandhara' School of Art was influenced by the art from Greece.

- Gandhara art, a style of Buddhist visual art that developed in what is now northwestern Pakistan and eastern Afghanistan between the 1st century BCE and the 7th century CE.
- The style, of Greco-Roman origin, seems to have flourished largely during the Kushan dynasty and was contemporaneous with an important but dissimilar school of Kushan art at Mathura (Uttar Pradesh, India).
- The Gandhara school incorporated many motifs and techniques from classical Roman art, including vine scrolls, cherubs bearing garlands, tritons, and centaurs. The basic iconography, however, remained Indian.

Hence, the correct option is (D).

**17.** Bhand Pather theatre is a tradition primarily of Jammu and Kashmir.

- Bhand pather, folk theatre of Kashmir. The bhand pather is a popular form of folk theatre and the word bhand stands for 'jester' while pather means 'drama'.
- It is exclusively associated with the community of bhands or folk theatre actors.
- The bhands enact around twelve types of bhand pather and across the valley, the bhands form a well-organized folk theatre community

Hence, the correct option is (C).

**18.** 'Aloo Posto' is a traditional delicacy of West Bengal.

- Bengali Aloo Posto is a simple dish made with spiced potatoes and cooked in chillies, turmeric, and poppy seeds. A great side dish or meal for any occasion.
- Some other famous dishes of West Bengal- Luchi-Alur Dom, Kosha Mangsho, Daab Chingri, Keemar Doi Bora, Bhetki Macher Paturi, Shukto etc.

Hence, the correct option is (D).

**19.** Kanada was associated with Vaisheshika School of Philosophy.

- The Sanskrit philosopher Kanada Kashyapa (2nd–3rd century) expounded its theories and is credited with founding the school.
- Vaisheshika, one of the six systems (darshans) of Indian philosophy, significant for its naturalism.
- The Vaisheshika school attempts to identify, inventory, and classify the entities and their relations that present themselves to human perceptions.

Hence, the correct option is (A).

**20.** Madhubani paintings depict nature and Hindu religious figure.

Madhubani painting is one of the many famous Indian art forms. As it is practised in the Mithila region of Bihar and Nepal, it is called Mithila or Madhubani art.

The colours used in Madhubani paintings are usually derived from plants and other natural sources. Women usually paint their homes to celebrate festivals and theme of the painting can be varied from nature to myths.

Hence, the correct option is (C).

**21.** Mohini Attam form of dance developed in Kerala.

Mohiniattam is among the two popular dance arts of the state, the other being Kathakali. Mohiniyattam is considered as a very graceful form of dance meant to be performed as solo recitals by women.

It believed to have originated in the 16th century. It is one of the eight Indian classical dance forms recognized by the Sangeet Natak Akademi.

Hence, the correct option is (D).

**22.** The famous Brihadeshwara Temple is located in thanjavur.

Brihadeshwara Temple is a Hindu temple dedicated to Shiva. It is located in Thanjavur in Tamil Nadu. It was built by Tamil King

Raja Raja Chola I. It is also known as Periya Kovil, RajaRajeswara Temple and Rajarajeswaram. It is one of the largest temples in India.

Hence, the correct option is (B).

**23.** 'Ghoomar' is a folk-dance form from the state of Rajasthan.

Ghoomar is a traditional folk dance of Rajasthan, India, and Sindh, Pakistan. The dance is chiefly performed by veiled women who wear flowing dresses called Ghaghara.

The dance typically involves performers pirouetting while moving in and out of a wide circle. The word ghoomna describes the twirling movement of the dancers and is the basis of the word Ghoomar.

Hence, the correct option is (D).

**24.** Kamakhya Temple is situated at Assam state of India.

The Kamakhya Temple is also called as Kamrup - Kamakhya is one of the oldest among the Shakti Pithas.

It is situated on the Nilachal Hill in the city of Guwahati in Assam. The deity of the temple, Kamakhya Devi is revered as the 'Bleeding Goddess'.

Hence, the correct option is (C).

**25.** The paintings of Ajanta belongs to buddhism religion.

It is located in Aurangabad, Maharashtra. It is an ancient rock-cut cave built in the 2nd century BC to the 5th century AD. There is a total of 29 caves in Ajanta related to Buddhist which were decorated with sculptures and paintings.

Hence, the correct option is (C).

**26.** In Haryana state Surajkund festival is celebrated.

The Surajkund Fair is organised in the month of February. It is observed in the Faridabad district of Haryana. It is the largest crafts fair in the World and the biggest cultural Fair in India. It is held for fifteen days every year.

Hence, the correct option is (C).

**27.** Pongal and Onam is a harvest festival celebrated in South India.

Pongala is a harvest festival of Kerala and Tamil Nadu. The name 'Pongala' means 'to boil over' and refers to the ritualistic offering of porridge made of rice, sweet brown molasses, coconut gratings, nuts and raisins. Generally women devotees participate in this ritual. Tamil people celebrate as Pongal. Onam is a major festival of Kerala. Onam is celebrated every year in the month of Chingam (Singham/Simham) to mark the birth anniversary of Lord Vamana and welcome King Bali, which lasts for ten days.

Hence, the correct option is (C).

**28.** Shanti Devi, Phulwa Filma are related to chakri dance forms of Rajasthan.

It is performed in the Hadoti region of Bundi, Kota & Baran District by women of Kanjar tribe on the occasions of marriages & festivals. Chakri dance is believed as same as the Raai dance of 'Beriyas' tribe of Madhya Pradesh. Devi Lal Sagar made this dance popular. Shanti Devi and Phulwa Filma are associated with Chakri Dance.

Hence, the correct option is (A).

**29.** Dhol Folk Dance belongs to Jalore area.

It is performed on marriages by only men in Jalore. In this dance, five men beat huge drums that are tied around their necks. One dancer holding a huge cymbal in their hands, also accompany the drummers. One dancer holds a naked sword on his mouth and juggles with the other three dancers.

Hence, the correct option is (C).

**30.** Kachi ghodi dance form of Rajasthan is performed by Bhambi communities.

The dancers ride on the dummy horses and move on the beats of drums. The dance form is prevalent in the Kamdholi, Sarghara, Bhambi tribe communities. The Kachchhi Ghodi dance form is famous in the Shekhawati region of Rajasthan.

Hence, the correct option is (D).

**Q.1** The maximum loan amount that can be granted under priority sector for building social infrastructure is _______ per borrower.

**A.** Rs 1 crore

**B.** Rs 20 crores

**C.** Rs 25 crores

**D.** Rs 5 crores

**Q.2** Which of the following is true about KYC?

A. The Reserve Bank of India advises banks to make it mandatory while opening and operating accounts.

B. It is a full form of Know Your Customer.

C. Low-income group customers are exempted from submitting KYC.

**A.** Only A

**B.** Only B

**C.** Only C

**D.** All of these

**Q.3** Which of the following is NOT correct about the banking ombudsman?

**A.** It is to resolve customer complaints

**B.** RBI directly monitors the ombudsman

**C.** It was launched in 2006

**D.** It charges nominal fees for resolving complaints

**Q.4** Under which among the following Acts, Co-operative Banks are registered?

**A.** Cooperative Societies Act, 1912

**B.** Cooperative Societies Act, 1950

**C.** Cooperative Societies Act, 1987

**D.** Cooperative Societies Act, 2000

**Q.5** When a bank borrower or counterparty fails to meet its payment obligation regarding the terms agreed with the bank, it is called _____.

**A.** Market Risk

**B.** Operational Risk

**C.** Liquidity Risk

**D.** Credit Risk

**Q.6** Which bank has launched a campaign 'DIGITAL APNAYEN' to encourage customers to use digital banking channels?

**A.** Axis Bank

**B.** Punjab National Bank

**C.** ICICI Bank

**D.** Yes Bank

**Q.7** Which of the following motifs is printed in 500 rupees note?

**A.** Sun Temple of Konark

**B.** Sanchi Stupa

**C.** Red Fort with Indian Flag

**D.** Hampi with Chariot

**Q.8** Which of the following motifs is printed in 20 rupees note?

**A.** Sanchi stupa

**B.** Ellora caves

**C.** Hampi with chariot

**D.** Red Fort with Indian Flag

**Q.9** The Government of India has approved a scheme for improving the short-term liquidity position of NBFCs/HFCs through a SPV in the form of Special Liquidity Scheme Trust. Which among the following entities set up the SLS trust?

**A.** RBSA Advisors

**B.** Caston Corporate Advisory Services

**C.** SBI Capital Markets Limited

**D.** HDFC Capital Markets Limited

**Q.10** Digital currency ABER was launched recently by which of the following?

**A.** UAE and Qatar

**B.** UAE and Saudi Arabia

**C.** Japan and China

**D.** China

**Q.11** Which of the following digital initiative has been launched by Lakshmi Vilas Bank (LVB) to enable the opening of savings account instantly?

**A.** Lakshmi InstaCash

**B.** Lakshmi DigiGo

**C.** Lakshmi QuickAccount

**D.** Lakshmi GoQuick

**Q.12** In August 2020, which of the following banks has waived off SMS charges in addition to its penalty waiver on non-maintenance of minimum balance for all its Savings Accounts?

**A.** Yes Bank

**B.** State Bank of India

**C.** HDFC Bank

**D.** Union Bank of India

**Q.13** In August 2020, Deutsche Bank has introduced a capital infusion of how many rupees (in crores) into its India department operations to fund its progress plans within the nation?

**A.** 1,500      **B.** 2,100      **C.** 2,700      **D.** 3,300

**Q.14** Which bank has launched another green initiative, IB-eNote that enables a totally paperless working environment?

**A.** Canara Bank

**B.** Indian Bank

**C.** Axis Bank

**D.** HDFC Bank

**Q.15** What is the full form of REITs?

**A.** Real Estate Income Trusts

**B.** Reserve Exchange Initial Trusts

**C.** Real Exchange Income Time

**D.** Real Estate Investment Trusts

**Q.16** Which of the following statements is/are correct with respect to the Lokpal Bill?

I. The Lokpal will consist of a chairperson and a maximum of ten members of which fifty percent shall be judicial members.

II. Prime minister has been brought under the purview of the Lokpal with specific exclusions.

III. All entities receiving donations from foreign sources in the context of the Foreign Contribution Regulation Act (FCRA) in excess of Rs. 20 lakhs per year are brought under the jurisdiction of the Lokpal.

IV. Lokpal will not be able to initiate 'suo moto' inquiries.

**A.** Only I & II

**B.** Only II & IV

**C.** Only I, II & III

**D.** Only I, III & IV

**Q.17** Urban cooperative bank with business size more than _____ be allowed to convert into universal commercial banks.

**A.** Rs. 10,000 cr.

**B.** Rs. 20,000 cr.

**C.** Rs. 30,000 cr.

**D.** Rs. 40,000 cr

**Q.18** "Vulture funds" are generally invested in _______

**A.** Upcoming start-ups in the sunrise sector

**B.** Institutions that promote organized crime

**C.** Distressed assets

**D.** Large cap segment of the stock markets

**Q.19** The mechanism through which the banks are allowed to borrow money through repurchase agreements are called a________.

**A.** Marginal standing facility

**B.** Liquidity Adjustment facility

**C.** Treasury bills

**D.** Open Market operations

**Q.20** Which of the following are the instruments of Credit Control in the hands of the RBI?

(A) Lowering or raising the discount and interest rates.

(B) Raising the minimum support price of the major agro products.

(C) Lowering or raising the minimum cash reserves maintained by the commercial banks.

**A.** Only (A)

**B.** Only (B)

**C.** Only (C)

**D.** Both (A) and (C) only

**Q.21** Under Basel, _______ is designed to ensure that banks build up capital buffers during normal times which can be drawn down as losses are incurred during a stressed period.

**A.** Capital Conservation Buffer

**B.** Counter Cycle Buffer

**C.** Leverage Ratio

**D.** All of the above

**Q.22** What purpose does the MICR number, which is present on a cheque, serve?

**A.** It is used to identify the genuineness of the cheque

**B.** It is used to identify the bank branch

**C.** It is nothing but a type of cheque number

**D.** Both (A) and (B)

**Q.23** Consider the following statements regarding Monetary Policy.

1. The primary objective of monetary policy is to maintain price stability while keeping in mind the objective of growth.

2. Open Market Operations is the instrument of Monetary Policy in which RBI buys and sells government securities in the open market.

Which among the above statements is/are correct?

**A.** 1 only

**B.** 2 only

**C.** Both 1 and 2

**D.** Neither 1 nor 2

**Q.24** Consider the following pairs.

| S. No | Type of Inflation | Definition |
|---|---|---|
| 1. | Reflation | It is when the prices of goods and services rise uncontrollably |
| 2. | Stagflation | It is deliberately introduced by the government. |
| 3. | Hyperinflation | When inflation and unemployment both are at higher levels |

Which among the above pairs is/are correct?

**A.** Only 1

**B.** 1 and 2 only

**C.** 1, 2, and 3 only

**D.** None of the above

**Q.25** The risk related to the bank's inability to generate profits at its target level is known as ______.

**A.** Business Risk

**B.** Reputational Risk

**C.** Credit Risk

**D.** Systematic Risk

**Q.26** SDDS is an International Monetary Fund standard to guide member countries in the dissemination of national statistics to the public. SDDS stands for-

**A.** Special Data Dissemination Service

**B.** Special Data Dissemination Standard

**C.** Special Data Dissemination System

**D.** Special Durable Dissemination Standard

**Q.27** ___________ is responsible for discharging certain core traditional central banking functions, viz., acting as bankers to the Government and banks and managing public debt of both, central and state governments.

**A.** CDBS

**B.** FISIM

**C.** DEIO

**D.** DGBA

**Q.28** Which Payments bank has launched Aadhaar Enabled Payment System(AEPS) service?

**A.** Airtel

**B.** Mobikwik

**C.** Idea

**D.** PayTm

**Q.29** IFCI is an Indian government-owned development bank to cater to the long-term finance needs the industrial sector. IFCI stands for-

**A.** Industrial Finance Company of India

**B.** Industrial Finance Corporation of Investment

**C.** Industrial Finance Corporation of India

**D.** International Finance Corporation of India

**Q.30** DCB Bank Limited is a private sector scheduled commercial bank in India. Where is the head office of DCB Bank Limited?

**A.** Bengaluru

**B.** Pune

**C.** New Delhi

**D.** Mumbai

# // Smart Answer Sheet //

**Correct** Indicates percentage of students who answered questions correctly.

**Skipped** Indicates percentage of students who skipped questions.

| Q. | Ans. | Correct / Skipped |
|----|------|-------------------|
| 1 | D | 28.08 % / 69.91 % |
| 2 | D | 24.12 % / 69.21 % |
| 3 | D | 32.31 % / 67.37 % |
| 4 | A | 10.72 % / 84.65 % |
| 5 | D | 66.49 % / 33.23 % |
| 6 | B | 66.2 % / 31.61 % |

| Q. | Ans. | Correct / Skipped |
|----|------|-------------------|
| 7 | C | 60.9 % / 38.34 % |
| 8 | B | 48.68 % / 48.34 % |
| 9 | C | 31.21 % / 67.56 % |
| 10 | B | 61.1 % / 38.18 % |
| 11 | B | 43.95 % / 30.75 % |
| 12 | B | 59.55 % / 40.07 % |

| Q. | Ans. | Correct / Skipped |
|----|------|-------------------|
| 13 | C | 29.59 % / 67.41 % |
| 14 | B | 60.33 % / 35.49 % |
| 15 | D | 49.33 % / 33.32 % |
| 16 | B | 68.99 % / 30.74 % |
| 17 | B | 59.16 % / 39.8 % |
| 18 | C | 40.48 % / 30.1 % |

| Q. | Ans. | Correct / Skipped |
|----|------|-------------------|
| 19 | B | 48.06 % / 31.27 % |
| 20 | C | 64.12 % / 33.9 % |
| 21 | A | 81.91 % / 14.71 % |
| 22 | D | 67.72 % / 30.6 % |
| 23 | C | 48.56 % / 44.74 % |
| 24 | D | 55.84 % / 32.17 % |

| Q. | Ans. | Correct / Skipped |
|----|------|-------------------|
| 25 | A | 65.81 % / 30.43 % |
| 26 | B | 46.97 % / 44.48 % |
| 27 | D | 64.24 % / 33.07 % |
| 28 | A | 86.0 % / 12.55 % |
| 29 | C | 59.81 % / 32.47 % |
| 30 | D | 69.15 % / 30.82 % |

| Performance Analysis | |
|----------------------|--------|
| Avg. Score (%) | 50.0% |
| Toppers Score (%) | 63.33% |
| Your Score | |

# //Hints and Solutions//

**1.** The maximum amount of loan that can be granted under priority sector for building social infrastructure such as schools etc. is Rs 5 crores.

Priority Sector areas are such that they need special focus by the banks in order to grow and it includes agriculture and allied sectors, housing, education, social infrastructure, etc.

Banks are required to fulfill the target of at least 40% of the total bank credit in a year to the priority sectors specified by the RBI.

Hence, the correct option is (D).

**2.** KYC is an acronym for 'Know Your Customer'.

The Reserve Bank of India advises banks to make the Know Your Customer procedures mandatory while opening and operating the accounts.

Low-income group customers are exempted from submitting KYC.

Hence, the correct option is (D).

**3.** There is no fee for filing and resolving customer's complaints with the banking ombudsman.

The Banking Ombudsman Scheme was introduced under Section 35 A of the Banking Regulation Act, 1949 by RBI in 2006. A banking ombudsman is introduced for the resolution of complaints relating to certain services rendered by banks.

Hence, the correct option is (D).

**4.** Co-operative banks are registered under the Cooperative Societies Act, 1912.

A cooperative bank is an institution established on a cooperative basis and dealing in the ordinary banking business. Like other banks, the Cooperative banks are founded by collecting funds through shares, accept deposits, and grant loans.

They issue shares of unlimited liability, while the joint-stock banks issue shares of limited liability.

Hence, the correct option is (A).

**5.** When a bank borrower or counterparty fails to meet its payment obligation regarding the terms agreed with the bank, it is called Credit Risk.

Credit risk is the possibility of a loss resulting from a borrower's failure to repay a loan or meet contractual obligations.

Traditionally, it refers to the risk that a lender may not receive the owed principal and interest, which results in an interruption of cash flows and increased costs for collection.

Hence, the correct option is (D).

**6.** Punjab National Bank has launched a campaign to encourage customers to use digital banking channels.

Under the campaign 'DIGITAL APNAYEN', the bank will contribute Rs 5 towards the **PM CARES** Fund on behalf of each customer conducting the first financial transaction to activate their RuPay Debit card either on point of sale (PoS) or e-commerce platform.

The campaign is on till March 31, 2021.

Hence, the correct option is (B).

**7.**

| Denomination | Motifs |
|---|---|
| Rs. 10 | Sun Temple of Konark |
| Rs. 20 | Ellora caves |
| Rs. 50 | Hampi with Chariot |
| Rs. 100 | Rani Ki Vav |
| Rs. 200 | Sanchi Stupa |
| **Rs. 500** | **Red Fort with Indian Flag** |
| Rs. 2000 | Mangalayan |

Hence, the correct option is (C).

**8.**

| Denomination | Motifs |
|---|---|
| Rs. 10 | Sun Temple of Konark |
| **Rs. 20** | **Ellora caves** |
| Rs. 50 | Hampi with Chariot |
| Rs. 100 | Rani Ki Vav |
| Rs. 200 | Sanchi Stupa |
| Rs. 500 | Red Fort with Indian Flag |
| Rs. 2000 | Mangalayan |

Hence, the correct option is (B).

**9.** The Government of India has approved a scheme for improving the short-term liquidity position of NBFCs/HFCs through a SPV in the form of Special Liquidity Scheme Trust. SBI Capital Markets Limited set up the SLS trust.

SPV-Special Purpose Vehicle

SBI Capital Markets Limited (SBICAP) is a subsidiary of the State Bank of India.

This Special Liquidity Scheme of Rs. 30,000 crore was announced by Smt Nirmala Sitharaman, Union Minister for Finance & Corporate Affairs.

Please note that the finances provided to the NFBCs/HFCs under this scheme should be used to repay existing liabilities and not to expand assets.

The Scheme would be open for three months for making subscriptions by the Trust.

The period of lending by the Trust shall be for a period of up to 90 days.

Commercial papers and Non-Convertible Debentures are the instruments used in this scheme.

Any NBFC including Microfinance Institutions registered with RBI under the Reserve Bank of India Act, 1934 (excluding those registered as Core Investment Companies) and any HFC registered with the National Housing Bank under the National Housing Bank Act, 1987 would be eligible to raise funding.

Capital to Risk (Weighted) Assets Ratio/ Capital adequacy Ratio of eligible NBFCs/HFCs should not be below the regulatory minimum, i.e., 15% and 12% respectively as on March 31, 2019.

RBI would be providing funds for the Scheme by subscribing to government-guaranteed special securities issued by the Trust.

The Government of India would be providing an unconditional and irrevocable guarantee to the special securities issued by the Trust.

Hence, the correct option is (C).

**10.** The digital currency ABER was launched recently by the central banks of UAE and Saudi Arabia.

- ABER is a common digital currency for the UAE and Saudi Arabia.

- It was released jointly by the Saudi Arabian monetary authority and the United Arab Emirates central bank.

- It was officially launched on 29th January 2019.

- It was launched to study the impact on the improvement and reduction of remittance costs and the assessments of risks.

- In its initial phase, the use of the ABER currency will be restricted to a limited number of banks in each state.

- The ABER currency will be used in financial statements between UAE and Saudi Arabia through Blockchains and Distributed Ledgers technologies.

- It is the first time when the monetary authorities of the UAE and Saudi Arabia are cooperating to use blockchain technology.

Hence, the correct option is (B).

**11.** Lakshmi Vilas Bank (LVB) has launched Lakshmi DigiGo, a digital initiative to enable the opening of savings account instantly.

Lakshmi DigiGo is a savings account with select features, including internet and mobile Banking.

LVB's new initiative will help people to onboard themselves and avail the most required banking services instantly through the website.

Hence, the correct option is (B).

**12.** State Bank of India has waived off SMS charges in addition to its penalty waiver on non-maintenance of minimum balance for all its Savings Accounts.

SBI has over 44 crore savings accounts.

Earlier, SBI customers had to maintain an average monthly balance of 3000, 2000, and 1000 rupees in metro, semi-urban and rural areas respectively.

Hence, the correct option is (B).

**13.** Deutsche Bank has introduced a capital infusion of ₹2,700 crores into its India department operations to fund its progress plans within the nation.

With this, the full capital deployed in India branches has now elevated to ₹18,200 crores.

These funds will likely be used to help the additional enlargement of Deutsche Bank India throughout all of its companies.

Hence, the correct option is (C).

**14.** Indian Bank has launched another green initiative, IB-eNote that enables a totally paperless working environment.

The IB e-Note is a tool that enables the processing and tracking of notes put up by various offices digitally.

This green initiative is expected to improve Turnaround Time considerably, besides saving on the cost of paper, printing and other administrative expenses.

Hence, the correct option is (B).

**15.** Real Estate Investment Trusts (REITs)

A real estate investment trust (REIT) is a company that owns, and in most cases operates, income-producing real estate. REITs own many types of commercial real estate, ranging from office and apartment buildings to warehouses, hospitals, shopping centers, hotels and even timberlands.

Currently, as per the REIT guidelines, the minimum investment has been kept at Rs. 2 lakh per investor. However, once they get listed on the stock exchanges, trading will be allowed for a minimum lot of Rs. 1 lakh.

Hence, the correct option is (D).

**16.** The correct options are –

II. Prime minister has been brought under the purview of the Lokpal with specific exclusions.

IV. Lokpal will not be able to initiate suo moto inquiries.

In first option - The Lokpal will consist of a chairperson and a maximum of eight members of which fifty percent shall be judicial members.

In second option - All entities receiving donations from foreign sources in the context of the Foreign Contribution Regulation Act (FCRA) in excess of Rs. 10 lakhs per year are brought under the jurisdiction of the Lokpal.

On 15 May 2018, Former Attorney General of India Mukul Rohatgi appointed as 'eminent jurist' in the Lokpal selection committee.

Note:

The selection of chairperson and members of Lokpal shall be through a selection committee consisting of

• Prime Minister,

• Speaker of Lok Sabha,

• Leader of Opposition in the Lok Sabha,

• Chief Justice of India or a sitting Supreme Court judge nominated by CJI,

• eminent jurist.

Hence, the correct option is (B).

**17.** To overhaul and strengthen the urban cooperative bank (UCB) structure, an internal committee of the Reserve Bank of India (RBI) chaired by deputy governor R Gandhi has recommended that UCBs with business size more than Rs. 20,000 crore be allowed to convert into universal commercial banks while those with a lower size be converted to small finance banks.

Hence, the correct option is (B).

**18.** It is a fund that buys securities in distressed investments, such as high-yield bonds in or near default, or equities that are in or near bankruptcy. These funds are like circling vultures patiently waiting to pick over the remains of a rapidly weakening company. The goal is high returns at bargain prices. Investors in the fund profit by buying debt at a discounted price on a secondary market and then using numerous methods to gain a larger amount than the purchasing price. Debtors include companies, countries, and individuals.

Hence, the correct option is (C).

**19.** Liquidity Adjustment Facility (LAF): is a monetary policy which allows banks to borrow money through repurchase agreements.

– LAF consists of repo and reverses repo operations.

LAF is a facility extended by the Reserve Bank of India to the scheduled commercial banks (excluding RRBs) and primary dealers to avail of liquidity in case of requirement or park excess funds with the RBI in case of excess liquidity on an overnight basis against the collateral of Government securities including State Government securities. Basically, LAF enables liquidity management on a day to day basis.

Liquidity adjustment facility (LAF) is a monetary policy tool which allows banks to borrow money through repurchase agreements or repos. LAF is used to aid banks in adjusting the day to day mismatches in liquidity (frictional liquidity deficit/surplus). Liquidity of a more durable nature are managed with other instruments like cash reserve ratio

Through LAF, banks are permitted to borrow only a certain percentage of its Net Demand and Time Liabilities (NDTL).In case the Bank requires more funds, beyond what is permissible under LAF, it can access another window called the Marginal Standing Facility (MSF)

In the LAF for overnight drawings, both the reverse repo and repo operations are conducted at a fixed rate.

Hence, the correct option is (B).

**20.** Credit control is the most important function of Reserve Bank of India (RBI). By using credit control methods, RBI tries to maintain monetary stability.

There are two types of methods for credit control: Qualitative methods and Quantitative methods. Under quantitative methods, certain percentage of deposit liabilities of banks is impounded in cash form with RBI and/or to be maintained in liquid assets like government securities.

Hence, the correct option is (C).

**21.** The capital conservation buffer (CCB) is designed to ensure that banks build up capital buffers during normal times (i.e. outside periods of stress) which can be drawn down as losses are incurred during a stressed period. The requirement is based on simple capital conservation rules designed to avoid breaches of minimum capital requirement

Hence, the correct option is (A).

**22.** MICR number is used to identify the genuineness of cheque.

MICR Code: Magnetic Ink Character recognition code. Magnetic Ink Character Recognition (MICR) is a 9-digit code that helps identify a particular bank branch that is part of the Electronic Clearing System (ECS) which is used to clear cheques on a routine basis.

Hence, the correct option is (D).

**23.** Monetary policy refers to the policy of the central bank with regard to the use of monetary instruments under its control to achieve the goals specified in the Act.

The Reserve Bank of India (RBI) is vested with the responsibility of conducting monetary policy. This responsibility is explicitly mandated under the Reserve Bank of India Act, 1934.

The primary objective of monetary policy is to maintain price stability while keeping in mind the objective of growth. Price stability is a necessary precondition to sustainable growth. So, statement 1 is correct.

There are several direct and indirect instruments that are used for implementing monetary policy-

- Repo Rate
- Reverse Repo Rate
- Liquidity Adjustment Facility
- Marginal Standing Facility
- Corridor
- Bank Rate
- Cash Reserve Ratio
- Statutory Liquidity Ratio
- Open Market Operations
- Market Stabilisation Scheme

In order to control the money supply, the RBI buys and sells government securities in the open market. These operations conducted by the Central Bank in the open market are referred to as Open Market Operations. So, statement 2 is correct.

The objective of OMOs is to keep a check on temporary liquidity mismatches in the market, owing to foreign capital flow.

When the RBI sells government securities, the liquidity is sucked from the market, and the exact opposite happens when RBI buys securities. The latter is done to control inflation.

Hence, the correct option is (C).

**24.** Reflation:

It is a situation deliberately brought by the government to reduce unemployment and increase demand by going for higher levels of economic growth. So, pair 1 is not correct.

Governments go for higher public expenditures, tax cuts, interest rate cuts, etc.

Fiscal deficit rises, extra money is printed at a higher level of growth, wages increase.

Stagflation:

It occurs when inflation and unemployment both are at higher levels. So, pair 2 is not correct.

It is a combination of high inflation and low growth.

When the economy is passing through stagnation and the government shuffles with the economic policy, a sudden and temporary price rise is seen in some of the goods.

Hyperinflation:

This type of inflation is 'large and accelerating'.

It is when the prices of goods and services rise uncontrollably. So, pair 3 is not correct.

In this inflation, not only the range of increase is very large but also the increase takes place in a very short span of time.

Such inflation quickly leads to a complete loss of confidence in the domestic currency and people start opting for other forms of money- gold, physical assets, etc.

Hence, the correct option is (D).

**25.** Business risk arises from the bank's inability to generate profits at its target levels.

For Bank, Business Risk is the risk associated with the failure of a bank's long-term strategy, estimated forecasts of revenue, and a number of other things related to profitability.

Business risk is the risk arising from a bank's long-term business strategy. It deals with a bank not being able to keep up with the changing competition dynamics, losing market share over time, and being closed or acquired.

Hence, the correct option is (A).

**26.** Special Data Dissemination Standard (SDDS) is an International Monetary Fund standard to guide member countries in the dissemination of national statistics to the public.

Hence, the correct option is (B).

**27.** The Department of Government and Bank Accounts (DGBA) is responsible for discharging certain core traditional central banking functions, viz., acting as bankers to the Government and banks and managing the public debt of both, central and state governments. It is also responsible for the maintenance of the Reserve Bank's internal accounts and the compilation of its weekly and annual accounts.

Hence, the correct option is (D).

**28.** Airtel Payments Bank rolls out "Aadhaar Enabled Payment System" service.

The AEPS is a bank-led model which allows online interoperable financial transactions at a Point of Sale(PoS) through business correspondent of any bank using Aadhaar authentication.

It will help people to do transactions at over 2,50,000 of its banking points across India.

It allows customers to carry out transactions by using their Aadhaar number or virtual ID to access their bank accounts.

The AEPS allows six types of transactions, including deposit and withdrawal.

The AEPS platform offers ease of secured banking to everyone by using only their Aadhaar.

COO- Ganesh Ananthanarayanan

Hence, the correct option is (A).

**29.** IFCI stands for Industrial Finance Corporation of India. The Government of India established The Industrial Finance Corporation of India (IFCI) on July 1, 1948, by way of an IFC Act 1948.

Hence, the correct option is (C).

**30.** DCB Bank Ltd. is a private sector scheduled commercial bank in India. The head office of DCB Bank Limited is in Mumbai.

Hence, the correct option is (D).

**Q.1** Who wrote the book "A Passage to India"?

*[Uttarakhand Public Service Commission (UKPSC), 2011]*

**A.** Jawaharlal Nehru
**B.** Minoo Masani
**C.** E.M. Forster
**D.** None of them

**Q.2** Al-Biruni's Kitab-ul-Hind was written in which language?

*[Indian Military Academy (IMA), 2020], [Officers Training Academy (OTA), 2020]*

**A.** Arabic
**B.** Persian
**C.** Urdu
**D.** Turkish

**Q.3** Uttarakhand Assembly Speaker Premchand Aggarwal released a book "Kamdhenu Samhita". It was written by whom?

**A.** Ramesh Semwal
**B.** Satpal Maharaj
**C.** Harak Singh Rawat
**D.** Ajay Bhatt

**Q.4** Which of the following is the composition of Banabhatta?

*[HSSC Canal Patwari, 2019]*

**A.** Sur Sagar
**B.** Harshacharita
**C.** Geetha Ramayan
**D.** Bhagavad Geeta

**Q.5** Who is the author of the book "War and Diplomacy in Kashmir"?

**A.** G. Parthasarathy
**B.** Sir Owen Dixon
**C.** C. Dasgupta
**D.** Kuldeep Nayar

**Q.6** The author of the book 'Flood of Fire' is:

**A.** Jai Ram Ramesh
**B.** George Saunders
**C.** Amitav Ghosh
**D.** Satya nadella

**Q.7** Who is the author of the book titled "Crunch Time: Narendra Modi's National Security Crises"?

**A.** Sreeram Chaulia
**B.** Tarun Das
**C.** Kaushik Basu
**D.** V. R. Panchamukhi

**Q.8** Who is the author of the book "Unfilled Barrels: India's Oil Story" (Bloomsbury)?

**A.** Richa Mishra
**B.** Sucheta Dalal
**C.** Ayesha Faridi
**D.** Tanvir Gill

**Q.9** Who is the author of the book 'Cooking to Save Your Life'?

**A.** Nandan Nilekani
**B.** Amartya Sen
**C.** Raghuram Rajan
**D.** Abhijit Banerjee

**Q.10** Who among the following is the author of the book titled 'Rewinding the first 25 years of MeitY'?

**A.** Dr. Shashi Tharoor
**B.** S S Oberoi
**C.** Prabhat Kumar
**D.** Venkaiah Naidu

**Q.11** Who wrote the book "Udaan Ek Majboor Bachhe Ki"?

**A.** Deepam Chatterjee
**B.** Mithilesh Tiwari
**C.** Amitabh Kumar
**D.** Bhupendra Yadav

**Q.12** Who is the author of the book "The Boy Who Wrote a Constitution"?

**A.** Uma Das Gupta
**B.** Jimmy Sonic

**C.** Anirudh Suri
**D.** Rajesh Talwar

**Q.13** Who has come up with a new work of fiction, 'In An Ideal World'?

**A.** Kunal Basu
**B.** Amitav Ghosh
**C.** Pankaj Kapur
**D.** Kunal Deshmukh

**Q.14** Who is the author of the book "A Little Book of India: Celebrating 75 years of Independence", released in January, 2022?

**A.** Shubira Prasad
**B.** Anukrti Upadhyay
**C.** Rahul Rawail
**D.** Ruskin Bond

**Q.15** Name the Autobiography written by Shane Warne?

**A.** Playing It My Way
**B.** Wide Angle
**C.** No Spin
**D.** The Test of My Life

**Q.16** Who is the author of the book 'The Founders: The Story of Paypal and the Entrepreneurs Who Shaped Silicon Valley'?

**A.** Chetan bhagat
**B.** Kiran Desai
**C.** Jimmy Soni
**D.** Shashi Tharoor

**Q.17** Who is the author of Ramayana in Rajasthani language?

**A.** Manihar
**B.** Jinadaat Suri
**C.** Sitaram Lalas
**D.** Hanuwant Kinkar

**Q.18** Which state governor released the book titled 'Making of a General-A Himalayan Echo'?

**A.** Tripura
**B.** Meghalaya
**C.** Manipur
**D.** West Bengal

**Q.19** Who wrote the famous poetry book 'Do Chattane'?

**A.** Mohan Rakesh
**B.** Sumitranandan Pant
**C.** Krishna Sobti
**D.** Harivansh Rai Bachchan

**Q.20** The book "Letters from a Father to Daughter" was written by

**A.** Mahatma Gandhi
**B.** V.B. Patel
**C.** Jawaharlal Nehru
**D.** S. Radhakrishnan

**Q.21** Who wrote the novel "A Passage to India" ?

**A.** Salman Rushdie
**B.** Edward Morgan Forster
**C.** Jonathan Swift
**D.** Daniel Defoe

**Q.22** Who is the author of the book named "Man Eaters of Kumaon"?

**A.** Thomas Mann
**B.** Romain Rolland
**C.** Jim Corbett
**D.** Philip Roth

**Q.23** Who is the author of Yuganta: The End of an Epoch?

*[UGC NET Sociology, 2020]*

**A.** David G. Mandelbaum

**B.** G.S. Ghurye
**C.** Irawati Karve
**D.** Leela Dube

**Q.24** Which of the following books are authored/co-authored by Stanley Cohen?

A. Folk, Devils and Moral Panics : The creation of Mods and Rockers

B. Frontiers of Identity : The British and others

C. Visions of Social control

D. The Urban Question

E. The Manfacture of News

Choose the most appropriate answer from the options given below.

*[UGC NET Sociology, 2020]*

**A.** A, B, C only
**C.** A, C, E only
**B.** B, C, D only
**D.** C, D, E only

**Q.25 Direction:** Match List-I with List-II.

| | List-I (Authors) | | List-II (Published work) |
|---|---|---|---|
| (a) | Rosa Hartmut and William Scheuerman | (i) | Television and Social Change in Rural India |
| (b) | Kirk Johnson | (ii) | The Fastfood Nation |
| (c) | Eric Schlossere | (iii) | High Speed Society |
| (d) | Dona Haraway | (iv) | Simians, Cyborgs and Women: Reinvention of Nature |

Choose the correct answer from the options given below.

*[UGC NET Sociology, 2020]*

**A.** (a)-(ii), (b)-(iii), (c)-(iv), (d)-(i)
**B.** (a)-(iii), (b)-(i), (c)-(ii), (d)-(iv)
**C.** (a)-(i), (b)-(iii), (c)-(iv), (d)-(ii)
**D.** (a)-(iv), (b)-(i), (c)-(ii), (d)-(iii)

**Q.26 Direction:** Match List-I with List-II.

| List-I (Authors) | | | List-II (Books) |
|---|---|---|---|
| (a) | A. Agarwal | (i) | Sacred Ecology |
| (b) | J.M. Acheson | (ii) | Cows, Kin and Globalization |
| (c) | S.A. Crate | (iii) | Capturing the commons |
| (d) | F. Berkes | (iv) | Environmentality |

Choose the correct answer from the options given below.

*[UGC NET Sociology, 2020]*

**A.** (a)-(iii), (b)-(ii), (c)-(i), (d)-(iv)
**B.** (a)-(iv), (b)-(iii), (c)-(ii), (d)-(i)
**C.** (a)-(ii), (b)-(iv), (c)-(iii), (d)-(i)
**D.** (a)-(i), (b)-(iii), (c)-(ii), (d)-(iv)

**Q.27** Who is the author of the book 'Crossed Swords: Pakistan, Its Army and the War Within'?

*[SSC Sub Inspector (CPO), 2020]*

**A.** Shuja Nawaz
**C.** Shashi Tharoor
**B.** JN Dixit
**D.** SD Muni

**Q.28** Soj-e-Vatan is the book written by:

*[Uttarakhand Public Service Commission (UKPSC), 2011]*

**A.** Mahadevi Verma
**B.** Premchand
**C.** Sumitranandan Pant
**D.** Suryakant Tripathi 'Nirala'

**Q.29** The timeless Indian novel 'Devdas' was written by:

**A.** Rabindranath Tagore
**B.** Bankim Chandra Chatterjee
**C.** Mirza Ghalib
**D.** Sarat Chandra Chattopadhyay

**Q.30** The author of world famous Harry Potter series is

**A.** Arundhati Roy
**B.** J K Rowling
**C.** Taslima Nasrin
**D.** Salman Rushdie

# // Smart Answer Sheet //

**Correct**  Indicates percentage of students who answered questions correctly.

**Skipped**  Indicates percentage of students who skipped questions.

| Q. | Ans. | Correct / Skipped | Q. | Ans. | Correct / Skipped | Q. | Ans. | Correct / Skipped | Q. | Ans. | Correct / Skipped | Q. | Ans. | Correct / Skipped |
|----|------|-------------------|----|------|-------------------|----|------|-------------------|----|------|-------------------|----|------|-------------------|
| 1 | C | 27.49 % / 71.98 % | 7 | A | 68.38 % / 31.43 % | 13 | A | 76.71 % / 12.15 % | 19 | D | 43.09 % / 39.89 % | 25 | B | 26.95 % / 70.75 % |
| 2 | A | 28.95 % / 71.03 % | 8 | A | 43.11 % / 31.53 % | 14 | D | 46.45 % / 47.54 % | 20 | C | 61.2 % / 34.27 % | 26 | B | 28.12 % / 69.52 % |
| 3 | A | 78.98 % / 12.35 % | 9 | D | 57.21 % / 33.46 % | 15 | C | 53.1 % / 44.07 % | 21 | B | 52.1 % / 44.46 % | 27 | A | 25.91 % / 70.25 % |
| 4 | B | 77.66 % / 15.98 % | 10 | B | 46.8 % / 52.11 % | 16 | C | 16.24 % / 79.06 % | 22 | C | 12.42 % / 84.62 % | 28 | B | 23.38 % / 72.18 % |
| 5 | C | 60.96 % / 34.66 % | 11 | B | 67.13 % / 30.75 % | 17 | D | 53.14 % / 33.04 % | 23 | C | 24.33 % / 68.41 % | 29 | D | 30.38 % / 68.56 % |
| 6 | C | 61.78 % / 37.93 % | 12 | D | 56.08 % / 37.3 % | 18 | C | 46.15 % / 46.56 % | 24 | C | 20.63 % / 78.69 % | 30 | B | 14.46 % / 84.04 % |

## Performance Analysis

| | |
|---|---|
| Avg. Score (%) | 36.67% |
| Toppers Score (%) | 53.33% |
| Your Score | |

# //Hints and Solutions//

**1.** E.M. Forster wrote the book "A Passage to India".

Edward Morgan Forster (E.M. Forster) was an English fiction writer, essayist and librettist. Many of his novels examine class difference and hypocrisy, including A Room with a View, Howards End and A Passage to India. The last brought him his greatest success.

This is the first edition of E M Forster's A Passage to India, which was published in 1924. It is widely considered to be Forster's finest work and it became his last novel, despite the fact that he remained active as a writer and critic for more than four decades after its publication.

Hence, the correct option is (C).

**2.** Al-Biruni's Kitab-ul-Hind was written in the Arabic language.

- It is a comprehensive treatise divided into eighty chapters on the basis of topics like religion and philosophy, festivals, astronomy, alchemy, customs and practices, social life-weight and measurement methods, sculpture and law of sciences, etc.

- Al-Bruni was an Iranian scholar during the Islamic golden age.

- He had good knowledge of Mathematics, Physics, Natural Sciences, and astronomy which distinguished him from other historians.

Hence, the correct option is (A).

**3.** "Kamdhenu Samhita" book is written by Ramesh Semwal who is president of the Uttarakhand Astrology Council. This book is based on the scientific, economic, social importance of Cows. This book is released by Uttarakhand Assembly Speaker Premchand Aggarwal.

Hence, the correct option is (A).

**4.** Harshacharita is the composition of Banabhatta.

In the first half of the seventh century, this book, composed by Banabhatta, a scholar of Sanskrit prose literature, sheds abundant light on the life of Harsha and the history of India during the time of Harsha. 'Harshacharita' is the historical epic of Vanabhatta. Baan has called it a story. In this story divided into eight exhalations, Banabhatta has described the life story of Harshavardhana, the Maharaja of Sthanavisvara. In the first three Uchhavas, Baan has described his lineage and his biography in detail. The real story of Harshachachit begins with the fourth exhalation. In this, a sublime description of the energetic character of Harshavardhana has been given from Pushpabhuti, the originator of Harshavardhana to Emperor Harshavardhana. 'Harshachit' is the first attempt to write prose on a historical subject. The language of this historical poem is completely poetic.

Hence, the correct option is (B).

**5.** C. Dasgupta is the author of the book "War and Diplomacy in Kashmir"

Based on declassified documents, the book throws new light on the roles played by Mountbatten and the British service chiefs in the Kashmir war of 1947-48 and explains why India took the Kashmir issue to the UN, why it did not carry the war into Pakistan and why it accepted a ceasefire. Examining archival material that has not been looked at previously and attempting an important reassessment of Mountbatten's role, the book highlights the fact that India's first Governor-General was not a mere constitutional figurehead. The book shows that he used and abused this authority to ensure that the conflict in Kashmir did not escalate into a full-scale inter-dominion war.

Hence, the correct option is (C).

**6.** Booker Prize awarded Amitabh Ghosh released his new novel 'Flood of Fire' on 7 June 2015 The novel is based on the major events of the first opium war (1839-42), which was concluded by the author through fictional entertainment The 'Food of Fire' covers the opium trade between India and China run by the East India Company in the mid-19th century, as well as incidents related to the smuggling of coolies to Mauritius by the British.

Hence, the correct option is (C).

**7.** A new book authored by Dr Sreeram Chaulia titled "Crunch Time: Narendra Modi's National Security Crises" was released on March 31 by the Minister of State for External Affairs, Meenakshi Lekhi. He is the Dean of the Jindal School of International Affairs of OP Jindal Global University.

Hence, the correct option is (A).

**8.** Financial journalist Richa Mishra's "Unfilled Barrels: India's Oil Story" (Bloomsbury) is the story of the growth of India's oil and gas sector over the past half a century. The book recounts India's upstream journey in a systematic manner.

Hence, the correct option is (A).

**9.** Economist Abhijit Banerjee has come up with his new book 'Cooking to Save Your Life'. He explores the social dimension of food through this book.

Abhijit Banerjee shared the 2019 Nobel Memorial Prize in Economic Sciences with Esther Duflo and Michael Kemer for their experimental approach to alleviating global poverty.

Hence, the correct option is (D).

**10.** Ministry of Electronics and Information Technology (MeitY) on 14 December 2021 launched the book — Rewinding of the first 25 years of MeitY. It has been authored by S S Oberoi, a former adviser at MeitY.

Hence, the correct option is (B).

**11.** The book "Udaan Ek Majboor Bachcha Ki" is written by Mithilesh Tiwari. This book is about the life journey of Captain Eddie Manek and how he went from zero to peak in his career graph.

Hence, the correct option is (B).

**12.** "The Boy Who Wrote a Constitution", has been authored by noted playwright and author Rajesh Talwar, released on the occasion of Ambedkar's 131st birth anniversary of Dr. B.R Ambedkar. The book chronicles the challenging boyhood and growing up years of India's first law minister. The fact-based drama is largely based on Ambedkar's childhood memories. It is published by Ponytail Books.

Hence, the correct option is (D).

**13.** Kunal Basu has come up with a new work of fiction, 'In An Ideal World. The book is scheduled to release under Penguin Random House India's 'Viking' imprint. It is a "powerful and fast-paced literary novel" exploring a variety of themes relevant to the current times - college, politics, family, crime investigation, and fanaticism.

Hence, the correct option is (A).

**14.** Author Ruskin Bond has come up with his book, "A Little Book of India: Celebrating 75 years of Independence".

It pays homage to the country that has been his home for 84 years. It has been published by Penguin Random House India (PRHI).Ruskin is the recipient of the Sahitya Akademi Award, Sahitya Akademi's Bal Sahitya Puraskar, Padma Shri, and Padma Bhushan, among other prestigious awards.

Hence, the correct option is (D).

**15.** "No Spin" is an autobiography of Veteran Australian bowler Shane Warne.

It is the true story behind the headlines, in Warne's own voice, and challenges some of the enduring myths and untruths that surround him. He played his first Test match in 1992 and took over 1,000 international wickets (in Tests and One-Day Internationals).

Hence, the correct option is (C).

**16.** Jimmy Soni has come with his new book 'The Founders: The Story of Paypal and the Entrepreneurs Who Shaped Silicon Valley'. It has been published by Simon & Schuster. It highlights the story of multinational digital-payments company PayPal and how it covered the journey of a start-up that turned into one of the most successful companies of all time, worth over USD 70 billion.

Hence, the correct option is (C).

**17.** Hanuwant Kinkar was the author of the Ramayana composed in the Rajasthani language.

Mahakavi Hanwant Kinkar was a scholar of the Rajasthani language. Apart from this, he has previously written the book 'Hanumat Charitramrit Sagar', 'Ram Chalisa', 'Ramanand Charit', 'Gyan Gangeswari', 'Narsingh Chalisa' and 'Marudhar Kesari Mishrimal Charit'.

Hence, the correct option is (D).

**18.** Manipur Governor, Dr. Najma Heptulla released the book 'Making of a General-A Himalayan Echo'.

- It is written by retired Lt General Konsam Himalayan Singh.
- In this book, he has written about his journey from a small village in Manipur to be the first person from North East India to reach the rank of three-star General of the Indian Army.

- It also highlights the features of Manipur which is also called as 'Land of Emeralds'.

Hence, the correct option is (C).

**19.** 'Do Chattana' is a poetry book which was written by Harivansh Rai Bachchan in 1965.

- Harivansh Rai Bachchan was born on 27 November 1907 in Agra, Uttar Pradesh.
- In 1976, he received the Padma Bhushan for his service to Hindi literature.
- He was also a Member of Parliament (Rajya Sabha) from 3 April 1966 – 2 April 1972.
- Some other famous works of Harivansh Rai Bachchan are - Madhukalash, Milan Yamini, Neeli Chidhiya, etc.

Hence, the correct option is (D).

**20.** The book "Letters from a Father to Daughter" was written by Jawaharlal Nehru.

Letters from a Father to his Daughter is a collection of letters written by Jawaharlal Nehru to his daughter Indira Priyadarshini, originally published in 1929 by Allahabad law journal press at Nehru's request and consisting of only the 30 letters sent in the summer of 1928 when Indira was 10 yearsअतः विकल्प (C) सही है।

Letters from a Father to his Daughter is a collection of letters written by Jawaharlal Nehru to his daughter Indira Priyadarshini, originally published in 1929 by Allahabad law journal press at Nehru's request and consisting of only the 30 letters sent in the summer of 1928 when Indira was 10 years.

Hence, the correct option is (C).

**21.** The novel "A Passage to India" was written by Edward Morgan Foster.

**Salman Rushdie:** The Midnight's Children Satanic Verses  Joseph Anton: A Memoir

**Edward Morgan Forster**: A Passage to India Howards End A Room with a View

**Jonathan Swift**: Gulliver's Travels A Tale of a Tub A Modest Proposal An Argument against Abolishing Christianity

Hence, the correct option is (B).

**22.** Jim Corbett, a hunter-nationalist is the author of the book "Man-Eaters of Kumaon" written in 1944. This book gives details about the experiences that Corbett had in the Kumaon region of India from the 1900s to the 1930s. During this period, he was hunting man-eating Bengal tigers and Indian leopards. It contains ten fascinating stories of tracking and shooting man-eaters in the Indian Himalayas. The stories also contain incidental information on flora, fauna and village life.

Hence, the correct option is (C).

**23.** The End of an Epoch is a book written by anthropologist Irawati Karve. It is called Yuganta for short. It is a critical analysis of the Mahabharata. The book was written in Marathi originally but later it was translated into English by W. Norman Brown. Its Nepali translation by Sujit Mainali was published in October 2020 by Kathmandu-based publishing house Book Hill.

This book is a study of the main protagonists of the Mahabharata. These character studies treat the protagonists of the book as historical figures rather than as mythical characters. In this book the author has attempted to interpret many of the events of the Mahabharata in a socio-political context. According to Karve's analysis, the Mahabharata is not really a myth but is an account of historical events that actually took place many thousands of years ago, in the nation of India. In this context, the author provides the readers with in-depth insight into the political and social situations that were prevalent during that period in Indian history.

Hence, the correct option is (C).

**24.** The books authored/co-authored by Stanley Cohen are:

- Folk, Devils and Moral Panics : The creation of Mods and Rockers
- Visions of Social control
- The Manfacture of News

Stanley Cohen (23 February 1942 – 7 January 2013) was a sociologist and criminologist, Professor of Sociology at the London School of Economics, known for breaking academic ground on "emotional management", including the mismanagement of emotions in the form of sentimentality, overreaction, and emotional denial. He had a lifelong concern with human rights violations, first growing up in South Africa, later studying imprisonment in England and finally in Palestine. He founded the centre for the Study of Human Rights at the London School of Economics.

Hence, the correct option is (C).

**25.**

| | List-I (Authors) | | List-II (Published work) |
|---|---|---|---|
| (a) | Rosa Hartmut and William Scheuerman | (iii) | High Speed Society |
| (b) | Kirk Johnson | (i) | Television and Social Change in Rural India |
| (c) | Eric Schlossere | (ii) | The Fastfood Nation |
| (d) | Dona Haraway | (iv) | Simians, Cyborgs and Women: Reinvention of Nature |

**High Speed Society** - It was published by Penn state press in 2010. It was edited by Hartmut Rosa.

**Television and Social Change in Rural India -** This book examines the social environment of village life in India and looks at the impact of television on the aspirations, values, ideas, relationships, and traditions of the villagers themselves.

**The Fastfood Nation -** The Dark Side of the All-American Meal is a 2001 book by Eric Schlosser. First serialized by Rolling Stone in 1999, the book has drawn comparisons to Upton Sinclair's 1906 muckraking novel The Jungle. The book was adapted into a 2006 film of the same name, directed by Richard Linklater.

**Simians, Cyborgs and Women: Reinvention of Nature -** Collection of essays from 1978 to 1989. Traces the gendered roots of primate studies, examines the contested terms of reference of existing feminist scholarship, and proposes the

concept of the cyborg as a metaphor for creating new visions and discourse.

Hence, the correct option is (B).

**26.**

| | List-I (Authors) | | List-II (Books) |
|---|---|---|---|
| (a) | A. Agarwal | (iv) | Environmentality |
| (b) | J.M. Acheson | (iii) | Capturing the commons |
| (c) | S.A. Crate | (ii) | Cows, Kin and Globalization |
| (d) | F. Berkes | (i) | Sacred Ecology |

**Environmentality** - Agrawal brings environment and development studies, new institutional economics, and Foucauldian theories of power and subjectivity to bear on his ethnographical and historical research. He visited nearly forty villages in Kumaon, where he assessed the state of village forests, interviewed hundreds of Kumaonis, and examined local records. Drawing on his extensive fieldwork and archival research, he shows how decentralization strategies change relations between states and localities, community decision makers and common residents, and individuals and the environment. In exploring these changes and their significance, Agrawal establishes that theories of environmental politics are enriched by attention to the interconnections between power, knowledge, institutions, and subjectivities.

**Capturing the commons** - James M. Acheson, author of the best-selling Lobster Gangs of Maine (the seminal work on the culture and economics of lobster fishing), here turns his attention to the management of the lobster industry. In this illuminating new book, he shows that resource degradation is not inevitable. Indeed, the Maine lobster fishery is one of the most successful fisheries in the world. Catches have been stable since World War II, and record highs have been achieved since the late 1980s. According to Acheson, these high catches are due, in part, to the institutions generated by the lobster-fishing industry to control fishing practices. These rules are effective.

**Cows, Kin and Globalization -** Cows, Kin, and Globalization. An Ethnography of Sustainabilityby Susan. A Crate primarily deals with the cultural ecologyof the indigenous Sakha in the Viliui area of the subarcticSakha Republic in Russia. It describes how the Viliui Sakhahave adapted to and continue to make a living in a marginalarea characterized by extreme temperatures ranging from40°C (summer) to –60°C (winter). Moreover, the bookdiscuss the political ecology of the Viliui Sakha and howthey have dealt with, and continue to deal with majorpolitical and economical changes caused by outside interests.

**Sacred Ecology** - Sacred Ecology examines bodies of knowledge held by indigenous and other rural peoples around the world, and asks how we can learn from this knowledge and ways of knowing. Berkes explores the importance of local and indigenous knowledge as a complement to scientific ecology, and its cultural and political significance for indigenous groups themselves. With updates of relevant links for further learning and over 180 new references, the fourth edition gives increased voice to indigenous authors, and reflects the remarkable increase in published local observations of climate change.

Hence, the correct option is (B).

**27.** Shuja Nawaz is the author of the book 'Crossed Swords: Pakistan, Its Army and the War Within'.

Shuja Nawaz is a political and strategic analyst from Pakistan. The second edition of the book named 'The Battle for Pakistan – The Bitter US Friendship and a Tough Neighbourhood' published in 2019.

Hence, the correct option is (A).

**28.** Soj-e-Vatan is the book written by Premchand.

Dhanpat Rai Srivastava, better known by his pen name Premchand, was an Indian writer famous for his modern Hindustani literature. Munshi Premchand was a pioneer of Hindi and Urdu social fiction.

Premchand was a pioneer of Hindi and Urdu social fiction. He was one of the first authors to write about caste hierarchies and the plights of women and labourers prevalent in the society of late 1880s. He is one of the most celebrated writers of the Indian subcontinent, and is regarded as one of the foremost Hindi writers of the early twentieth century. He published his first collection of five short stories in 1907 in a book called Soz-e-Watan.

Hence, the correct option is (B).

**29.** The timeless Indian novel 'Devdas' was written by Saratchandra Chattopadhyay.

- Sarat Chandra Chattopadhyay (1876-1938) wrotes Devdas in 1901 at the age of 17.
- His other famous novels are Pather Dabi, Srikanta, Parineeta, Datta, etc.
- His nickname is Nyarha.
- He is also known as Anila Devi.

Hence, the correct option is (D).

**30.** JK Rowling is the author of the world famous Harry Potter.

J.K. Rowling first had the idea for Harry Potter while delayed on a train traveling from Manchester to London King's Cross in 1990.

Over the next five years, she began to plan out the seven books of the series.

Hence, the correct option is (B).

**Q.1** BIOS is used by:
A. Compiler
B. Interpreter
C. Operating system
D. Application software

**Q.2** What is a background image mounted on a desktop?
A. Wallscreen
B. Wallpaper
C. Screensaver
D. None of these

**Q.3** Which of the following is an output device?
A. MIC
B. Mouse
C. Speaker
D. Keyboard

**Q.4** The value of a Terabyte is:
A. 1024 Petabytes
B. 1024 Megabytes
C. 1024 Gigabytes
D. 1024 Kilobytes

**Q.5** Which process checks to ensure the components of the computer are operating and connected properly?
A. Booting
B. Processing
C. Saving
D. None of these

**Q.6** A collection of programs that controls how the computer system runs and processes information is called?
A. Computer
B. Operating system
C. Office
D. Compiler

**Q.7** What is the file extension of MS-Powerpoint?
A. .exe
B. .xlsx
C. .pptx
D. .pst

**Q.8** What menu is selected to cut, copy and paste?
A. File
B. Edit
C. Too ls
D. Table

**Q.9** Which among the following is NOT a database software in computers?

*[UPSSSC Forest Guard, 2018]*

A. MS. Access
B. Foxpro
C. Oracle
D. MS Word

**Q.10** Which of the following is not a pointing input device?

*[Rajasthan Police Constable, 2020]*

A. Track Ball
B. Joystick
C. Digitizing Tablet
D. Scanner

**Q.11** Currently which generation computers are were using?

*[Allahabad High Court Review Officer (RO), 2019]*

A. 2nd
B. 5th
C. 6th
D. 3rd

**Q.12** Restarting a computer already started is called:
A. Warm booting
B. Cold booting
C. Logging Off
D. Shut down

**Q.13** What is called from F1 to F12 (KEY)?
A. Alphabetical key
B. Special Key
C. Function Key
D. Numeric key

**Q.14** The earliest calculating device is____.
A. Abacus
B. Clock
C. Difference Engine
D. Calculator

**Q.15** Viruses, Trojan horses and Worms are ____.
A. able to harm computer system
B. unable to be detected if present on computer
C. user-friendly applications
D. harmless applications resident on computer

**Q.16** The process of copying files to a CD-ROM is known as:
A. Burning
B. Zipping
C. Digitizing
D. Ripping

**Q.17** Which of the following is the first electronic computer?
A. ENIAC
B. UNIVAC
C. ADVAC
D. None of these

**Q.18** All data in the computer system is represented as ________.

*[KVS Trained Graduate Teacher, 2018]*

A. only two numbers - 0 and 1
B. numbers and alphabets
C. numbers, alphabets and symbols like =, -, *, $ etc.
D. numbers and alphabets of all languages that appear on the keyboard

**Q.19** ______ devices that enter information into the computer and communicate with it are called devices.

*[KVS Trained Graduate Teacher, 2018]*

A. Output
B. Input
C. Hardware
D. Storage

**Q.20** A disruptive program that spreads from program to program or from disk to disk is known as a ______.

*[KVS Trained Graduate Teacher, 2018]*

A. Time bomb
B. Trojan horse
C. Virus
D. Time - related bomb sequence

**Q.21** Action of using the mouse to move an item on computer screen to a new location is called:

*[KVS Trained Graduate Teacher, 2018]*

A. Copy and Paste
B. Cut and Paste
C. Drag and Drop
D. Plug and Play

**Q.22** What will be the full form of GIF?
A. Graphic Interchange Format
B. Global Information Forum
C. Graphic Information Format
D. Global Interchange File

**Q.23** Bar charts can be plotted on:

A. Multiple data series
B. Only two data series
C. Only one data series
D. None of the above

**Q.24** Storage that stores or retains data after power off is called____.

A. Volatile storage
B. Non Volatile storage
C. Sequential storage
D. Direct storage

**Q.25** In a Windows-based computer, two files cannot be in the same folder if:

*[RRB (NTPC), 2017]*

A. They have different names, but same creation date.
B. They have different names, but are of same file type.
C. They have the same name, and are of the same file type.
D. They have the same name, but are of different file type.

**Q.26** Which of the following is an input device of a computer?

A. Scanner    B. Printer    C. Speaker    D. Monitor

**Q.27** Which of the following is NOT a portable device?

A. iPods
B. Thumb drives
C. Desktop computers
D. Laptops

**Q.28** What is the data that goes into a computer?

A. Algorithm
B. Input
C. Output
D. Calculation

**Q.29** A scanner is which type of device?

A. Input
B. Output
C. Input and output both
D. None of these

**Q.30** To close a selected drop-down list; cancel a command and close a dialog box _____ is used.

A. Esc key
B. Enter key
C. Alt key
D. Tab key

# // Smart Answer Sheet //

**Correct**    Indicates percentage of students who answered questions correctly.

**Skipped**    Indicates percentage of students who skipped questions.

| Q. | Ans. | Correct / Skipped | Q. | Ans. | Correct / Skipped | Q. | Ans. | Correct / Skipped | Q. | Ans. | Correct / Skipped | Q. | Ans. | Correct / Skipped |
|----|------|-------------------|----|------|-------------------|----|------|-------------------|----|------|-------------------|----|------|-------------------|
| 1 | C | 83.64 % / 15.73 % | 7 | C | 83.19 % / 10.66 % | 13 | C | 84.78 % / 11.86 % | 19 | B | 81.57 % / 16.95 % | 25 | C | 80.76 % / 18.77 % |
| 2 | B | 89.84 % / 10.15 % | 8 | B | 82.11 % / 17.28 % | 14 | A | 77.8 % / 15.24 % | 20 | C | 83.28 % / 15.71 % | 26 | A | 86.3 % / 12.11 % |
| 3 | C | 89.72 % / 10.1 % | 9 | D | 77.15 % / 22.12 % | 15 | A | 84.68 % / 10.5 % | 21 | C | 80.14 % / 15.69 % | 27 | C | 89.15 % / 10.29 % |
| 4 | C | 85.0 % / 10.43 % | 10 | D | 79.73 % / 12.69 % | 16 | A | 81.07 % / 11.19 % | 22 | A | 86.95 % / 11.4 % | 28 | B | 76.25 % / 22.77 % |
| 5 | A | 84.07 % / 14.55 % | 11 | B | 84.29 % / 10.25 % | 17 | A | 89.77 % / 10.08 % | 23 | A | 79.0 % / 11.74 % | 29 | A | 76.39 % / 18.61 % |
| 6 | B | 88.02 % / 11.72 % | 12 | A | 82.93 % / 13.44 % | 18 | A | 78.99 % / 17.9 % | 24 | B | 81.52 % / 14.33 % | 30 | A | 81.37 % / 10.12 % |

| Performance Analysis | |
|---|---|
| Avg. Score (%) | 43.33% |
| Toppers Score (%) | 56.67% |
| Your Score | |

# //Hints and Solutions//

**1.** The BIOS is a critical bit of low-level code that is stored in non-volatile memory. This is used by the computer system for managing the hardware and for loading the particular operating system on another operating system.

Hence, the correct option is (C).

**2.** A wallpaper or background (also known as a desktop wallpaper, desktop background, desktop picture or desktop image on computers) is a digital image (photo, drawing etc.) used as a decorative background of a graphical user interface on the screen of a computer, smartphone or other electronic device.

Hence, the correct option is (B).

**3.** Computer speakers are output device that transforms the signal from the computer's sound card into audio. Speakers create sound using internal amplifiers that vibrate at different frequencies according to data from the computer. This produces sound.

- An output device is a piece of computer hardware that receives data from a computer and then translates that data into another form. That form may be audio, visual, textual, or hard copy such as a printed document.

- The key distinction between an input device and an output device is that an input device sends data to the computer, whereas an output device receives data from the computer.

Hence, the correct option is (C).

**4.** The smallest unit of memory is called a bit.

- Bit stands for binary digit.
- The memory of a computer is measured in Bytes
- The storage capacity of a hard disk is measured in Megabytes, Gigabytes, and Terabytes.
- The terabyte is a multiple of the unit byte for digital information.
- The value of a Terabyte is 1024 Gigabytes.
- 1 TB = 1000000000000 bytes = $10^{12}$ bytes

Hence, the correct option is (C).

**5.** Alternatively referred to as boot-up or sometimes startup, booting is the process of powering on a computer and getting into the operating system.

During the boot process, the computer goes through multiple steps, to ensure the computer hardware works correctly, and the necessary software can be loaded.

Hence, the correct option is (A).

**6.** An operating system (OS) is system software that manages computer hardware and software resources and provides common services for computer programs.

Hence, the correct option is (B).

**7.** .pptx is a file extension for a presentation file format used by Microsoft PowerPoint, the popular presentation software commonly used for office and educational slide shows.

Hence, the correct option is (C).

**8.** The edit menu as its name suggests, includes commands relating to the editing of your document. It includes important editing features such as undo, repeat, cut, copy,paste, select all, find, replace and more.

Hence, the correct option is (B).

**9.** MS Word since it's a word processor.

Microsoft Word is a word processor developed by Microsoft. It was first released on October 25, 1983, under the name Multi-Tool Word for Xenix systems.

Hence, the correct option is (D).

**10.** Scanner is not a pointing input device.

- A scanner is a device usually connected to a computer.
- Its main function is to scan or take a picture of the document, digitize the information and present it on the computer screen.

Hence, the correct option is (D).

**11.** The period of fifth-generation is the 1980-till date.

- In the fifth generation, VLSI technology became ULSI (Ultra Large Scale Integration) technology, resulting in the production of microprocessor chips having ten million electronic components.
- This generation is based on parallel processing hardware and AI (Artificial Intelligence) software.

Second Generation

- It is a computer that uses discrete transistors instead of vacuum tubes.
- In this generation, transistors were used that were cheaper, consumed less power, more compact in size, more reliable, and faster than the first-generation machines made of vacuum tubes.

Third Generation

- It is marked by the use of Integrated Circuits (IC's) in place of transistors.
- In this generation, remote processing, time-sharing, multiprogramming operating systems were used.

Sixth Generation

- These computers are called intelligent computers based on artificial intelligence or artificial brains.
- Complex problem solving is possible and researches are ongoing to find ways to solve the problems more efficiently and easily.

Hence, the correct option is (B).

**12.** A warm booting is the process of restarting a computer. It may be used in contrast to a cold boot, which refers to starting up a computer that has been turned off. Warm boots are typically initiated by a "Restart" command in the operating system.

Hence, the correct option is (A).

**13.** The function keys or F-keys on a computer keyboard, labeled F1 through F12, are keys with a special function defined by the operating system or the active program.

Hence, the correct option is (C).

**14.** The abacus is a calculating tool that was in use centuries before the adoption of the written modern numeral system and is still widely used by merchants, traders and clerks in Asia, Africa, and elsewhere.

Hence, the correct option is (A).

**15.** Viruses, Trojan horses and Worms are technically different and refer to different types of malicious software that can damage your PC or laptop.

Hence, the correct option is (A).

**16.** The process of copying files to a CD-ROM is known as Burning.

- The term burn describes the action of creating a CD or other recordable discs.
- Burning refers to the process of copying files to a CD-ROM.
- You can identify a burned or recordable disc by looking at the bottom of the disc.
- Any blank disc or recordable disc can be used in a burner to create a new disc or copy an existing disc.

Hence, the correct option is (A).

**17.** ENIAC (Electronic Numerical Integrator and Computer) was the first programmable, electronic, general-purpose digital computer. It was Turing-complete and able to solve "a large class of numerical problems" through reprogramming.

Hence, the correct option is (A).

**18.** All of the data stored and transmitted by digital devices is encoded as bits.

Computers use binary - the digits 0 and 1 - to store data. It is represented by a 0 or a 1. Binary numbers are made up of binary digits (bits), eg the binary number 1001. The circuits in a computer's processor are made up of billions of transistors.

Hence, the correct option is (A).

**19.** In computing, an input device is a piece of equipment used to provide data and control signals to an information processing system such as a computer or information appliance. Examples of input devices include keyboards, mouse, scanners, cameras, joysticks, and microphones.

Hence, the correct option is (B).

**20.** An intentionally disruptive program that spreads from program to program or from disk to disk is known as a Virus.

Hence, the correct option is (C).

**21.** Drag and drop (also "drag-and-drop") is a common action performed within a graphical user interface. It involves moving the cursor over an object, selecting it, and moving it to a new location.

Hence, the correct option is (C).

**22.** GIF stands for Graphics Interchange Format.

It is a bitmap image format that was developed by a US-based software writer Steve Wilhite while working at the internet service provider CompuServe.

Hence, the correct option is (A).

**23.** Bar charts can be plotted on multiple data series.

A bar chart uses bars to show comparisons between categories of data. These bars can be displayed horizontally or vertically. A bar graph will always have two axis. One axis will generally have numerical values, and the other will describe the types of categories being compared.

Hence, the correct option is (A).

**24.** Non-volatile memory (NVM) or non-volatile storage is a type of computer memory that can retain the stored information even after power is removed. In contrast, volatile memory needs constant power in order to retain data.
Hence, the correct option is (B).

**25.** If the two files have the same name and are of the same file type then the files cannot be saved in the same folder but they can be stored in a different folder with the same name and file type.

Hence, the correct option is (C).

**26.** Scanner is an input device of a computer.

Input devices are used to enter data or instructions into a computer.

- Keyboard
- Mouse
- Digital camera
- Scanner
- Mic
- Barcode reader
- Joystick

Hence, the correct option is (A).

**27.** Portable devices are any devices that can easily be carried. We can not carry Desktop computers anywhere, so it is not a portable device. iPods, Thumb drives, Laptops are portable devices as they are easy to carry.

Hence, the correct option is (C).

**28.** Any device through which we give any data to a computer or personal computer, it is called input and the device is called input device. Some examples of this are: keyboard, mouse, scanner, all these input devices we input something inside the computer.ng inside the computer with input devices.

Hence, the correct option is (B).

**29.** A scanner is an input device that scans documents such as photographs and pages of text. When a document is scanned, it is converted into a digital format. This creates an electronic version of the document that can be viewed and edited on a computer.

Hence, the correct option is (A).

**30.** The Esc key can often be used to get you out of dialogs or dropdown lists - it generally represents the pressing of the cancel button in these cases.

To close a selected drop-down list; cancel a command and close a dialog box Esc key shortcut key is used.

Hence, the correct option is (A).

**Q.1** Which of the following is the capital of china ?
A. Wuhan
B. Beijing
C. Shanghai
D. Shenzhen

**Q.2** San Jose is the capital of which of the following countries?
A. Jamaica
B. Guinea-Bissau
C. Moldova
D. Costa Rica

**Q.3** What is the capital of Qatar?
A. Russia
B. USA
C. Sweden
D. Doha

**Q.4** What is the Capital of Cambodia?
A. Phnom Penh
B. Phnom Kravanh
C. Krong Kampot
D. Bakan

**Q.5** What is the capital of Paraguay?
A. Ankara
B. Russia
C. London
D. Asuncion

**Q.6** The capital of Afghanistan ______.
A. Kabul
B. Herat
C. Kandahar
D. Ghazni

**Q.7** The capital of Austria is:
A. Canberra
B. Vienna
C. Jakarta
D. Tokyo

**Q.8** What is the currency of Egypt?
A. Euro
B. Pound
C. Dollar
D. Dinar

**Q.9** The Capital of Lebanon is:
A. Beirut
B. Tripoli
C. Sidon
D. Tyre

**Q.10** Madrid is the Capital City of ____.
A. Philippines
B. Maldives
C. Spain
D. United Kingdom

**Q.11** The official currency of Nepal is called____.
A. Nepalese taka
B. Loti
C. Nepalese rupee
D. Birr

**Q.12** What is the capital of Japan?
A. Tokyo
B. Osaka
C. Fukuoka
D. None of these

**Q.13** What is the currency of France?
A. Euro
B. Dollar
C. Renminbi
D. Taka

**Q.14** Which among the following is the capital of France?
A. Vaduz
B. Baku
C. Paris
D. Libya

**Q.15** The Capital of Manipur is?
A. Aizwal
B. Imphal
C. Kohima
D. Shillong

**Q.16** What is the capital of Saudi Arabia?
*[RBI Office Attendant, 2017]*
A. Kabul
B. Yerevan
C. Riyadh
D. Helsinki

**Q.17** What is the capital of Zimbabwe?
*[RBI Office Attendant, 2017]*
A. Abuja
B. Makati
C. Nairobi
D. Harare

**Q.18** What is the Currency of Malaysia?
*[RBI Office Attendant, 2017]*
A. Ringgit
B. Koruna
C. Litas
D. Rufiy

**Q.19** Which of the following is the currency of Japan?
*[RBI Office Attendant, 2017]*
A. Yen
B. Yuan
C. Won
D. Dinar

**Q.20** What is the currency of Indonesia?
*[RBI Office Attendant, 2017]*
A. Rufiyaa
B. Rial
C. Yen
D. Rupiah

**Q.21** What is the currency of Malaysia?
A. Malaysian Dinar
B. Malaysian Dollars
C. Malaysian Euro
D. Malaysian Ringgit

**Q.22** What is the currency of Iran?
A. Iranian Rial
B. Iranian Rubel
C. Iranian Diner
D. Iranian Dollar

**Q.23** ______ is the capital of South Africa.
A. London
B. New York
C. Moscow
D. Cape Town

**Q.24** What is the currency of Sweden?
A. Krona
B. Euro
C. Krone
D. Franc

**Q.25** What is the capital of Iraq?
A. Baghdad
B. Tehran
C. Berlin
D. Riyadh

**Q.26** Which of the following country-capital pair is not correctly matched?
A. Iran - Tehran
B. Israel - Amman
C. Iraq - Baghdad
D. Lebanon - Beirut

**Q.27** Krone is the official currency of which among the following countries?
A. Denmark
B. Turkey
C. Chile
D. Paraguay

**Q.28** What is the currency of Indonesia called?
A. Baht
B. Dinar
C. Rial
D. Rupiah

**Q.29** What is the capital of Chile?
A. Tehran
B. Santiago
C. Bishkek
D. Phnom penh

**Q.30** Which of the following is the currency of Bangkok?
A. Dollar
B. Baht
C. Yen
D. Euro

# // Smart Answer Sheet //

**Correct** Indicates percentage of students who answered questions correctly.

**Skipped** Indicates percentage of students who skipped questions.

| Q. | Ans. | Correct / Skipped | Q. | Ans. | Correct / Skipped | Q. | Ans. | Correct / Skipped | Q. | Ans. | Correct / Skipped | Q. | Ans. | Correct / Skipped |
|----|------|------|----|------|------|----|------|------|----|------|------|----|------|------|
| 1 | B | 78.76 % / 18.23 % | 7 | B | 84.4 % / 11.22 % | 13 | A | 89.63 % / 10.16 % | 19 | A | 85.87 % / 12.6 % | 25 | A | 84.18 % / 11.64 % |
| 2 | D | 77.63 % / 10.6 % | 8 | B | 86.79 % / 13.12 % | 14 | C | 85.85 % / 11.58 % | 20 | D | 76.87 % / 17.59 % | 26 | B | 83.89 % / 12.44 % |
| 3 | D | 77.66 % / 21.08 % | 9 | A | 80.67 % / 12.9 % | 15 | B | 83.42 % / 13.76 % | 21 | D | 84.89 % / 12.43 % | 27 | A | 78.06 % / 11.55 % |
| 4 | A | 88.01 % / 10.3 % | 10 | C | 86.99 % / 10.48 % | 16 | C | 79.19 % / 15.05 % | 22 | A | 88.0 % / 11.78 % | 28 | D | 88.33 % / 10.25 % |
| 5 | D | 88.24 % / 10.22 % | 11 | C | 79.41 % / 11.99 % | 17 | D | 83.83 % / 12.63 % | 23 | D | 79.91 % / 17.16 % | 29 | B | 82.39 % / 12.48 % |
| 6 | A | 77.26 % / 14.27 % | 12 | A | 79.17 % / 12.09 % | 18 | A | 86.85 % / 10.56 % | 24 | A | 81.96 % / 12.82 % | 30 | B | 89.68 % / 10.19 % |

## Performance Analysis

| | |
|----|----|
| Avg. Score (%) | 63.33% |
| Toppers Score (%) | 73.33% |
| Your Score | |

# //Hints and Solutions//

**1.** Beijing is the capital of the People's Republic of China. It is the world's most populous capital city.

Hence, the correct option is (B).

**2.** San Jose is the capital of Costa Rica.

| Country | Costa Rica |
|---|---|
| Capital | San Jose |
| President | Carlos Alvarado Quesada |
| Currency | Costa Rican colón |

Hence, the correct option is (D).

**3.** Doha is the capital of Qatar.

Qatar is a World Bank high-income economy, backed by the world's third-largest natural gas reserves and oil reserves.

Hence, the correct option is (D).

**4.** Cambodia is largely a land of plains and great rivers and lies amid important overland and river trade routes linking China to India and Southeast Asia. The Capital of Cambodia is Phnom Penh.

Hence, the correct option is (A).

**5.** The capital city of Paraguay is Asuncion. The city is located on the left bank of the Paraguay River, it is also the largest city in the country.

Hence, the correct option is (D).

**6.** The capital and currency of Afghanistan are Kabul and Afghani respectively. Afghanistan is a land-based country in South Asia. Afghanistan became the eighth member of SAARC in April 2007.

Hence, the correct option is (A).

**7.** Vienna is the capital and largest city of Austria, and one of the nine states of Austria. Vienna is Austria's most populous city, with about 2 million inhabitants (2.6 million within the metropolitan area, nearly one-third of the country's population), and its cultural, economic, and political center. It is the 6th-largest city by population within city limits in the European Union.

Hence, the correct option is (B).

**8.** The currency of Egypt is the Egyptian Pound which is divided into 100 piastres. It is abbreviated as LE which means livre egyptienne (French for Egyptian pound). Cairo is the capital of Egypt and Arabic is its official language.

Hence, the correct option is (B).

**9.** Lebanon is a country in the Levant region of Western Asia. Lebanon is officially known as the Lebanese Republic. Beirut is the Capital of Lebanon. Lebanon is bordered by Syria to the north and east, Israel to the south.

Cyprus to the west across the Mediterranean Sea. It is one of the smallest sovereign states on the Asian mainland covers an area of 10,400 km².

Lebanon achieved independence in 1943. Lebanese pound is the currency of Lebanon.

Hence, the correct option is (A).

**10.** Madrid is the capital of Spain. It is the third-largest city in the European Union (EU) after London and Berlin.

Hence, the correct option is (C).

**11.** The Nepalese rupee is the official currency of the Federal Democratic Republic of Nepal. The Nepalese rupee is subdivided into 100 paise. The issuance of the currency is controlled by the Nepal Rastra Bank, the central bank of Nepal.

Hence, the correct option is (C).

**12.** Tokyo is the capital of Japan. The area covered by Tokyo is 2194 square kilometers. It is the safest of all the large metropolitan cities.

Hence, the correct option is (A).

**13.** Euro is the currency of France. Euro is the official currency of 19 of the 27 member states of the European Union.

Hence, the correct option is (A).

**14.** Paris is the capital of France.

| Country | France |
|---|---|
| Capital | Paris |
| President | Emmanuel Macron |
| Prime Minister | Jean Castex |
| Currency | Euro, CFP franc |

Hence, the correct option is (C).

**15.** Imphal is the capital of the Indian state of Manipur. In the center of this historic city are the ruins of the Kangla Mahal, the seat of the former Manipur state. The city of Imphal extends into both Imphal West district and Imphal East district, and most of the city's population resides in its western part.

Hence, the correct option is (B).

**16.** Riyadh is the capital of Saudi Arabia.

Riyadh is Saudi Arabia's largest city and country's administrative capital. The name Riyadh was derived from the plural form of the Arabic word "rawḍah," meaning gardens or meadows. Riyadh rapidly grew from an enclosed desert village into a modern cosmopolitan city, and later became the capital of Saudi Arabia in 1932.

Hence, the correct option is (C).

**17.** Harare is the capital and most populous city of Zimbabwe. It is situated in north-eastern Zimbabwe in the country's Mashonaland region, Harare is a metropolitan province, which also incorporates the municipalities of Chitungwiza and Epworth.

Hence, the correct option is (D).

**18.** The Malaysian ringgit is the currency of Malaysia.

The currency abbreviation for the currency is RM, and the currency code is MYR. This is the code seen when requesting a currency quote, such as USD/MYR which shows the rate of exchange between the U.S. dollar (USD) and the Malaysian ringgit.

Hence, the correct option is (A).

**19.** The yen is the official currency of Japan. It is the third most traded currency in the foreign exchange market, after the United States dollar and the Euro. It is also widely used as a third reserve currency after the United States dollar and the Euro.

Hence, the correct option is (A).

**20.** The rupiah (Rp) is the official currency of Indonesia. Issued and controlled by Bank Indonesia, its ISO 4217 currency code is IDR. The name "rupiah" is derived from the Sanskrit word for silver, rupyakam. Sometimes, Indonesians also informally use the word "Perak" ("silver" in Indonesian) in referring to rupiah in coins. The rupiah is divided into 100 sen, although high inflation has rendered all coins and banknotes denominated in sen obsolete.

Hence, the correct option is (D).

**21.** The currency of Malaysia is the Malaysian ringgit. It is further divided into 100 sen. The Malaysian ringgit is issued by the central bank of Malaysia (Bank Negara Malaysia). Dinar is a monetary unit used in several Middle Eastern countries, including Algeria, Bahrain, Iraq, Jordan, Kuwait, Libya, and Tunisia.

Hence, the correct option is (D).

**22.** The Parliament of Iran has decided to change its currency from Rial to Toman. But, the decision has not been implemented yet. Thus, currently, Rial is the official currency of Iran.

Hence, the correct option is (A).

**23.** Cape Town is the legislative capital of South Africa. It is home to the country's legislative parliament, including the National Assembly and National Council of Provinces.

Hence, the correct option is (D).

**24.** The monetary unit in Sweden is the krona SEK (plural "kronor") and equals 100 öre. Banknotes are printed in values of 20, 50, 100, 200, 500, and 1,000 kronor. The coin is available as 1, 2, 5, and 10 kronor.

Hence, the correct option is (A).

**25.** Baghdad is the capital of Iraq and the country's largest city. It is the home to more than 7.6 million inhabitants. It is located along the Tigris River and at the junction of historic trade roads.

Hence, the correct option is (A).

**26.** "Israel - Amman" does not correctly match.

The capital of Israel is Jerusalem and Amman is the capital of Jordon.

Hence, the correct option is (B).

**27.** Krone is the official currency of Denmark.

The currency of Turkey is Lira.

The currency of Chile is Peso.

The currency of Paraguay is Guarani.

Hence, the correct option is (A).

**28.** The rupiah (Rp) is the official currency of Indonesia. Issued and controlled by Bank Indonesia. The name "rupiah" is derived from the Sanskrit word for silver, rupyakam. Sometimes, Indonesians also informally use the word "Perak" ("silver" in Indonesian) in referring to rupiah in coins.

Hence, the correct option is (D).

**29.** Santiago de Chile or simply Santiago is the capital and largest city of Chile. It is the center of Chile's largest and most densely populated conurbation. Chile is situated in the South American continent. This country shares its borders with Bolivia, Peru, and Argentina. The national language of Chile is Spanish.
Hence, the correct option is (B).

**30.** Bangkok is the capital of Thailand.

The currency used in Bangkok is the Baht.

The 10th Mekong Ganga Cooperation (MGC) Ministerial Meeting was held in Bangkok, Thailand in August 2019.

India was represented by External Affairs Minister S Jaishankar.

During this meeting, the new MGC Plan of Action 2019-2022 was adopted.

Hence, the correct option is (B).

**Q.1** Which country has signed a $ 2.25 billion deal with a Russian state-run nuclear energy company 'ASE' in August 2022?

*[RBI Assistant, 2020], [UPSSSC Rajasva Lekhpal, 2015]*

**A.** India
**B.** China
**C.** Japan
**D.** South Korea

**Q.2** Who among the followings has been elected as the 15 th President of India in July 2022 ?
**A.** Nirmala Sitharaman
**B.** Swati Piramal
**C.** Hima Kohli
**D.** Droupadi Murmu

**Q.3** Who has been appointed as a director in the Prime Minister's Office (PMO) in August 2022?
**A.** Shweta Singh
**B.** Ravi Kumar
**C.** Ruchi Mishra
**D.** Anoop Kumar Pathak

**Q.4** The Union Government has authorised which bank for issue and encash Electoral Bonds through its 29 Authorized Branches from 1–10 th of July 2022?
**A.** State Bank of India
**B.** Axis Bank
**C.** ICICI Bank
**D.** HDFC Bank

**Q.5** Who has been appointed as the new Director-General of the Sashastra Seema Bal on June 2022?
**A.** Sujoy Lal Thaosen
**B.** Sanjay Arora
**C.** Sanjeev Sharma
**D.** Ranjeet Singh Rana

**Q.6** Abhijit Sen, who passed away on August 29, 2022, was related to which field?
**A.** Geography
**B.** Psychology
**C.** Biology
**D.** Economics

**Q.7** In August 2022, which state has recognised 'Dahi-Handi' as an official sport in the state?
**A.** Maharashtra
**B.** Gujarat
**C.** Punjab
**D.** Haryana

**Q.8** When 'India Water Week' 2019 was celebrated?

*[Haryana Primary Teacher (PRT), 2020]*

**A.** 15 January to 21 January
**B.** 22 March to 26 March
**C.** 2 October to 8 October
**D.** 24 September to 28 September

**Q.9** The theme of World Environment Day 2019 was:

*[Haryana Primary Teacher (PRT), 2020]*

**A.** Beat Water pollution
**B.** Beat Sound pollution
**C.** Beat Air pollution
**D.** Soil conservation

**Q.10** Which medal did Devendra Jhajharia win in World Para Athletics Grand Prix 2022?
**A.** Gold
**B.** Silver
**C.** Bronze
**D.** None of the above

**Q.11** In July 2022 Elon Musk, CEO of Tesla, is terminating his 44 billion dollar deal to buy _________ because the social media company had breached multiple provisions of the merger agreement.
**A.** Facebook
**B.** Tagged
**C.** Goodreads
**D.** Twitter

**Q.12** Which is the first e-commerce company to set up solar farms in India?
**A.** Walmart
**B.** Amazon
**C.** Flipkart
**D.** ebay

**Q.13** Which Union Minister launched the 'Bal Raksha' mobile app at the All India Institute of Ayurveda (AIIA) on 24 July 2022?
**A.** Sarbananda Sonowal
**B.** Anurag Thakur
**C.** Amit Shah
**D.** Rajnath Singh

**Q.14** In August 2022, India has nominated which dance form to be inscribed on UNESCO's intangible cultural heritage list?
**A.** Loor
**B.** Garba
**C.** Khor
**D.** Ghoomar

**Q.15** In which of the following national parks the eight African cheetahs is shifted?

*[Delhi Forest Guard, 2020]*

**A.** Kuno Palpur National Park
**B.** Jim Corbett National Park
**C.** Ranthambore National Park
**D.** Kaziranga National Park

**Q.16** The 'National Anti-Corruption Commission Bill' is related to which country?
**A.** USA
**B.** India
**C.** Australia
**D.** Pakistan

**Q.17** Vinesh Phogat is recently honouredwith which National Award ?

*[HTET PGT - Computer Science, 2020]*

**A.** Dronacharya Award
**B.** Arjuna Award
**C.** Rajiv Gandhi Khel Ratna Award
**D.** Dhyanchand Award

**Q.18** Special ASEAN-India Foreign Ministers' Meeting (SAIFMM) will be held on the 16th and 17th June 2022 in ______________.

**A.** New Delhi, India
**B.** Islamabad, Pakistan
**C.** Dhaka, Bangladesh
**D.** Colombo, Sri Lanka

**Q.19** What is the contribution of India to the UN Women Core budget in 2022?

*[HSSC Canal Patwari, 2021], [Delhi Forest Guard, 2021]*

**A.** USD 10,000
**B.** USD 50,000
**C.** USD 100,000
**D.** USD 500,000

**Q.20** In which city, Union Minister Nitin Gadkari has unveiled India's first Electric Double Decker bus on 18 August 2022?

**A.** Bengaluru
**B.** Bhopal
**C.** Mumbai
**D.** Nagpur

**Q.21** The $8th$ Meeting of BRICS Communications Ministers was held in virtual mode in July $2022$ under the presidency of________________.

**A.** Brazil
**B.** Russia
**C.** China
**D.** South Africa

**Q.22** Which country has won gold medal in men's table tennis event at the 2022 Commonwealth Games in Birmingham on 2 August 2022 ?

**A.** Malaysia
**B.** Canada
**C.** India
**D.** South Africa

**Q.23** Which edition of Chartered Accountant's Day was observed on 1 July 2022?

**A.** 70th
**B.** 72th
**C.** 74th
**D.** 76th

**Q.24** In which Indian Institute of Technology (IIT) campus, Union Minister Jitendra Singh inaugurated India's first Autonomous Navigation facility, 'TiHAN' on 4 July 2022?

**A.** IIT Guwahati
**B.** IIT Jodhpur
**C.** IIT Madras
**D.** IIT Hyderabad

**Q.25** Which state launched the Mukhya Mantri Bagwani Bima scheme portal on April 2022 To compensate for the damage caused to the crops due to adverse weather and natural calamities?

**A.** Uttar Pradesh
**B.** Tamil Nadu
**C.** Gujarat
**D.** Haryana

**Q.26** What was the theme of International Girls in ICT Day 2022 which is observed annually on the fourth Thursday in April?

**A.** Access and safety
**B.** Inspiring the Next Generation
**C.** Case For Change, Connected Women, IoT and Tech4Girls
**D.** Powering Change: Women in Innovation and Creativity

**Q.27** In which of the following states/union territories was an election NOT held during MarchApril 2021?

*[SSC CGL, 2022]*

**A.** West Bengal
**B.** Bihar
**C.** Tamil Nadu
**D.** Puducherry

**Q.28** Chief of Army Staff (COAS) General Manoj Pande proceeded on a 3-day visit to which country in July 2022?

**A.** Bangladesh
**B.** Myanmar
**C.** Bhutan
**D.** Thailand

**Q.29** In August 2022, who has become first Indian player to have played 100 matches each in all three formats of the game?

**A.** MS Dhoni
**B.** Virat Kohli
**C.** Rohit Sharma
**D.** Shikhar Dhawan

**Q.30** The Department of Food and Public Distribution will organize a National Conference on Food and Nutrition Security in India in July $2022$ in ___________.

**A.** New Delhi
**B.** Pune
**C.** Hyderabad
**D.** Mumbai

# // Smart Answer Sheet //

**Correct** Indicates percentage of students who answered questions correctly.

**Skipped** Indicates percentage of students who skipped questions.

| Q. | Ans. | Correct / Skipped |
|---|---|---|
| 1 | D | 76.0 % / 15.53 % |
| 2 | D | 82.07 % / 12.76 % |
| 3 | A | 86.84 % / 11.04 % |
| 4 | A | 86.93 % / 10.64 % |
| 5 | A | 89.81 % / 10.11 % |
| 6 | D | 79.72 % / 17.63 % |

| Q. | Ans. | Correct / Skipped |
|---|---|---|
| 7 | A | 79.82 % / 17.22 % |
| 8 | D | 86.51 % / 12.01 % |
| 9 | C | 80.11 % / 14.07 % |
| 10 | B | 78.66 % / 13.69 % |
| 11 | D | 77.21 % / 15.32 % |
| 12 | B | 79.27 % / 18.92 % |

| Q. | Ans. | Correct / Skipped |
|---|---|---|
| 13 | A | 76.54 % / 17.46 % |
| 14 | B | 76.62 % / 21.04 % |
| 15 | A | 85.34 % / 11.43 % |
| 16 | C | 81.15 % / 17.16 % |
| 17 | C | 86.94 % / 10.43 % |
| 18 | A | 79.26 % / 20.47 % |

| Q. | Ans. | Correct / Skipped |
|---|---|---|
| 19 | D | 87.86 % / 11.11 % |
| 20 | C | 82.09 % / 16.63 % |
| 21 | C | 80.48 % / 17.49 % |
| 22 | C | 85.94 % / 10.73 % |
| 23 | C | 78.51 % / 19.53 % |
| 24 | D | 82.46 % / 13.02 % |

| Q. | Ans. | Correct / Skipped |
|---|---|---|
| 25 | D | 86.66 % / 11.08 % |
| 26 | A | 84.53 % / 10.06 % |
| 27 | B | 81.27 % / 13.65 % |
| 28 | A | 76.76 % / 16.56 % |
| 29 | B | 80.42 % / 13.87 % |
| 30 | A | 88.79 % / 10.38 % |

| Performance Analysis | |
|---|---|
| Avg. Score (%) | 33.33% |
| Toppers Score (%) | 60.0% |
| Your Score | |

# //Hints and Solutions//

**1.** South Korea has signed a $ 2.25 billion deal with a Russian state-run nuclear energy company 'ASE'in August 2022.

- It has been signed to provide components for Egypt's first nuclear power plant.
- ASE is a subsidiary of Rosatom, a state-owned Russian nuclear conglomerate.
- South Korea has also signed a $ 20 billion contract to build nuclear power reactors in the UAE.

Hence, the correct option is (D).

**2.** Former Jharkhand Governor and National Democratic Alliance candidate Droupadi Murmu has been elected as the 15th President of India on 21 July 2022.

She is the first tribal woman to be elected to the position & the youngest as well.

She defeated opposition candidate Yashwant Sinha by bagging 64.03% of the electoral college votes.

Hence, the correct option is (D).

**3.** Indian Foreign Service (IFS) officer Shweta Singh was on 2 August 2022 appointed as a director in the Prime Minister's Office (PMO).

- She is a 2008-batch IFS officer.
- The Appointments Committee of the Cabinet (ACC) approved Singh's appointment for a period of three years from the date of her joining.

Hence, the correct option is (A).

**4.** The Union Government has authorized the State Bank of India to issue and encashes Electoral Bonds through its 29 Authorized Branches from 1–10 th of July 2022.

The Electoral Bonds will be valid for fifteen calendar days from the date of issue and no payment will be made to any payee Political Party if the Electoral Bond is deposited after the expiry of the validity period.

Hence, the correct option is (A).

**5.** Sujoy Lal Thaosen has been recently appointed as the new Director-General of the Sashastra Seema Bal.

New Delhi, June 2022 (PTI) IPS officer Sujoy Lal Thaosen took charge as the new director-general (DG) of the Sashastra Seema Bal (SSB), which guards Indian frontiers with Nepal and Bhutan. Thaosen, a 1988-batch Indian Police Service (IPS) officer of the Madhya Pradesh cadre, was handed over the baton by officiating DG and ITBP chief Sanjay Arora at the headquarters of the force in R K Puram.

Hence, the correct option is (A).

**6.** Abhijit Sen, one of India's leading agricultural economists passed away on August 29, 2022 at the age of 72. Abhijit Sen was a member of the Planning Commission of India from 2004 to 2014 during the tenure of former Prime Minister Manmohan Singh.

Hence, the correct option is (D).

**7.** 'Dahi-Handi' will now be recognised as an official sport in Maharashtra in August 2022.

- "Pro-Dahi-Handi" competitions will also be organised in the state.
- Dahi-Handi will be recognised under the sports category in Maharashtra.
- The 'Govindas' will get jobs under the sports category.
- "Dahi Handi", meaning "curd in an earthen pot", is a popular event in the state associated with Janmashtami.

Hence, the correct option is (A).

**8.** The 6th India Water Week-2019 (IWW-2019) is to be held at Vigyan Bhawan, New Delhi from 24 to 28 September 2019.

- It is organised by the Ministry of Jal-Shakti, Department of Water Resources, River Development and Ganga Rejuvenation, Government of India.
- The IWW-2019 is being organised with the theme of "Water Cooperation - Coping with 21st Century Challenges".
- The objective of bringing new ideas for mutual cooperation for sustainable water management in the context of changing basin dynamics across administrative boundaries.

Hence, the correct option is (D).

**9.** World Environment Day is observed every year on 5th June.

- It was first held in 1974(first theme- "Only One Earth") by the United Nations (established in 1972 on the first day of the Stockholm Conference on the Human Environment).
- It is observed every year with a new theme and a new Host Country.
- Its objective is to raise awareness and bring down the negative impact of uncontrolled human interventions in nature, such as Global Warming, Wildlife Crime, Sustainable consumption, Marine Pollution, etc.
- In 2019 the theme was "Beat Air Pollution", the Host country was China. Air pollution is the cause of major environmental concerns at present, as it kills more than 7 billion people per year, causes long term ailments like asthma, and reduces cognitive development in kids.

Hence, the correct option is (C).

**10.** Indian javelin thrower, Devendra Jhajharia has clinched a silver medal in the World Para Athletics Grand Prix 2022 in Morocco.

Paralympics gold medalist Devendra Jhajharia threw the javelin to a distance of 60.97 meters to capture the silver. He is a three-time Paralympics medalist.

Hence, the correct option is (B).

**11.** In July 2022 Elon Musk, CEO of Tesla, is terminating his 44 billion dollar deal to buy Twitter because the social media

company had breached multiple provisions of the merger agreement.

Twitter had failed or refused to respond to multiple requests for information on fake or spam accounts on the platform, which is fundamental to the company's business performance.

Twitter fired high-ranking executives and one-third of the talent acquisition team, breaching Twitter's obligation to preserve substantially intact the material components of its current business organization.

Hence, the correct option is (D).

**12.** Amazon announced its first solar project in India with three new solar farms in Rajasthan, with a combined energy capacity of 420 megawatts.

Amazon aims to use 100% renewable energy across its business by 2025. The Indian project includes a 210-MW project to be developed by ReNew Power, a 100-MW project to be developed by Amp Energy India, and a 110-MW project to be developed by Brookfield Renewable Partners.

Hence, the correct option is (B).

**13.** Union Minister of Ayush, Sarbananda Sonowal on $24$ July $2022$ launched Bal Raksha mobile app at the All India Institute of Ayurveda (AIIA).

The app aims to raise parental awareness of paediatric preventive healthcare through Ayurvedic intervention. Mr Sonowal also inaugurated the 'Vaccination Centre for Children' at the AIIA.

AIIA Founded: $2015$

Director: Dr Tanuja Nesari

Hence, the correct option is (A).

**14.** India has nominated the dance form Garba to be inscribed on UNESCO's intangible cultural heritage list in August 2022.

In 2021, 'Durga Puja' was included in the UNESCO intangible cultural heritage representative.

India was elected by UNESCO to serve on the distinguished Intergovernmental Committee of the 2003 Convention for the Safeguarding of the Intangible Cultural Heritage in July 2022.

Hence, the correct option is (B).

**15.** Eight African cheetahs from Namibia in South Africa have been relocated to Kuno Palpur National Park in Madhya Pradesh.

After the Cheetahs arrive in the National Park, they will stay in smaller enclosures during the quarantine phase before being shifted to the bigger ones. From 1952 onwards, cheetahs gradually started becoming extinct in India, then in 2009 the 'African Cheetah Introduction Project in India' was started.

Hence, the correct option is (A).

**16.** The 'National Anti-Corruption Commission Bill' is related to Australia.

Australia's attorney general recently introduced the National Anti-Corruption Commission bill. The National Anti-Corruption Commission is a body to investigate and report on serious or systemic corruption in the public sector.

It will be led by a commissioner, who will serve one fixed term of five years. NACC has a broad jurisdiction to investigate commonwealth ministers, parliamentarians, staff, the heads and employees of commonwealth agencies, government contractors and their employees, defence force members, statutory office holders among others.

Hence, the correct option is (C).

**17.** Major Dhyan Chand Khel Ratna:

Major Dhyan Chand Khel Ratna Award (formerly Rajiv Gandhi Khel Ratna) is the highest sports award given in India. The award has been named after the best player of India and world hockey, who was a member of the Indian hockey team that won three Olympic gold medals.

Vinesh Phogat:

Vinesh Phogat (born 25 August 1994) is an Indian wrestler. She became the first Indian female wrestler to win gold in both the Commonwealth and Asian Games. She is the only Indian female wrestler to have won multiple medals at the World Wrestling Championships.

Hence, the correct option is (C).

**18.** Special ASEAN-India Foreign Ministers' Meeting (SAIFMM) will be held on the 16th and 17th June 2022 in New Delhi, India to commemorate 30 years of ASEAN-India Dialogue Relations. In recognition of this milestone, the year 2022 is being celebrated as the ASEAN-India Friendship Year as announced by ASEAN and Indian leaders at the 18th ASEAN-India Summit in October 2021.

Hence, the correct option is (A).

**19.** India has contributed USD 500,000 to the UN Women, the United Nations agency for gender equality and women empowerment for their core budget.

India's Permanent Representative to the United Nations T.S.Tirumurti announced that India reaffirmed its partnership of women-led development and gender parity. UN Women Executive Director, Sima Bahous thanked India for its contribution.

Hence, the correct option is (D).

**20.** Highways and Road Transport Minister Nitin Gadkari on 18 August 2022 unveiled India's first Electric Double Decker bus in Mumbai.

Switch Mobility Ltd, a subsidiary of Ashok Leyland, has manufactured this unique electric double-decker bus called 'Switch EiV 22.'

The Switch electric double-decker can carry nearly twice the number of seated passengers compared to a single-decker bus.

Hence, the correct option is (C).

**21.** The $8th$ Meeting of BRICS Communications Ministers was held in virtual mode on $6$ July $2022$ under the presidency of China.

Minister of Railways, Communications, Electronics and Information Technology Ashwini Vaishnav, participated in the meeting. The Ministers decided to work in the field of ICTs in areas identified at the $14th$ BRICS Summit. The Ministers also adopted a Declaration.

Additional Information:

BRICS:

BRICS is a grouping of five major emerging economies - Brazil, Russia, India, China, and South Africa.

Since $2009$ , the governments of the BRICS states have met annually at formal summits.

India hosted the most recent $13th$ BRICS summit on $9$ September $2021$ virtually.

Originally the first four were grouped as "BRIC" before the induction of South Africa in $2010$.

Hence, the correct option is (C).

**22.** The Indian men's table tennis team clinched the gold medal at the 2022 Commonwealth Games in Birmingham on 2 August 2022.

- India defeated Singapore by 3-1 in the final.
- This is India's third gold medal at the CWG in the men's team event having earlier won in 2010 and 2018.
- On 2 August 2022 , the Indian women's lawn bowls team also won its first-ever gold at the Commonwealth Games.

Hence, the correct option is (C).

**23.** 74th edition of Chartered Accountant's Day was observed on 1 July 2022.

The day is celebrated by Institute of Chartered Accountants of India (ICAI). ICAI was established by the Parliament of India in 1949. It is the second-largest accounting and statutory body across the globe. In India, ICAI is the only licensing and regulatory body for the financial audit and accounting profession.

Hence, the correct option is (C).

**24.** Union Minister Jitendra Singh inaugurated India's first Autonomous Navigation facility, TiHAN at the IIT Hyderabad campus on 4 July 2022.

TiHAN (Technology Innovation Hub on Autonomous Navigation) has been developed by the Union Ministry of Science & Technology.

Hence, the correct option is (D).

**25.** To compensate for the damage caused to the crops due to adverse weather and natural calamities, Haryana has launched the Mukhya Mantri Bagwani Bima scheme portal on April 2022 with an initial corpus of Rs 10 crore for the scheme. The scheme compensates a sum of Rs 30,000 per acre for vegetables and Spices and Rs 40,000 per acre for fruits, which will be compensated to the farmers upon claim via four categories such as 25 per cent, 50 per cent, 75 per cent and 100 per cent based

on the survey. The farmer's contribution will be only 5 per cent of the insured amount i.e., Rs 750 per acre for vegetables and Spices and Rs 1000 per acre for fruits.

Hence, the correct option is (D).

**26.** The theme of International Girls in ICT Day 2022 was Access and Safety. It is celebrated every year on the fourth Thursday in April. International Girls in ICT Day aims to inspire a global movement to increase the representation of girls and women in technology.

Hence, the correct option is (A).

**27.** The election was not held in Bihar during March-April 2021.

- Members of the Seventeenth Bihar Legislative Assembly were elected in three parts from October to November.
- The previous Bihar Sixteenth Legislative Assembly's tenure concluded on November 29, 2020.
- Following the elections, incumbent Chief Minister Nitish Kumar was re-sworn in as Chief Minister after being chosen as the leader of the National Democratic Alliance in Bihar, and two new deputy Chief Ministers, Tarkishore Prasad, and Renu Devi were recruited into the new administration.

Hence, the correct option is (B).

**28.** Chief of Army Staff (COAS) General Manoj Pande has proceeded on a 3-day visit to Bangladesh from 18-20 July 2022.

This is the first foreign visit of General Manoj Pande since his assumption as Army Chief. He will be carrying out multiple meetings with senior officials of the security establishment and exchange views on various defence related issues.

Hence, the correct option is (A).

**29.** Virat Kohli has become the first Indian and the second player overall in international cricket history to have played 100 matches each in all three formats of the game in August 2022.

Kohli has now 100 T20's to his name in addition to 102 Tests and 262 ODIs since he made his international debut in August 2008. The first player with the record was New Zealand batter Ross Taylor who retired recently.

Hence, the correct option is (B).

**30.** The Department of Food and Public Distribution will organize a National Conference on Food and Nutrition Security in India on $5$ July $2022$ in New Delhi.

It is aimed at facilitating cross-learning, disseminating best practices for schemes under Public Distribution System, and strengthening the focus on nutritional security. Consumer Affairs Minister Piyush Goyal will address the one-day conference.

Hence, the correct option is (A).

**Q.1** Consider the following statements regarding Bound rates or Bound Tariffs.

1. Bound rate is the maximum rate of duty (tariff) that can be imposed by the importing country on an imported commodity.

2. Bound rate agreed for any commodity at WTO is same for all the members of WTO.

Which of the above statements is/are incorrect?

**A.** 1 only
**B.** 2 only
**C.** Both 1 and 2
**D.** Neither 1 nor 2

**Q.2** The reference to 'primary deficit' in the annual budget documents of the Government of India is:

**A.** Difference between budget deficit and capital deficit of the current financial year

**B.** Difference between current year's revenue deficit and grant for capital formation

**C.** Difference between current year's fiscal deficit and interest payment on previous borrowings

**D.** Difference between revenue deficit and grants to states and local bodies of the current financial year

**Q.3** Which of the following is incorrect regarding the Revenue Budget?

**A.** It details the sources of revenue for the government.

**B.** Corporate tax and excise duty are important constituent of tax revenue of government.

**C.** Mostly the difference between revenue receipts and revenue expenditure is positive.

**D.** Revenue expenditure does not result in the creation of assets.

**Q.4** Consider the following statements:

(1) Headline inflation is a measure of the total inflation within an economy.

(2) Headline inflation is affected by areas of the market which may experience sudden inflationary spikes such as food, vegetables or energy.

Which of the statements given above is/are correct?

**A.** Only 1
**B.** Only 2
**C.** Both 1 and 2
**D.** Neither 1 nor 2

**Q.5** Three of the following statements correctly describe the duties of the Competition Commission of India. Find out the false statement.

**A.** Limiting freedom of trade
**B.** Eliminating practices that adversely affect competition
**C.** Promote and maintain competition
**D.** Protect the interests of consumers

**Q.6** Which of the following can become a part of the National Pension Scheme (NPS)?

**A.** Central government employees
**B.** State government employees
**C.** Unorganized sector workers
**D.** All of the above

**Q.7** Who among the following, first mooted the idea of the Liquidity Trap?

**A.** Alfred Marshall
**B.** John Maynard Keynes
**C.** Milton Friedman
**D.** Adam Smith

**Q.8** Which of the taxes are not covered under Goods and Service Tax (GST)?

*[Territorial Army Officer, 2017]*

**A.** Octrio Tax
**B.** Value added tax
**C.** Central sales tax
**D.** Customs Tax

**Q.9** With reference to Foreign Direct Investment in India, which one of the following is considered its major characteristic?

*[UPSC Prelims, 2020]*

**A.** It is the investment through capital instruments essentially in a listed company.

**B.** It is a largely non-debt creating capital flow.

**C.** It is the investment which involves debt-servicing.

**D.** It is the investment made by foreign institutional investors in the Government securities.

**Q.10** The income elasticity of demand for inferior goods is:

**A.** Less than one
**B.** Less than zero
**C.** Equal to one
**D.** Greater than one

**Q.11** Which of the following factors signifies Perfect competition?

1. All firms produce an identical or homogeneous product

2. There is perfect information and knowledge

3. Large number of buyers and seller.

4. Each firm earns normal profits and no firms can earn super-normal profits.

Select the correct answer using the code given below:

**A.** 1, 2, and 3 only
**B.** 2, and 3 only
**C.** 2, 3, and 4 only
**D.** 1, 2, 3, and 4

**Q.12** Which one of the following cities has emerged as the 'electronic capital' of India?

*[CBSE Class X, 2012]*

**A.** Delhi
**B.** Kolkata
**C.** Bangalore
**D.** Hyderabad

**Q.13** Bank notes and Cheques are examples of which type of money?

**A.** Commodity Money
**B.** Fiat Money
**C.** Fiduciary Money
**D.** Commercial Bank Money

**Q.14** The rate at the Central Bank of a country (Reserve Bank of India) lends money to Commercial Banks in the event of any shortfall of funds is refers to:

**A.** Bank rate      **B.** Repo rate
**C.** Reverse Repo rate      **D.** None of the above

**Q.15** The main focus of the First Five-Year Plan was on the _______.

**A.** service sector
**B.** agricultural and industrial sector
**C.** agricultural sector
**D.** industrial sector

**Q.16** Who is the determinant of the minimum support price?

**A.** Indian Council of Agricultural Research
**B.** State government
**C.** Agricultural Costs and Prices Commission
**D.** None of these

**Q.17** Which of the following statements are correct?

1. When marginal revenue is positive, total revenue increases with an increase in output.
2. When marginal revenue is zero, the total revenue is maximum.
3. When marginal revenue becomes negative, total revenue falls with an increase in output.

Select the correct answer using the code given below:

**A.** 1 and 2 only      **B.** 2 and 3 only
**C.** 1 and 3 only      **D.** 1, 2, and 3

**Q.18** Which of the statements given below is/are not correct with regard to measuring National Income:

**A.** In the product method, the net value added by each component in production is emphasised.
**B.** As per the Consumption method, National income is the summation of total consumption and savings.
**C.** The retirement pension is not included in the National Income.
**D.** The Sale and Purchase of old items are included while measuring the National income.

**Q.19** Which of the following is correct regarding the Revenue Budget?

**A.** It comprises the capital receipts of the government.
**B.** Borrowings and loans of a government are included in revenue receipts.
**C.** Mostly the difference between revenue receipts and revenue expenditure is positive.
**D.** The difference between revenue receipts and revenue expenditure is termed as the revenue deficit.

**Q.20** Auckland in New Zealand has been named the most livable city globally by which of the following?

**A.** International Monetary Fund
**B.** Economist Intelligence Unit
**C.** Organization for Economic Co-operation and Development
**D.** Freedom House

**Q.21** Which country has surpassed China to become India's biggest trading partner in 2021-22?

**A.** USA      **B.** Saudi Arabia
**C.** UAE      **D.** Russia

**Q.22** Which bank has partnered with Hindustan Petroleum Corporation Limited (HPCL) to launch cobranded contactless RuPay Credit Card?

**A.** Bank of Baroda
**B.** State Bank of India
**C.** Punjab National Bank
**D.** Axis Bank

**Q.23** The Reserve Bank of India (RBI) has imposed a penalty of Rs. 45 lakh on _______ for non-compliance with the directions.

**A.** Axis Bank
**B.** Kotak Mahindra Bank
**C.** State Bank of India
**D.** MUFG Bank

**Q.24** The Cabinet Committee on Economic Affairs (CCEA) on May 25, 2022 has cleared the government's 29.5% stake sale in _________.

**A.** Chambal Fertilisers & Chemicals
**B.** Coromandel International
**C.** Allwin Chemical & Fertilizer Ltd
**D.** Hindustan Zinc Ltd (HZL)

**Q.25** Which company has become the first crypto firm to enter the prestigious Fortune 500 list?

**A.** Bitfinex      **B.** BitGo
**C.** BitMain      **D.** Coinbase

**Q.26** Which country has extended a credit line with India by $200 million in order to procure emergency fuel stocks in May 2022?

**A.** Bangladesh      **B.** Myanmar
**C.** Thailand      **D.** Sri Lanka

**Q.27** Which regulatory body imposed a penalty on Daimler Financial Services India and KKR India Financial Services for non-compliance of laws?

**A.** Securities and Exchange Board of India (SEBI)
**B.** Insurance Regulatory and Development Authority
**C.** Competition Commission of India (CCI)
**D.** Reserve Bank of India (RBI)

**Q.28** Which bank has launched an end-to-end digital platform to facilitate co-lending of loans in partnership with NBFCs (Non-Banking Financial Companies)?

**A.** State Bank of India
**B.** Punjab National Bank
**C.** Bank of Baroda
**D.** Bank of India

**Q.29** Which bank has partnered with Worldline India to digitise the e-challan system in May 2022?

**A.** Bank Of India
**B.** State Bank of India
**C.** Punjab National Bank

**D.** Axis Bank

**Q.30** Which bank has signed an MoU with the Central Board of Direct Taxes (CBDT) and Central Board of Indirect Taxes and Customs (CBIC) for tax collection?

**A.** Kotak Mahindra Bank
**B.** Dhanlaxmi Banka
**C.** Federal Bank
**D.** DCB Bank

# // Smart Answer Sheet //

**Correct**    Indicates percentage of students who answered questions correctly.

**Skipped**    Indicates percentage of students who skipped questions.

| Q. | Ans. | Correct / Skipped |
|---|---|---|
| 1 | B | 40.5 % / 37.11 % |
| 2 | C | 66.58 % / 30.58 % |
| 3 | C | 78.17 % / 21.04 % |
| 4 | C | 57.09 % / 31.02 % |
| 5 | A | 45.53 % / 46.31 % |
| 6 | D | 48.19 % / 42.72 % |

| Q. | Ans. | Correct / Skipped |
|---|---|---|
| 7 | B | 63.7 % / 32.73 % |
| 8 | D | 83.73 % / 12.27 % |
| 9 | B | 44.43 % / 43.04 % |
| 10 | B | 69.89 % / 30.09 % |
| 11 | D | 11.58 % / 67.81 % |
| 12 | C | 81.39 % / 17.19 % |

| Q. | Ans. | Correct / Skipped |
|---|---|---|
| 13 | C | 58.77 % / 32.0 % |
| 14 | B | 54.55 % / 34.92 % |
| 15 | C | 58.12 % / 41.82 % |
| 16 | C | 52.97 % / 37.35 % |
| 17 | D | 25.67 % / 70.3 % |
| 18 | D | 20.13 % / 67.11 % |

| Q. | Ans. | Correct / Skipped |
|---|---|---|
| 19 | D | 18.04 % / 78.99 % |
| 20 | B | 22.29 % / 73.76 % |
| 21 | A | 25.86 % / 73.8 % |
| 22 | A | 31.39 % / 67.57 % |
| 23 | D | 26.84 % / 73.08 % |
| 24 | D | 18.25 % / 75.85 % |

| Q. | Ans. | Correct / Skipped |
|---|---|---|
| 25 | D | 15.78 % / 76.81 % |
| 26 | D | 30.94 % / 67.78 % |
| 27 | D | 23.88 % / 74.85 % |
| 28 | C | 16.84 % / 70.66 % |
| 29 | A | 28.1 % / 68.54 % |
| 30 | B | 17.39 % / 70.01 % |

## Performance Analysis

| | |
|---|---|
| Avg. Score (%) | 66.67% |
| Toppers Score (%) | 70.0% |
| Your Score | |

# //Hints and Solutions//

**1.** Bound rate agreed for any commodity at WTO is same for all the members of WTO is incorrect regarding Bound rates or Bound Tariffs.

Bound rate is the maximum rate of duty (tariff) that can be imposed by the importing country on an imported commodity. Here, each country commits itself to a ceiling on customs duties (tariff) on a certain number of products.

These rates vary from country to country and commodity to commodity.

Hence, the correct option is (B).

**2.** Primary deficit refers to the difference between the current year's fiscal deficit and interest payments on previous borrowings. It indicates the borrowing requirements of the government, excluding interest. It also shows how much of the government's expenditure can be met through borrowing, apart from interest payments. Primary deficit indicates the amount of borrowing that the government requires excluding the interest component. Fiscal deficit is the difference between total expenditure and total income of the government. In other words, the primary deficit is the difference between the government's income-expenditure gap and its interest payments on past borrowings.

Hence, the correct option is (C).

**3.** 'Mostly the difference between revenue receipts and revenue expenditure is positive' is incorrect.

The revenue budget comprises the revenue receipts of the government and the expenditure incurred in utilising the revenues. It gives the details of the sources from where the revenue is coming to the government.

- Revenue receipts are divided into tax and non-tax revenue. Tax revenues are taxes such as income tax, corporate tax, excise and other duties that the government levy. While non-tax revenue comprises the disinvestments that the government does in the companies where it is a stakeholder.

- Revenue expenditure is expenditure done for the normal running of government departments and other services etc. It is the expenditure that does not result in the creation of assets. All grants given to state governments and other parties are also treated as revenue expenditure.

- The difference between revenue receipts and revenue expenditure is usually negative because the government spends more than it earns. It is termed as the revenue deficit.

Hence, the correct option is (C).

**4.** Headline inflation encompasses all commodities and is a measure of the total inflation in the economy. Commodities such as food or energy which are much volatile and exhibit inflationary spikes compared to other commodities are also included in this measure. Headline inflation is commonly known as the CPI and includes more volatile food and energy price data, whereas the core inflation index excludes it.

Hence, the correct option is (C).

**5.** Among the given options, limiting freedom of trade is a false statement.

- Competition Commission of India is a statutory body responsible for enforcing the objectives of the Competition Act, 2002.

- CCI was established by the Central Government with effect from 14th October 2003, but it became fully functional on 20th May, 2009.

- Composition- A Chairperson and 6 Members appointed by the Central Government.

- It aims at establishing a competitive environment in the Indian economy through proactive engagement with all the stakeholders, the government, and international jurisdiction.

Hence, the correct option is (A).

**6.** The National Pension System was launched with the objective of providing retirement income to all citizens. The National Pension System aims to usher in pension reforms and promote the habit of saving for retirement among citizens.

- The National Pension Scheme is applicable to all new employees of Central Government Services (other than Armed Forces) and Central Autonomous Bodies joining Government service on or after 1st January, 2004.

- The National Pension Scheme is applicable to all the employees of the State Governments, who join the State Autonomous Bodies services after the date of notification of the respective State Governments.

- Citizens of India must be between the age of 18 to 60 years on the date of submission of their applications, who belong to the unorganized sector or who do not have regular employment in the Central or State Government or an autonomous body of the Central or State Government / If employed in a Public Sector Undertaking, they can open an NPS - Swavalamban - External website that opens in a new window account.

So we can conclude that central government employees, state government employees and unorganized sector employees can become part of the National Pension Scheme (NPS).

Hence, the correct option is (D).

**7.** John Maynard Keynes first mooted the idea of the Liquidity Trap.

A liquidity trap is a contradictory economic situation in which interest rates are very low and savings rates are high, rendering monetary policy ineffective. It was first described by economist John Maynard Keynes. A liquidity trap is when monetary policy becomes ineffective due to very low interest rates combined with consumers who prefer to save rather than invest in higher-yielding bonds or other investments.

Hence, the correct option is (B).

**8.** Customs Tax is not covered under Goods and Service Tax (GST).

Customs Duty is a tax imposed on imports and exports of goods. The rates of customs duties are either specific or on ad valorem basis, that is, it is based on the value of goods.

Hence, the correct option is (D).

**9.** With reference to Foreign Direct Investment in India, it is a largely non-debt creating capital flow is considered its major characteristic.

Foreign Direct Investment (FDI) is the investment by a non-resident entity/person resident outside India in the capital of an Indian company under Foreign Exchange Management (Transfer or Issue of Security by a Person Resident Outside India) Regulations, 2017.

FDI's are long term investment. It is also nondebt creating capital flow as it has no direct repayment obligation for the residents.

Hence, the correct option is (B).

**10.** The income elasticity of demand for inferior goods is less than zero.

Income elasticity of demand is the change in the quantity demanded of a commodity with respect to the percentage change in income. Income elasticity of demand is referred to as the corresponding change in the demand of a product in response to the change in a consumer's income. It can also be defined as the ratio of change in the quantity demanded by the change in the customer's income.

Hence, the correct option is (B).

**11.** From the given statement all the statement is correct.

The term perfect competition is used to describe a market scenario where there are a large number of sellers and buyers who are selling and buying similar goods and services. Since the products and services bought or sold in this market scenario, there are no barriers to entry or exit and the prices are almost identical.

It is difficult to have a market with characteristics that demonstrate perfect competition:

Features:

- Large number of buyers and sellers
- Homogenous product is produced by every firm
- Free entry and exit of firms
- Consumers have perfect knowledge about the market and are well aware of any changes in the market. Consumers indulge in rational decision making
- No government intervention
- Each firm earns normal profits and no firm can earn super-normal profits.

Hence, the correct option is (D).

**12.** Bangalore has emerged as the electronic capital of India.

It plays the maximum role as the country's leading information technology (IT) exporter. It is said to be one of India's largest electronic/IT industrial parks, stretching over 800 acres (3.2 km$^2$).

Hence, the correct option is (C).

**13.** Bank notes and Cheques are examples of fiduciary money.

Fiduciary Money refers to money that is conventionally possessed in trust or promises between Issuer and Bearer. Fiduciary money depends for its value on the confidence that it will be generally accepted as a medium of exchange. It means that fiduciary money are accepted as a means of payment on the basis of trust but not on the basis of any order of the government.

Hence, the correct option is (C).

**14.** The rate at the Central Bank of a country (Reserve Bank of India) lends money to Commercial Banks in the event of any shortfall of funds is refers to Repo rate.

- It is the rate at which the Reserve Bank Of India lends money to commercial banks in India if they face a scarcity of funds.
- It is a rate on short-term, collateral-backed borrowing.
- The Repo rate is used by monetary authorities to control inflation.

Hence, the correct option is (B).

**15.** The main focus of the First Five-Year Plan was on the agricultural sector.

- The First Five Year Plan in India was active between 1951 and 1956.
- The plan was based on the Harrod-Domar model.
- The First Five-Year Plan was presented before the parliament by Jawaharlal Nehru.
- Gulzarilal Nanda was the first Deputy Chairman of the Planning Commission of India.
- Economist K N Raj is known as the architect of this plan.
- It was quasi-successful for the government.
- The target growth rate of the First Five Year Plan was 2.1% annual gross domestic product (GDP) growth.

Hence, the correct option is (C).

**16.** The minimum support prices are announced by the Government of India at the beginning of the sowing season for certain crops on the basis of the recommendations of the Commission for Agricultural Costs and Prices (CACP).

- It may be noted that the cost of production is an important factor that goes as an input in the determination of MSP, but it is certainly not the only factor that determines MSP.
- The Indian government sets the price for 23 commodities twice a year.
- MSP is fixed on the recommendations of the Commission for Agricultural Costs and Prices (CACP) since 2009.

- MSP stands for "Minimum Support Price".

Hence, the correct option is (C).

**17.** The correct answer using the code given below is 1, 2, and 3.

1. Marginal revenue follows the law of diminishing returns, which states that any production increases will result in smaller increases in output.

2. The profit-maximizing quantity and price can be determined by setting marginal revenue equal to zero, which occurs at the maximal level of output.

3. Marginal revenue can even become negative – that is, the total revenue decreases from one output level to the next.

Hence, the correct option is (D).

**18.** Methods of Measuring the National Income:

Product Method:

- It calculates the aggregate value of final goods & services produced in a year.

- It emphasises a calculation of the net contribution at every stage of production.

- This method focuses on the net value added by each of the components in production.

- While calculating National income, the following elements should be excluded from the output of the enterprise:

- Consumption of raw materials.

- Capital consumption.

- Net Indirect Taxes.

Consumption Method:

- Also known as the Expenditure method.

- According to it, Income is either spent on consumption or spent.

- National income is the addition of total consumption & total savings.

- In India, a combination of the Production method & Income method is used to estimate National income.

- National Income = Total expenditure on consumption + Total savings.

- Items not included while measuring the National income are the following:

- Sale and Purchase of Old Items: It is not included in measuring the National Income as they may be included when they were produced.

- Gains from goods & services that are achieved due to inflationary effects.

- Gains from illegal activities are also not included.

- Prohibited items.

- The retirement pension is not included as it is not the subject of final goods & services.

Hence, the correct option is (D).

**19.** The revenue budget comprises the revenue receipts of the government and the expenditure incurred in utilising the revenues. Thus, option 1 is incorrect.

It gives the details of the sources from where the revenue is coming to the government. Revenue receipts are divided into tax and non-tax revenue. Tax revenues are taxes such as income tax, corporate tax, excise, and other duties that the government levy.

While non-tax revenue comprises the disinvestments that the government does in the companies where it is a stakeholder. Revenue expenditure is expenditure done for the normal running of government departments and other services etc.

It is the expenditure that does not result in the creation of assets. All grants given to state governments and other parties are also treated as revenue expenditure.

The difference between revenue receipts and revenue expenditure is usually negative because the government spends more than it earns. Thus, option 3 is incorrect. It is termed the revenue deficit. Thus, option 4 is correct.

Hence, the correct option is (D).

**20.** Auckland in New Zealand has been named the most livable city globally by The Economist Intelligence Unit (EIU).

The livability index ranks cities based on more than 30 qualitative and quantitative factors across five broad categories: stability, health care, culture and environment, education, and infrastructure.

Auckland is followed by Osaka, Adelaide, Wellington, Tokyo, Perth, Zurich, etc.

The Economist Intelligence Unit is the research and analysis division of Economist Group providing forecasting and advisory services through research and analysis.

Hence, the correct option is (B).

**21.** USA has surpassed China to become India's biggest trading partner in 2021-22.

The US has surpassed China to become India's top trading partner in 2021-22. According to the data of the Commerce Ministry, in 2021-22, the bilateral trade between the US and India stood at USD 119.42 billion as against USD 80.51 billion in 2020-21. During 2021-22, India's two-way commerce with China aggregated at USD 115.42 billion as compared to USD 86.4 billion in 2020-21.

Hence, the correct option is (A).

**22.** Bank of Baroda has partnered with Hindustan Petroleum Corporation Limited (HPCL) to launch cobranded contactless RuPay Credit Card.

In partnership with the National Payments Corporation of India (NPCI), BOB Financial and Hindustan Petroleum have launched the HPCL BoB co-branded contactless RuPay Credit Card. The card comes with various features including rewards for spending on utilities, grocery and departmental stores. BOB Financial is a wholly-owned subsidiary of the Bank of Baroda.

Hence, the correct option is (A).

**23.** The Reserve Bank of India (RBI) has imposed a penalty of Rs. 45 lakh on MUFG Bank for non-compliance with the directions.

RBI on May 27, 2022, imposed a penalty of Rs 45 lakh on Japan-based MUFG Bank for non-compliance with the directions on "time-bound implementation and strengthening of SWIFTrelated operational controls'. MUFG Bank is the largest bank in Japan. It was established on January 1, 2006. It is one of the three so-called Japanese "megabanks".

Hence, the correct option is (D).

**24.** The Cabinet Committee on Economic Affairs (CCEA) on May 25, 2022, cleared the government's 29.5% stake sale in Hindustan Zinc Ltd (HZL).

The Cabinet Committee on Economic Affairs (CCEA) on May 25, 2022, cleared the government's 29.5% stake sale in Hindustan Zinc Ltd (HZL), which could fetch around Rs. 38,000 crore to the exchequer. The decision would give a push to the government's disinvestment drive. In 2002, the govt. offloaded a 26% stake in HZL to Sterlite Opportunities and Ventures Ltd for Rs. 445 crore.

Hence, the correct option is (D).

**25.** Coinbase has become the first crypto firm to enter the prestigious Fortune 500 list.

Retail giant Walmart topped the ranking for the 10th straight year, followed by Amazon and Apple. The Fortune 500 is an annual list published by Fortune magazine that ranks 500 of the largest United States corporations by total revenue for their respective fiscal years.

Hence, the correct option is (D).

**26.** Sri Lanka has extended a credit line with India by $200 million in order to procure emergency fuel stocks in May 2022.

Sri Lanka has extended a credit line with India by $200 million in order to procure emergency fuel stocks. Four shipments are due to arrive in May 2022. Sri Lanka's overall inflation surged to nearly 30% in April from 18.7% recorded in March 2022. Sri Lanka has used $400 million, on multiple shipments in April, of the $500 million credit line extended by India earlier in 2022.

Hence, the correct option is (D).

**27.** The RBI on 6 May 2022 imposed a penalty of Rs 5 lakh each on Daimler Financial Services India and KKR India Financial Services. They have been fined for non-compliance with directions related to 'monitoring of frauds in NBFCS". RBI conducted a statutory inspection of the two companies with reference to their financial position as on March 31, 2020.

Hence, the correct option is (D).

**28.** Bank of Baroda has announced the launch of an end-to-end digital platform to facilitate the co-lending of loans in partnership with NBFCs (Non-Banking Financial Companies). It will provide seamless integration between the bank and multiple NBFC partners to accelerate and simplify the co-lending process. It uses rule-based algorithms for underwriting, enables credit assessment checks, etc.

Hence, the correct option is (C).

**29.** Worldline, a payment services firm, has partnered with the Bank of India. A Memorandum of Association was signed between BOI and the police department to integrate Point of Sale (POS) terminals with the e-challan portal of the police department on 10 May 2022. Three zones namely Jabalpur, Rewa, and Shahdol covering 12 districts in MP will be covered in this initiative.

Hence, the correct option is (A).

**30.** Dhanlaxmi Bank has signed a pact with the Central Board of Direct Taxes (CBDT) and Central Board of Indirect Taxes and Customs (CBIC) for tax collection on April 2022. This MoU will help customers to pay their direct taxes and GST payments and other indirect taxes through the branch network and digital platforms of the bank. The bank has been authorized by the Reserve Bank of India (RBI) based on a recommendation from the Controller General of Accounts for the collection of various taxes.

Hence, the correct option is (B).

**Q.1** As per Freud's theory the fundamental technique people use to allay anxiety caused by conflicts:

**A.** Projection       **B.** Reaction Formation
**C.** Repression       **D.** Regression

**Q.2** Introversion-Extraversion trait of personality is propounded by:

*[Rajasthan Teachers Eligibility Test - Level 1 Primary Level (RTET), 2017]*

**A.** Hans Eysenck       **B.** R.B. Cattle
**C.** Gordon Allport       **D.** Carl Jung

**Q.3** Who has classified introvert personality and extrovert personality?

**A.** Freud    **B.** Jung    **C.** Munn    **D.** Allport

**Q.4** Which of the following cannot be included under the concept of personality?

**A.** The way a person talks.
**B.** The way a person acts.
**C.** The way a person decides.
**D.** The way a person moves.

**Q.5** Which of the following is not an unstandardized test or subjective method for evaluating personality?

**A.** Graphology       **B.** Score card
**C.** Anecdotal Records       **D.** Sociometry

**Q.6** Your description of who you are as a person is your:

**A.** Self awareness       **B.** Self esteem
**C.** Self concept       **D.** Self disclose

**Q.7** In Carl Rogers' theory, the main structure of personality is the:

**A.** Ego       **B.** Superego
**C.** Self       **D.** None of the above

**Q.8** Which of the following is projective technique of personality measurement?

*[UPTET Science and Maths, 2019], [UPTET Social Studies, 2019]*

**A.** Rating scale
**B.** Observation
**C.** Interview
**D.** Thematic Apperception test

**Q.9** "The personality of an adopted child is influenced by his/her biological parents." This statement is:

**A.** True       **B.** False
**C.** Not indentified       **D.** None of the above

**Q.10** OCEAN theory is a:

**A.** Theory of perception
**B.** Theory of personality
**C.** Theory of intelligence
**D.** None of the above

**Q.11** Child Apperception Test (CAT) method of Personality measurement was given by:

**A.** Skinner    **B.** Bellak    **C.** Holland    **D.** Murray

**Q.12** A person with strong sexual urges channelizes the energy into religious fervour. He is using:

**A.** Projection       **B.** Reaction Formation
**C.** Rationalization       **D.** Regression

**Q.13** Projective tests are also called:

**A.** Death methods
**B.** Unstructured tests
**C.** Self report inventories
**D.** Both 1&2

**Q.14** According to Freud's recommended personality structure, which of the following would satisfy its fundamental urges immediately and reflexively as they arose, without regard to rules, the reality of life, or morals of any kind?

*[RTET - Level 2 (Social Studies), 2017]*

**A.** Superego
**B.** Both ego and Super-ego
**C.** Id
**D.** Ego

**Q.15** The determinants of personality are:

**A.** Social       **B.** Cultural
**C.** Biological       **D.** All of the above

**Q.16** Who has not given any trait theory of personality?

**A.** Kretschmer       **B.** Cattell
**C.** Allport       **D.** None of the above

**Q.17** Due to which development at the age 4 to 5 years male child shows affectionate behaviour towards his mother and opposite to his father?

*[Haryana Primary Teacher (PRT), 2019]*

**A.** Pituitary gland       **B.** Thyroid gland
**C.** Electra complex       **D.** Oedipus complex

**Q.18** Which type of learning mainly influences the personality of the child?

**A.** Trial and Error learning
**B.** Imitation learning
**C.** Insightful learning
**D.** Instructional learning

**Q.19** Phrenologists tried to find out about personality by:

**A.** Reading a person's horoscope
**B.** Feeling a person's skull
**C.** Looking at a person's hands
**D.** Asking people questions

**Q.20** Which of the following personality types is described as noisy, callous and fond of physical activity?

| | |
|---|---|
| **A.** Endomorph | **B.** Ectomorph |
| **C.** Mesomorph | **D.** None of the above |

**B.** Archetypes
**C.** Personal unconscious
**D.** Complex

**Q.21** The ego obeys the ___ principle.

| | |
|---|---|
| **A.** Pleasure | **B.** Reality |
| **C.** Moral | **D.** Perfection |

**Q.22** Which of the following systems the internalized representation of the values and morals of society is as taught to the child by the parents and others?

| | |
|---|---|
| **A.** Id | **B.** Ego |
| **C.** Super ego | **D.** Libido |

**Q.23** The method of reducing anxiety called _____ is to push the impulse out of awareness into the unconscious.

| | |
|---|---|
| **A.** Regression | **B.** Repression |
| **C.** Suppression | **D.** Ration |

**Q.24** _____ have been devised as one method for uncovering unconscious motives.

**A.** Inventory
**B.** Projective tests
**C.** Behavioural assessment
**D.** Situational tests

**Q.25** _____refers to the characteristic patterns of behaviour and way of thinking that determine a person's adjustment to his environment.

| | |
|---|---|
| **A.** Motivation | **B.** Personality |
| **C.** Development | **D.** Thinking |

**Q.26** ___ defined personality as the dynamic organization within the individual of those psycho-physical systems that determine his unique adjustment to his environment.

| | |
|---|---|
| **A.** Sheldon | **B.** Gordon Allport |
| **C.** Kwarren | **D.** Freud |

**Q.27** Which of the following scales has been useful in measuring anxiety, hostility, and hallucination, phobias and suicidal impulses?

| | |
|---|---|
| **A.** 16 PF | **B.** MMPI |
| **C.** TAT | **D.** Adjective checklist |

**Q.28** According to psycho-analytic theory, the sexual energy that underlines the biologically based urges is called the:

**A.** Ego
**B.** Defense mechanisms
**C.** Libido
**D.** Oedipus

**Q.29** Which of the following approaches of personality emphasizes on-going inter-actions among motives, impulses and psychological processes?

**A.** Type and trait approaches
**B.** Dynamic approach
**C.** Learning and behavioural approaches
**D.** None of the above

**Q.30** According to Jung _____ are inherited ways of organizing, or reacting to our experience with the world.

**A.** Collective unconscious

# // Smart Answer Sheet //

**Correct** Indicates percentage of students who answered questions correctly.

**Skipped** Indicates percentage of students who skipped questions.

| Q. | Ans. | Correct / Skipped |
|---|---|---|
| 1 | C | 66.62 % / 31.44 % |
| 2 | A | 88.64 % / 10.17 % |
| 3 | B | 57.7 % / 37.5 % |
| 4 | C | 63.77 % / 32.04 % |
| 5 | A | 45.09 % / 39.93 % |
| 6 | C | 48.46 % / 37.87 % |

| Q. | Ans. | Correct / Skipped |
|---|---|---|
| 7 | C | 61.63 % / 30.57 % |
| 8 | D | 63.86 % / 31.37 % |
| 9 | A | 81.11 % / 13.79 % |
| 10 | B | 69.45 % / 30.37 % |
| 11 | B | 84.34 % / 13.54 % |
| 12 | B | 77.46 % / 19.97 % |

| Q. | Ans. | Correct / Skipped |
|---|---|---|
| 13 | B | 44.55 % / 32.72 % |
| 14 | C | 61.9 % / 32.32 % |
| 15 | D | 67.95 % / 30.45 % |
| 16 | A | 54.83 % / 34.78 % |
| 17 | D | 64.27 % / 34.62 % |
| 18 | B | 82.22 % / 17.19 % |

| Q. | Ans. | Correct / Skipped |
|---|---|---|
| 19 | B | 82.56 % / 15.76 % |
| 20 | C | 86.89 % / 10.78 % |
| 21 | B | 79.33 % / 19.02 % |
| 22 | C | 51.51 % / 30.5 % |
| 23 | B | 80.43 % / 10.03 % |
| 24 | B | 47.3 % / 50.8 % |

| Q. | Ans. | Correct / Skipped |
|---|---|---|
| 25 | B | 77.82 % / 19.95 % |
| 26 | B | 66.86 % / 30.96 % |
| 27 | B | 55.48 % / 31.82 % |
| 28 | C | 68.56 % / 30.64 % |
| 29 | B | 28.85 % / 68.83 % |
| 30 | A | 43.83 % / 30.56 % |

## Performance Analysis

| | |
|---|---|
| Avg. Score (%) | 56.67% |
| Toppers Score (%) | 56.67% |
| Your Score | |

# //Hints and Solutions//

**1.** As per Freud's theory the fundamental technique people use to allay anxiety caused by conflicts Repression.

According to Freud, much of human behaviour reflects an attempt to deal with or escape from anxiety. Thus, how the ego deals with anxiety largely determines how people behave. Freud believed that people avoid anxiety mainly by developing defence mechanisms that try to defend the ego against the awareness of the instinctual needs. Thus, a defence mechanism is a way of reducing anxiety by distorting reality. The most important is repression, in which anxiety-provoking behaviours or thoughts are totally allayed by the unconscious. When people repress a feeling or desire, they become totally unaware of that wish or desire.
Hence, the correct option is (C).

**2.** Introversion-Extraversion trait of personality is propounded by Hans Eysenck.

Hans Eysenck (1916-1997): British psychologist Hans Eysenck developed a model of personality basic upon just three universal traits; Introversion/Extroversion, Neuroticism/Emotional stability, and Psychoticism. Eysenck sees only two major types or traits as underlying personality structure: introversion-extraversion and stability-neuroticism. Introversion involves directing attention to inner experiences. while extraversion relates to focusing attention outward on other people and the environment. So, a person high in introversion might be quiet and reserved, while an individual high in extraversion might be sociable and outgoing.
Hence, the correct option is (A).

**3.** Jung has classified introvert personality and extrovert personality.

Carl Jung personality theory is known as an analytic theory or analytical psychology. Carl Jung suggested that all human beings share certain unconscious ideas, because we are all human and were created from similar evolutionary circumstances and common ancestors. The unconscious that we all share is called the collective unconscious. Each individual has his own self-actualization. Jung expressed libido in a very comprehensive way, he equated libido as life energy. In light of libido, Jung proposed two types of personalities- extroverts and introverts. The persons in whom life energy (libido) flows inward are known as introvert, while, persons whom the life energy flows outward are termed as an extrovert.
Hence, the correct option is (B).

**4.** The way a person decides cannot be included under the concept of personality.

The term "personality" is derived from the Latin word "persona" which means the mask worn by the Roman actors? In this sense, personality means the individual as seen by others. Personality is the totality of everything about a person his/her physical, emotional, mental, social, ethical and spiritual make-up.

In simple terms, personality consists of the following:

- The way you look.
- The way you dress.
- The way you talk.
- The way you walk.
- The way you act.

Hence, the correct option is (C).

**5.** Graphology is not an unstandardized test or subjective method for evaluating personality.

Graphology is the analysis of handwriting with attempt to determine someone's personality traits. No scientific evidence exists to support graphology, and it is generally considered a pseudoscience or scientifically questionable practice. The term is sometimes incorrectly used to refer to forensic document examination, due to the fact that aspects of the latter dealing with the examination of handwritten documents are occasionally referred to as graphanalysis.
Hence, the correct option is (A).

**6.** Your description of who you are as a person is your Self concept.

Self-concept:

- It is used to refer to how someone thinks about, evaluates, perceives, or describes themselves. To be aware of oneself is to have a concept of oneself.
- The self-concept is the accumulation of knowledge about the self, such as. beliefs regarding personality traits, physical characteristics, abilities, values, goals, and roles.
- In an individual, the self-concept becomes more abstract, complex, and hierarchically organized into cognitive mental representations or self-schemas, which direct the processing of self-relevant information.
- The self-concept the way in which one perceives oneself-can be divided into categories, such as:
- personal self-concept (facts or one's own opinions about oneself, such as "II have brown eyes" or "I am attractive"); social self-concept (one's perceptions about how one is regarded by others: "people think I have a great sense of humor"); and self-ideals (what or how one would like to be: "I want to be a lawyer" or "I wish I were thinner").

Hence, the correct option is (C).

**7.** In Carl Rogers' theory, the main structure of personality is the Self.

Carl Rogers, an American humanistic psychologist belonged to the school of humanism. He propagated the humanistic theories of learning. He tried to distinguish two types of learning-cognitive and experiential. The theory of experiential learning by Carl Rogers: It is associated with the effective application of the acquired knowledge. It is self-initiated as the learner willingly takes the initiative to engage in such type of learning. The learner himself evaluates the results and outcomes of such learning by, applying it to the realization of learning objectives. It leaves a pervasive effect on the learner. Whatever is learned through this method can be made into use when and where he needs it.
Hence, the correct option is (C).

**8.** Thematic Apperception test is projective technique of personality measurement.

The Thematic Apperception Test, or TAT, is a type of projective test that involves describing ambiguous scenes. Popularly known as the "picture interpretation technique," it was developed by American psychologists Henry A. To date, the TAT is one of the most widely researched and clinically used personality tests. The TAT is a widely used projective test for the assessment of children and adults. It is designed to reveal an individual's perception of interpersonal relationships. Thirty-one picture cards serve as stimuli for stories and descriptions about relationships or social situations.
Hence, the correct option is (D).

**9.** "The personality of an adopted child is influenced by his/her biological parents." This statement is True.

Personality is something unique and specific. Each one of us is a unique person in oneself. Every one of us has specific characteristics for making adjustments. However, the uniqueness of an individual's personality does not mean that he has nothing to share with others in term of traits and characteristics of personality. Biological Determinants of Personality: Genetic Determinants,Heredity is of two types: Biological heredity which is the child inherits from his forefathers in the form of chromosome and second is social heredity, which means all that one generation gets from the preceding generation in the form of social tradition, customs, skills etc. Each generation transmits the acquired skills and knowledge to the succeeding generations.
Hence, the correct option is (A).

**10.** OCEAN theory is a Theory of personality.

It is described by the acronym OCEAN (openness, conscientiousness, extraversion, agreeableness and neuroticism).

- Openness includes traits related to intellect, imagination, insightful, artistic and creative.

- Conscientiousness includes being careful, thoughtful and organized. It includes paying attention to details, planning, goal-directed behaviour and impulse control.

- Extraversion includes traits like sociability, energetic, excitability, gregarious and assertive. There is high emotional expressiveness.

- Agreeableness refers to trustfulness, being helpful, kind, affection, prosocial and altruistic behaviour.

- Neuroticism refers to traits like being anxious, moody and irritability. There is lack of emotional stability. Each of these five traits are thus higher-order traits that consists of several inter-related lower-order traits.
Hence, the correct option is (B).

**11.** Child Apperception Test (CAT) method of Personality measurement was given by Bellak.

The CAT, developed by Bellak and Bellak (1949), is based on the adult Thematic Apperception Test. The TAT, created by psychologist Henry A. Murray uses a standard series of 31 picture cards in assessing the perception of interpersonal relationships.

- The main purpose of the CAT is to assess the personality, level of maturity, and, often, the psychological health of the children.

- The theory is that a child's responses to a series of drawings of animals in familiar situations are likely to reveal significant aspects of a child's personality.

- Some of these dimensions of personality include a level of reality testing and judgment, control and regulation of drives, defences, conflicts, and level of autonomy.

- The obtained responses are analysed and the personality of the child is delineated which may consist of dominant drives, emotions, sentiments, conflicts and complexes.

Hence, the correct option is (B).

**12.** A person with strong sexual urges channelizes the energy into religious fervour. He is using Reaction Formation.

In reaction formation, a person defends against anxiety by adopting behaviours opposite to her/his true feelings. A person with strong sexual urges, who channels her/his energy into religious fervour, presents a classical example of reaction formation.
Hence, the correct option is (B).

**13.** Projective tests are also called Unstructured tests.

With unstructured test cycles, QA engineers perform their own functional tests without the guidance of test cases or test scripts, experiencing and testing the application as end-users with no prior knowledge. In psychology, a projective test is a personality test designed to let a person respond to ambiguous stimuli, presumably revealing hidden emotions and internal conflicts projected by the person into the test.
Hence, the correct option is (B).

**14.** According to Freud's recommended personality structure, Id would satisfy its fundamental urges immediately and reflexively as they arose, without regard to rules, the reality of life, or morals of any kind.

Id is the unconscious part of the human personality that works to fulfill basic desires. It is based on the pleasure principle which aspires for the satisfaction of antisocial desires. It is the basic personality component that is present since birth and seeks to satisfy sexual wishes. The id would satisfy its fundamental urges immediately and reflexively as they arose without regard to rules, the realities of life, or morals of any kind.
Hence, the correct option is (C).

**15.** The determinants of personality are Social, Cultural, Biological.

Determinants of Personality:

Biological factors: An individual's physical attributes, inherited diseases, temperament level, heredity as well as the role of the brain makes up the biological factors.

Cultural factors: Culture is a combination of beliefs, values, norms, customs and techniques for dealing with the environment which is shared among a particular community and transmitted by one generation to the next.

Social factors: An individual's family and social groups, the status of the family, behavioural patterns, etc. constitute the social factors that determines the personality of an individual.
Hence, the correct option is (D).

**16.** Kretschmer has not given any trait theory of personality.

Personality traits are "enduring patterns of perceiving, relating to, and thinking about the environment and oneself that are exhibited in a wide range of social and personal contexts." Traits are the building blocks and human behavior can be described in terms of these traits. A trait is what we call a characteristic way in which an individual perceives, feels, believes, or acts.

Kretschmer was a German psychiatrist who on the basis of his observation of patients classified people into four types. He used the physical constitution and temperament for this purpose The four types he talked about included:

1. Piknik type

2. Asthenic type

3. Athletic type

4. Dysplastic type.
Hence, the correct option is (A).

**17.** Due to Oedipus complex at the age 4 to 5 years male child shows affectionate behaviour towards his mother and opposite to his father.

Oedipus complex: Boy's sense of affection for his mother. Feeling of rivalry for the father. A threat of getting punished by the father for having a desire for the mother.
Hence, the correct option is (D).

**18.** Imitation learning mainly influences the personality of the child.

Imitation learning techniques aim to mimic human behavior in a given task. An agent (a learning machine) is trained to perform a task from demonstrations by learning a mapping between observations and actions. Methods for designing and evaluating imitation learning tasks are categorized and reviewed.
Hence, the correct option is (B).

**19.** Phrenologists tried to find out about personality by Feeling a person's skull.

Phrenology is a process that involves observing and/or feeling the skull to determine an individual's psychological attributes. Franz Joseph Gall believed that the brain was made up of 27 individual organs that determined personality, the first 19 of these 'organs' he believed to exist in other animal species.
Hence, the correct option is (B).

**20.** Mesomorph personality types is described as noisy, callous and fond of physical activity.

Mesomorphs have large bone structure, well-defined muscles, broad shoulders, narrow waists, and attractive, strong bodies. According to Sheldon, mesomorphs are adventurous, assertive, competitive, and fearless. They are curious and enjoy trying new things, but can also be obnoxious and aggressive.
Hence, the correct option is (C).

**21.** The ego obeys the Reality principle.

In Freudian psychology and psychoanalysis, the reality principle is the ability of the mind to assess the reality of the external world, and to act upon it accordingly, as opposed to acting on the pleasure principle. Allowing the individual to defer (put off) instant gratification, the reality principle is the governing principle of the actions taken by the ego, after its slow development from a "pleasure-ego" into a "reality-ego".
Hence, the correct option is (B).

**22.** Super ego is representation of the values and morals of society is as taught to the child by the parents and others.

Superego, in the psychoanalytic theory of Sigmund Freud, the latest developing of three agencies (with the id and ego) of the human personality. The superego is the ethical component of the personality and provides the moral standards by which the ego operates. According to Sigmund Freud's psychoanalytic theory of personality, the superego is the component of personality composed of the internalized ideals that we have acquired from our parents and society.
Hence, the correct option is (C).

**23.** The method of reducing anxiety called Repression is to push the impulse out of awareness into the unconscious.

Repression is a psychological defense mechanism in which unpleasant thoughts or memories are pushed from the conscious mind. An example might be someone who does not recall abuse in their early childhood, but still has problems with connection, aggression and anxiety resulting from the unremembered trauma. Repression is the unconscious blocking of unpleasant emotions, impulses, memories, and thoughts from your conscious mind.
Hence, the correct option is (B).

**24.** Projective tests have been devised as one method for uncovering unconscious motives.

Projective tests are sets of ambiguous stimuli, such as ink blots or incomplete sentences, and the individual responds with the first thought or series of thoughts that come to mind or tells a story about each stimulus. Projective tests are used less often because they are more complicated to administer and score, and their results are viewed as less objective.
Hence, the correct option is (B).

**25.** Personality refers to the characteristic patterns of behaviour and way of thinking that determine a person's adjustment to his environment.

Personality is defined as the characteristic sets of behaviors, cognitions, and emotional patterns that evolve from biological and environmental factors. While there is no generally agreed upon definition of personality, most theories focus on motivation and psychological interactions with one's environment. A large new study published in Nature Human Behavior, however, provides evidence for the existence of at least four personality types: average, reserved, self-centered and role model.
Hence, the correct option is (B).

**26.** Gordon Allport defined personality as the dynamic organization within the individual of those psycho-physical

systems that determine his unique adjustment to his environment.

Gordon Allport (1961): Personality is a dynamic. organization, inside the person, of psychophysical. systems that create the person's characteristic. patterns of behavior, thoughts, and feelings. Gordon Allport was a pioneering psychologist often referred to as one of the founders of personality psychology. He rejected two of the dominant schools of thought in psychology at the time, psychoanalysis and behaviorism, in favor of his own approach that stressed the importance of individual differences and situational variables.
Hence, the correct option is (B).

**27.** MMPI scales has been useful in measuring anxiety, hostility, and hallucination, phobias and suicidal impulses.

The Minnesota Multiphasic Personality Inventory (MMPI) is one of the most commonly used psychological tests in the world. The MMPI-2 is designed with 10 clinical scales which assess 10 major categories of abnormal human behavior, and four validity scales, which assess the person's general test-taking attitude and whether they answered the items on the test in a truthful and accurate manner.
Hence, the correct option is (B).

**28.** According to psycho-analytic theory, the sexual energy that underlines the biologically based urges is called the Libido.

Libido is a person's overall sexual drive or desire for sexual activity. In psychoanalytic theory libido is psychic drive or energy, particularly associated with sexual instinct, but also present in other instinctive desires and drives. Libido is influenced by biological, psychological, and social factors.
Hence, the correct option is (C).

**29.** Dynamic approach of personality emphasizes on-going inter-actions among motives, impulses and psychological processes.

Dynamic systems approach theory, we present Personality Dynamics model – a novel framework that captures people's typical pattern of changes in personality states using three model parameters: baseline personality, reflecting the stable set point around which one's states fluctuate, per- sonality variability, or the extent to which one's personality states fluctuate across time and situations, and per- sonality attractor force, pertaining to the swiftness with which deviations of one's baseline are pulled back to the baseline.
Hence, the correct option is (B).

**30.** According to Jung Collective unconscious are inherited ways of organizing, or reacting to our experience with the world.

Collective unconscious refers to the unconscious mind and shared mental concepts. It is generally associated with idealism and was coined by Carl Jung. The collective unconscious is a concept originally defined by psychoanalyst Carl Jung. Sometimes referred to as the "objective psyche," it refers to the idea that a segment of the deepest unconscious mind is genetically inherited and is not shaped by personal experience.
Hence, the correct option is (A).

**Q.1** Which is the largest Mammal?

**A.** Blue Whale  **B.** African Elephant

**C.** Hippopotamus  **D.** Polar bear

**Q.2** Chemically silk fibers are predominantly_____.

**A.** Protein

**B.** Carbohydrate

**C.** Complex lipid

**D.** Mixture of polysaccharide and fat

**Q.3** The pressure exerted on the ground by a man is greatest:

**A.** When he lies down on the ground

**B.** When he stands on the toes of one foot

**C.** When he stands with both feet flat on the ground

**D.** All of the above yield the same pressure

**Q.4** Which one of the following is the best conductor of electricity?

**A.** Mica  **B.** Copper  **C.** Gold  **D.** Silver

**Q.5** The resistance of a semiconductor on heating:

**A.** Remains constant  **B.** Decreases

**C.** Increases  **D.** None of the above

**Q.6** Anemophily defines as:

**A.** It is the pollination by sunlight.

**B.** It is the pollination by wind.

**C.** It is the pollination by both wind and sunlight.

**D.** None of the above

**Q.7** Milk is a:

**A.** Emulsion  **B.** Suspension

**C.** Foam  **D.** Gel

**Q.8** Nylon is made up of:

**A.** Polyamide  **B.** Polyester

**C.** Polyethylene  **D.** Polypropylene

**Q.9** The casual organism of Polio is:

**A.** A fungi  **B.** A virus

**C.** A worm  **D.** A bacteria

**Q.10** The unit of electric power is:

*[Bihar PSC, 2019], [Bihar PSC, 2018]*

**A.** Ampere  **B.** Volt

**C.** Coulomb  **D.** Watt

**Q.11** Man perceives sound vibrations in the frequency ranges of:

**A.** 0 - 5 Hz  **B.** 6 - 10 Hz

**C.** 11-15 Hz  **D.** 20 - 20000 Hz

**Q.12** Blindspot in the human eye can be located at:

**A.** Left end of Ciliary muscles

**B.** Junction of the optic nerve and the retina

**C.** Centre of eye Lens

**D.** Both ends of Cornea

**Q.13** Which of the following raw materials is required in the largest quantity in the manufacture of Steel?

**A.** Coal  **B.** Iron Ore

**C.** Limestone  **D.** Potash

**Q.14** A plant that grows in waters of high salinity is called_____.

**A.** Halophytes  **B.** Oxylophytes

**C.** Psammophytes  **D.** Chasmophytes

**Q.15** Which of the following is the reason for orange color of Carrot?

**A.** It grows in the soil.

**B.** It contains carotene.

**C.** It is not exposed to sunlight.

**D.** The entire plant is orange in colour.

**Q.16** What happens to a helium atom when it loses an electron?

**A.** It becomes an alpha particle.

**B.** It becomes a negative helium Ion.

**C.** It becomes a positive Helium ion.

**D.** It becomes a proton.

**Q.17** Electron microscope works on which of the following principles?

**A.** Optical interference

**B.** Wave Nature of electrons

**C.** Motion of charged particle in electromagnetic fields

**D.** Faraday's law of Electromagnetic induction

**Q.18** The acceleration due to gravity on any planet does not depend on which of the following?

**A.** Radius of the planet

**B.** Mass of the planet

**C.** Density of the planet

**D.** Mass of the object

**Q.19** Which of the following phenomenon is the basis of an electric generator?

**A.** Electromagnetic Induction

**B.** Ferroelectric effect

**C.** Telluric currents

**D.** Electroluminescence

**Q.20** What is the susceptibility of a diamagnetic material?

**A.** Positive and small  **B.** Positive and large

**C.** Negative  **D.** None of these

**Q.21** Name the sugars present in honey ________.

**A.** Levulose  **B.** Maltose

**C.** Dextrose  **D.** All of the above

**Q.22** When the water is heated from 0°C to 10°C, its volume
_____________.

A. will increase
B. will decrease
C. first decreases, then increases
D. will remain constant

**Q.23** Plaster of Paris consists of a fine white powder of ______
sulphate.

A. Sodium
B. Calcium
C. Magnesium
D. Barium

**Q.24** The chemical used for making tooth pastes white is
_________.

A. Calcium carbon
B. Sodium carbonate
C. Titanium dioxide
D. Zinc oxide

**Q.25** Compressed Natural Gas (CNG) is mainly:

A. Ethane
B. Propane
C. Methane
D. Butane

**Q.26** Dioptre is unit of ________.

A. Power of a lens
B. The focal length of a lens
C. Intensity of light
D. Intensity of sound

**Q.27** The value of Avogadro constant is _____ $\times 10^{23}$.

A. 7.022
B. 5.022
C. 8.022
D. 6.022

**Q.28** Which glass is used to make spectacles?

A. Soda glass
B. Potash glass
C. Crookes glass
D. Jena glass

**Q.29** The acid present in soft drinks is:

A. Carbonic acid
B. Tartaric acid
C. Malic acid
D. Salicylic acid

**Q.30** A plant cell without cell wall is called:

A. Proplast
B. Protoplast
C. Nucleoplasm
D. Explant

# // Smart Answer Sheet //

**Correct**    Indicates percentage of students who answered questions correctly.

**Skipped**    Indicates percentage of students who skipped questions.

| Q. | Ans. | Correct / Skipped |
|----|------|-------------------|
| 1 | A | 77.46 % / 19.38 % |
| 2 | A | 77.8 % / 21.02 % |
| 3 | B | 80.54 % / 18.73 % |
| 4 | D | 85.27 % / 14.58 % |
| 5 | B | 88.96 % / 10.57 % |
| 6 | B | 77.15 % / 16.43 % |
| 7 | A | 77.96 % / 17.84 % |
| 8 | A | 84.07 % / 13.39 % |
| 9 | B | 80.11 % / 16.4 % |
| 10 | D | 88.36 % / 11.51 % |
| 11 | D | 86.27 % / 12.99 % |
| 12 | B | 85.23 % / 13.14 % |
| 13 | A | 88.43 % / 11.51 % |
| 14 | A | 79.89 % / 16.16 % |
| 15 | B | 86.63 % / 11.22 % |
| 16 | C | 87.93 % / 10.02 % |
| 17 | B | 81.01 % / 17.65 % |
| 18 | D | 89.83 % / 10.05 % |
| 19 | A | 78.24 % / 11.8 % |
| 20 | C | 85.29 % / 10.66 % |
| 21 | D | 85.62 % / 14.2 % |
| 22 | C | 87.23 % / 11.6 % |
| 23 | B | 89.53 % / 10.3 % |
| 24 | C | 89.54 % / 10.19 % |
| 25 | C | 83.74 % / 13.64 % |
| 26 | A | 78.54 % / 14.1 % |
| 27 | D | 89.15 % / 10.82 % |
| 28 | C | 89.12 % / 10.57 % |
| 29 | A | 80.95 % / 19.01 % |
| 30 | B | 81.74 % / 14.53 % |

## Performance Analysis

| | |
|---|---|
| **Avg. Score (%)** | **46.67%** |
| **Toppers Score (%)** | **66.67%** |
| **Your Score** | |

# //Hints and Solutions//

**1.** The Blue whale is a marine mammal. Its length has been seen at 30 meters. It is the largest animal in present-day animals.
Hence, the correct option is (A).

**2.** Silk is a natural protein fiber, some forms of which can be woven into textiles.

The protein fiber of silk is composed mainly of fibroin and is produced by certain insect larvae to form cocoons.
Hence, the correct option is (A).

**3.** The pressure exerted on the ground will be largest if the area in contact with the ground is the smallest.

So, when a person stand on his toes, the pressure will be greatest.
Hence, the correct option is (B).

**4.** Silver electrons are free to flow compared to other elements, hence the best conductor of electricity is silver.
Hence, the correct option is (D).

**5.** As the temperature of semiconductors increases, the valence band's electrons get enough energy to escape from the confines of their atoms. Consequently, Increasing the heat of the semiconductors, electrical conductivity increases, the resistance decreases.
Hence, the correct option is (B).

**6.** Anemophily or wind pollination is a form of pollination whereby pollen is distributed by wind. Almost all gymnosperms are anemophilous, as are many plants in the order Poales, including grasses, sedges and rushes.
Hence, the correct option is (B).

**7.** An emulsion is a mixture of two or more liquids that are normally immiscible (unblendable). The emulsion is used when both the dispersed and the continuous phase are liquid. Examples of emulsions include vinaigrettes, milk, and some cutting fluids for metalworking.
Hence, the correct option is (A).

**8.** Nylon is a generic designation for a family of synthetic polymers, more specifically aliphatic or semi-aromatic polyamides. They can be melt-processed into fibers, films, or shapes.
Hence, the correct option is (A).

**9.** Polio is a highly infectious disease caused by a virus. Its causative agent, poliovirus, was identified in 1908 by Karl Landsteiner. The polio virus invades the nervous system. And can cause total paralysis in a matter of hours.
Hence, the correct option is (B).

**10.** Electric power is defined as the rate, per unit time, at which electrical energy is transferred by an electric circuit.

The SI unit of power is the watt, one joule per second.

Ampere- Electric Current

Volt- Electric Potential (Voltage)

Coulomb- Electric Charge
Hence, the correct option is (D).

**11.** The frequencies at which a human being can perceive sound are between 20 Hertz and 20,000 Hertz. It is within these frequencies ranges that people can communicate with each other and listen to music.
Hence, the correct option is (D).

**12.** Blindspot in the human eye can be located at the junction of the optic nerve and the retina.

**Blindspot:** The eye lens focuses light on the back of the eye, on a layer called the retina. The retina contains several nerve cells. Sensations felt by the nerve cells are then transmitted to the brain through the optic nerve. At the junction of the optic nerve and the retina, there are no sensory cells, so no vision is possible at that spot. This is called the blind spot.

Hence, the correct option is (B).

**13.** Steelmaking is the process of producing steel from iron ore and scrap.

In steelmaking, impurities such as nitrogen, silicon, phosphorus, sulfur, and excess carbon are removed from the raw iron, and alloying elements such as manganese, nickel, chromium, and vanadium are added to produce different grades of steel.

Limiting dissolved gases such as nitrogen and oxygen, and entrained impurities (termed "inclusions") in the steel is also important to ensure the quality of the products cast from the liquid steel.

To manufacture one tonne of steel, the following are needed:

- 8 tonnes of coal
- 4 tonnes of iron ore
- 1 tonne of limestone.

Hence, the correct option is (A).

**14.** A halophyte is a plant that grows in waters of high salinity, coming into contact with saline water through its roots or by salt sprays, such as in saline semi-deserts, mangrove swamps, marshes and sloughs and seashores.

Hence, the correct option is (A).

**15.** Carrot is orange in color because it contains β-carotene. β-carotene is a strongly colored red-orange pigment abundant in plants and fruits. It is an organic compound.

Hence, the correct option is (B).

**16.** When a helium atom loses electrons, it get positive charge because the number of protons in the helium atom becomes greater than the number of electrons. When helium atom loses one electron it becomes positive ion with +1 charge.

Hence, the correct option is (C).

**17.** Electron microscope works on the principle of Wave Nature of electrons. Electron microscopes use an electron beam instead of visible light and an electron detector instead of our eyes. An electron beam allows us to see at very small scales because electrons can also behave as light due to its wave nature.

Hence, the correct option is (B).

**18.** The value of acceleration due to gravity on any planet depends upon the mass, radius and density of the planet and it is independent of the mass, shape and density of the object placed on the surface of the planet.

Hence, the correct option is (D).

**19.** Electromagnetic Induction is the phenomenon used for the electric generator. In an electric generator, mechanical energy is used to rotate a conductor in a magnetic field to produce electricity. Electromagnetic induction is a phenomenon in which a changing magnetic field across a loop of wire results in the generation of an induced emf. When there is relative motion between a magnet and the coil, magnetic flux changes and therefore an electromotive force is generated in the coil. This electromotive force generates induced current.

Hence, the correct option is (A).

**20.** Magnetic susceptibility is the degree to which a material can be magnetized in an external magnetic field. In terms of the susceptibility χ, a material is diamagnetic if χ is negative, paramagnetic if χ is positive and small, and ferromagnetic if χ is large and positive.

Hence, the correct option is (C).

**21.** The sugars present in honey levulose, maltose, and dextrose.

Honey is also rich in flavonoids, due to which the thick liquid exhibits excellent anti-inflammatory properties and provides great health benefits. Honey being a hyperosmotic agent removes fluid from the wound and also replenishes it quickly and harmful bacteria also die there.

Hence, the correct option is (D).

**22.** When the water is heated from 0°C to 10°C, its volume first decreases, then increases. Mostly on heating the liquids there is an increase in their volume and a decrease in density, but the behavior of water is exactly the opposite between 0°C to 4°C. If heated in a vessel with water, the volume decreases from 0°C to 4°C and the density increases.

Hence, the correct option is (C).

**23.** Plaster of Paris consists of a fine white powder of calcium sulphate.

Plaster of Paris is a white powdery chemical compound that is hydrated calcium sulfate that is usually obtained from calcining gypsum. Paris became the center of plaster production in the 18th century, thus, it is known as Plaster of Paris. Plaster of Paris is also known or called gypsum plaster.

Hence, the correct option is (B).

**24.** The chemical used for making toothpaste white is titanium dioxide. Titanium dioxide is having a "high refractive index" .Titanium oxide or titanium dioxide is a mineral that occurs naturally in crystalline form.The chemical properties of titanium oxide make it a viable ingredient of toothpaste as a "whitening agent".When used as a pigment, it is called titanium white, Pigment White 6 (PW₆).

TiO2 is the formula for Titanium dioxide.

Hence, the correct option is (C).

**25.** Compressed Natural Gas (CNG) is mainly Methane.

Compressed natural gas (CNG), is made by compressing natural gas which is mainly composed of methane, $CH_4$. It is a better fuel than petrol or diesel as its combustion produces fewer undesirable gases than petrol or diesel. The cost and placement of fuel storage tanks is the major barrier to the wider adoption of CNG as a fuel. CNG vehicles require a great amount of space for fuel storage than conventional gasoline-powered vehicles.

Hence, the correct option is (C).

**26.** Dioptre is unit of Power of a lens.

The SI unit of the focal length is the meter (m).

So the SI unit of power $= \dfrac{1}{\text{(SI unit of focal length)}} = m^{-1} =$ Dioptre (D).

$1\ m^{-1} = 1\ D$

Hence, the correct option is (A).

**27.** The value of Avogadro constant is 6.022 $\times$ $10^{23}$. A mole is a fundamental unit of measure of the amount of a substance. For atoms, the mass of Avogadro's number of particles is equal to their atomic mass in grams. For molecules, the mass of Avogadro's number of particles is equal to their molecular mass in grams.

Hence, the correct option is (D).

**28.** Crookes glass is used to make spectacles.Crookes glass contains cerium oxide which sharply absorbs the ultraviolet rays from the sunlight so utilized in making spectacles. The glass is the homogenous mixture of the silicates of various alkaline metals of non-crystalline and transparent or less transparent substances. The glass was manufactured first in Egypt. Crook's glass consists of Cesium oxide. It is also used in the making of Spectacles as it absorbs UV rays.

Hence, the correct option is (C).

**29.** The acid present in soft drinks is Carbonic acid.Citric, carbonic, and phosphoric acids are the three most common acids found in soft drinks. Carbonic acid is formed from dissolved carbon dioxide, which is found in nearly all soft drinks.

The chemical formula is simply a mixture of $H_2O$ and $CO_2$, resulting in $H_2CO_3$.

$CO_{2\,(g)} + H_2O\ (l) \rightarrow H_2CO_3(aq)$

To make soft drinks fizzy, carbonic acid is added. When the bottle is opened, the pressure drops and the carbonic acid dissolves into carbon dioxide and water, causing it to fizz.

Hence, the correct option is (A).

**30.** A plant cell without cell wall is called protoplasts.

Protoplasts are obtained from plant cells by dissolving the cell wall using enzymatic method - using enzymes cellulase and pectinase or by mechanical method. The cells are obtained from the mesophyll part of the leaf.

Protoplasts are mainly used for protoplast fusion or somatic hybridization, where conventional breeding methods cannot be applied.

Hence, the correct option is (B).

**Q.1** Arrange the layer of the atmosphere from top to bottom.
**A.** Troposphere - Stratosphere - Mesosphere - Ionosphere
**B.** Ionosphere - Troposphere - Stratosphere - Mesosphere
**C.** Ionosphere - Mesosphere - Stratosphere - Troposphere
**D.** Troposphere - Stratosphere - Ionosphere - Mesosphere

**Q.2** Which of the following is a erosional feature by river?
**A.** Loess
**B.** U-shaped valley
**C.** V-shaped valley
**D.** Natural levee

**Q.3** The invisible line joins the North pole to the South Pole is called:
**A.** Meridian
**B.** Latitude
**C.** Equator
**D.** Axial plane

**Q.4** Equinox is a state in which the duration of day and night is equal. It falls on:
**A.** 22th March and 31st September
**B.** 10th March and 13th September
**C.** 21st March and 23rd September
**D.** 21th June and 22nd December

**Q.5** GPS is an instrument used to capture the:
**A.** Cross sectional measurement of an area
**B.** Location of an area
**C.** Relative relief of an area
**D.** Graphical measurement and inclination

**Q.6** The difference in the duration of day and night increases as one moves from:
**A.** West to east
**B.** East and west of the prime meridian
**C.** Poles to equator
**D.** Equator to poles

**Q.7** The second-largest body of the solar system is:
**A.** Sun     **B.** Earth     **C.** Jupiter     **D.** Saturn

**Q.8** Which of the following planets are comes under the category of inner planet:
**A.** Earth, Mars, Saturn
**B.** Mercury, Venus, Jupitar
**C.** Mercury, Venus, Earth
**D.** Saturn, Mars, Uranus

**Q.9** Which of the following statement fulfill the condition related to Summer Solstice:
**A.** Most daylight hours people living in the southern hemisphere
**B.** Equal day and night of the people of northern hemisphere
**C.** Most daylight hours people living in the northern hemisphere
**D.** Smaller duration of the day at equator

**Q.10** Timber vegetation is generally not found in which of the following regions?

*[Indian Military Academy (IMA), 2020], [Officers Training Academy (OTA), 2020]*

**A.** Subtropical region          **B.** Temperate region
**C.** Alpine region               **D.** Tundra region

**Q.11** The largest geographical area of India is covered by which one of the following types of soils?

*[Indian Military Academy (IMA), 2020], [Officers Training Academy (OTA), 2020]*

**A.** Inceptisols                 **B.** Entisols
**C.** Alfisols                    **D.** Vertisols

**Q.12** Which one of the following cities is the closest to Equator?

*[Indian Military Academy (IMA), 2020], [Officers Training Academy (OTA), 2020]*

**A.** Mogadishu                   **B.** Singapore
**C.** Colombo                     **D.** Manila

**Q.13** Which one among the following is not a coral reef island?

*[Indian Military Academy (IMA), 2020], [Officers Training Academy (OTA), 2020]*

**A.** Great Barrier Reef, Australia
**B.** Rainbow Reef, Fiji
**C.** Swaraj Island, India
**D.** Kyushu Island, Japan

**Q.14** Sea of Azov is connected to _______.

*[Indian Military Academy (IMA), 2020], [Officers Training Academy (OTA), 2020]*

**A.** Black Sea                   **B.** Baltic Sea
**C.** Mediterranean Sea           **D.** North Sea

**Q.15** Climax mine, the largest producer of molybdenum, is located in _______.

*[Indian Military Academy (IMA), 2020], [Officers Training Academy (OTA), 2020]*

**A.** Canada                      **B.** USA
**C.** Australia                   **D.** South Africa

**Q.16** Which one among the following Union Territories of India is the smallest in geographical area?

*[Indian Military Academy (IMA), 2020], [Officers Training Academy (OTA), 2020]*

**A.** Chandigarh
**B.** Puducherry
**C.** Dadra and Nagar Haveli and Daman and Diu
**D.** Lakshadweep

**Q.17** Sri Lanka is separated from India by a narrow channel of sea formed by the Palk Strait and the _______.
**A.** Gulf of Sinhala             **B.** Gulf of Kuch
**C.** Gulf of Mannar              **D.** Gulf of Gibraltar

**Q.18** Which one of the following countries is the major producer of mica?

**A.** India          **B.** USA          **C.** Brazil          **D.** China

**Q.19** Which of the following is the second largest ocean in the world?

**A.** Atlantic Ocean          **B.** Pacific Ocean
**C.** Indian Ocean          **D.** Antarctic Ocean

**Q.20** The westerly disturbances causing winter rains in northern India originate in:

**A.**   The Himalayas
**B.**   The Arabian Sea
**C.**   The Indian Ocean
**D.**   The Mediterranean Region

**Q.21** Which is the coldest atmospheric layer?

**A.** Troposphere          **B.** Ionosphere
**C.** Exosphere          **D.** Mesosphere

**Q.22** Mangrove vegetation in India is most extensive in

________.

**A.** Malabar          **B.** Rann of Kutch
**C.** Sunderbans          **D.** None of these

**Q.23** The first four planets nearest from the Sun are known as:

**A.** Terrestrial Planets          **B.** Jovian Planets
**C.** Gaseous Planets          **D.** Gas-Giant Planets

**Q.24** Which is the largest island in the world?

**A.** Greenland          **B.** Madagaskar
**C.** Canada          **D.** Borneo

**Q.25** What is the name of mid latitude grassland in South America?

*[Super TET Paper - I, 2018], [Bihar PSC, 2017]*

**A.** Prairie          **B.** Pampas          **C.** Veld          **D.** Steppe

**Q.26** How many Indian states share border with Myanmar?

**A.** 4          **B.** 5          **C.** 3          **D.** 6

**Q.27** The Chilka Lake is located in which of the following states?

**A.** Odisha          **B.** West Bengal
**C.** Andhra Pradesh          **D.** Telangana

**Q.28** "Mumbai High" is asspciated with:

**A.** Steel          **B.** Petroleum
**C.** Mausoleum          **D.** Jute

**Q.29** The Rihand River Valley Project is in:

**A.** Himachal Pradesh          **B.** Haryana
**C.** Uttar Pradesh          **D.** Assam

**Q.30** Where is Rajiv Gandhi International Airport?

**A.**   Hyderabad, Telangana
**B.**   Lucknow, Uttar Pradesh
**C.**   Varanasi, Uttar Pradesh
**D.**   Kolkata, West Bengal

# // Smart Answer Sheet //

**Correct**    Indicates percentage of students who answered questions correctly.

**Skipped**    Indicates percentage of students who skipped questions.

| Q. | Ans. | Correct / Skipped |
|----|------|-------------------|
| 1 | C | 78.53 % / 13.79 % |
| 2 | C | 78.94 % / 19.92 % |
| 3 | A | 89.55 % / 10.08 % |
| 4 | C | 86.46 % / 10.4 % |
| 5 | B | 83.28 % / 15.95 % |
| 6 | D | 89.96 % / 10.0 % |

| Q. | Ans. | Correct / Skipped |
|----|------|-------------------|
| 7 | C | 83.45 % / 15.29 % |
| 8 | C | 82.48 % / 12.6 % |
| 9 | C | 78.77 % / 17.93 % |
| 10 | D | 78.29 % / 11.56 % |
| 11 | A | 83.41 % / 15.01 % |
| 12 | B | 79.67 % / 16.09 % |

| Q. | Ans. | Correct / Skipped |
|----|------|-------------------|
| 13 | D | 77.07 % / 16.26 % |
| 14 | A | 83.65 % / 12.79 % |
| 15 | B | 78.63 % / 16.28 % |
| 16 | D | 80.8 % / 15.3 % |
| 17 | C | 86.16 % / 12.61 % |
| 18 | D | 87.06 % / 12.08 % |

| Q. | Ans. | Correct / Skipped |
|----|------|-------------------|
| 19 | A | 86.56 % / 13.24 % |
| 20 | D | 78.81 % / 16.33 % |
| 21 | D | 83.8 % / 13.17 % |
| 22 | C | 78.39 % / 20.43 % |
| 23 | A | 89.88 % / 10.03 % |
| 24 | A | 77.6 % / 12.22 % |

| Q. | Ans. | Correct / Skipped |
|----|------|-------------------|
| 25 | B | 80.12 % / 14.74 % |
| 26 | A | 86.96 % / 11.02 % |
| 27 | A | 83.89 % / 12.08 % |
| 28 | B | 86.91 % / 12.22 % |
| 29 | C | 87.66 % / 11.68 % |
| 30 | A | 88.25 % / 10.01 % |

## Performance Analysis

| | |
|----|----|
| Avg. Score (%) | 43.33% |
| Toppers Score (%) | 70.0% |
| Your Score | |

# //Hints and Solutions//

**1.** The order of the layers of the atmosphere from top to bottom: Ionosphere - Mesosphere - Stratosphere - Troposphere

The space in which the air surrounds the earth is called the atmosphere.

The lower part of the atmosphere (which usually extends from four to eight miles) is called the troposphere, the upper part of it is called the stratosphere, and the part above it is called the mesosphere and the upper part from the mesosphere is called the ionosphere.

Hence, the correct option is (C).

**2.** The landscape is being continuously worn away by two processes – weathering and erosion. Erosion is the wearing away of the landscape by different agents like water, wind, and ice.

- At higher gradients, downward, vertical erosion is more dominant. This produces V-shaped valleys

- The V-shaped valley is typical of one that has been carved by flowing water.

- The erosion is more pronounced when the water flow is a heavy one, and the water carries suspended particles (sedimentary load).

Hence, the correct option is (C).

**3.** Both longitude and latitude are angles measured with the center of the earth as an origin. Longitude is an angle from the prime meridian, measured to the east (longitudes to the west are negative). Latitudes measure an angle up from the equator (latitudes to the south are negative).

- The line joining the north and south pole is called Prime Meridian.

- A (geographic) meridian (or line of longitude) is half of an imaginary great circle on the Earth's surface.

- It is a coordinate line terminated by the North Pole and the South Pole, connecting points of equal longitude, as measured in angular degrees east or west of the Prime Meridian.

Hence, the correct option is (A).

**4.** An equinox is an event in which a planet's subsolar point passes through its Equator. The equinoxes are the only time when both the Northern and Southern Hemispheres experience roughly equal amounts of daytime and nighttime.

- There are two equinoxes every year: one around March 21 and another around September 23.

- Sometimes, the equinoxes are nicknamed the "vernal equinox" (spring equinox) and the "autumnal equinox" (fall equinox).

- During the equinoxes, solar declination is 0°. Solar declination describes the latitude of the Earth where the sun is directly overhead at noon.

- The subsolar point is an area where the sun's rays shine perpendicular to the Earth's surface at a right angle.

- Only during equinox is the Earth's 23.5° axis not tilting toward or away from the sun: the perceived center of the Sun's disk is in the same plane as the Equator.

Hence, the correct option is (C).

**5.** The global positioning system (GPS) is a network of satellites and receiving devices used to determine the location of something on Earth. Some GPS receivers are so accurate they can establish their location within 1 centimeter (0.4 inches). GPS receivers provide location in latitude, longitude, and altitude.

Hence, the correct option is (B).

**6.** The Earth orbits the sun once every 365 days and rotates about its axis once every 24 hours. Day and night are due to the Earth rotating on its axis, not its orbit around the sun.

- Due to the rotation of the earth in its axis, the phenomena of day and night happens.

- To complete a complete rotation the earth takes 23 hours and 56 minutes.

- During the rotation in its axis (23.5° inclined) when a part of the come in front of the Sun, it considered as day time at that place, and night remains on the opposite side of that place.

- The inclination also causes variation in the energy received on the surface of the earth.

- The sun rays almost perpendicular to the equatorial region all over the year, but it becomes oblique towards the pole.

- The duration of the day and night is almost the same at the equator.

- So the difference in the duration of day and night increases as one moves from the Equator to poles.

- For most of us here on the planet Earth, sunrise, sunset, and the cycle of day and night (the diurnal cycle) are just simple facts of life.

- As a result of seasonal changes that happen with every passing year, the length of day and night can vary and be either longer or shorter by just a few hours.

Hence, the correct option is (D).

**7.** The correct sequence of planets from the distance from the Sun is, Mercury, Venus, Earth, Mars, Jupiter, Saturn, Uranus, Neptune

The correct sequence from smallest to largest is Mercury, Mars, Venus, Earth, Neptune, Uranus, Saturn, and Jupiter. Jupiter's diameter is about 11 times that of the Earth's and the Sun's diameter is about 10 times Jupiter's diameter.

Hence, the correct option is (C).

**8.** Mercury, Venus, and Earth, are known as inner planets.

The International Astronomical Union (IAU) downgraded the status of Pluto to that of a dwarf planet in 2006 because it did not meet the three criteria the IAU uses to define a full-sized planet.

Planets: A celestial body moving in an elliptical orbit around a star is known as a planet.

The planet of our solar system is divisible into two groups:

Inner planet or terrestrial planets: they are made up of rocks and metals and relatively have high density.

Hence, the correct option is (C).

**9.** The Earth rotates on its axis and revolves around the Sun in an elliptical orbit. For this rotation of the Earth, Sunrays never distributed equally over the globe. The circle that divides the day from night on the globe is called the circle of illumination. For a certain period of time, the Northern Hemisphere gets more light while the southern hemisphere gets less and vise versa.

**Summer Solstice:**

- The day that the Earth's the North Pole is tilted closest to the sun is called the summer solstice.

- This is the longest day (most daylight hours) of the year for people living in the northern hemisphere.

- It is also the day that the Sun reaches its highest point in the sky.

- A large portion of the Northern Hemisphere is getting light from the sun, it is summer in the regions north of the equator.

- The longest day and the shortest night at these places occur on 21st June.

Thus it is clear that most daylight hours people living in the northern hemisphere found during the Summer solstice.

Hence, the correct option is (C).

**10.** Timber vegetation is generally not found in Tundra region.

- Timber is a type of wood that has been processed into beams and planks.

- It is also known as 'lumber' in the US and Canada.

- Any wood capable of yielding a minimum dimensional size can be termed timber or lumber. It is a stage in the process of wood production.

- Timbers are used for structural purposes. Those woods which are adapted for building purposes are timbers. Finished timber is supplied in standard sizes for the industry.

- Timber is used for building houses and making furniture.

- The Timber vegetation is generally found in the Subtropical, Temperate, and Alpine regions.

- The tundra is a treeless polar desert found in the high latitudes in the polar regions, primarily in Alaska, Canada, Russia, Greenland, Iceland, and Scandinavia, as well as sub-Antarctic islands. The region's long, dry winters feature months of total darkness and extremely frigid temperatures.

Hence, the correct option is (D).

**11.** The largest geographical area of India is covered by Inceptisols soils.

Inceptisols:

- These are usually the weakly developed young soil though they are more developed than entisols.

- Area (in Thousand Hectares): 130372.9

- Percentage of the total area of India: 39.74.

Entisols:

- Usually young or underdeveloped. Lack vertical development of horizons. These are less fertile soils.

- Area (in Thousand Hectares): 92131.71

- Percentage of the total area of India: 28.08

Alfisols:

- Pale, greyish brown to reddish in color with moderate-to-high reserves of basic cations and are fertile. Although their productivity depends on moisture and temperature. They are supplemented by the moderate application of lime and other chemical fertilizers.

- Area (in Thousand Hectares): 44448.68

- Percentage of the total area of India: 13.55

Vertisols:

- These are expandable clay soils, formed of more than 30% clays. Vertisol clays are black when wet and become iron-hard when dry. When drying, Vertisols crack, and the cracks widen and deepen as the soil dries; this produces cracks 2 to 3 cm wide. These are productive soils. The regur soils of India are an example of vertisols.

- Area (in Thousand Hectares): 27960

- Percentage of the total area of India: 8.52.

Hence, the correct option is (A).

**12.** Among the given cities, Singapore is closest to the equator.

Singapore is a sovereign island city-state in maritime Southeast Asia. It lies about one degree of latitude (137 kilometres or 85 miles) north of the equator, off the southern tip of the Malay Peninsula, bordering the Straits of Malacca to the west, the Riau Islands (Indonesia) to the south, and the South China Sea to the east. Singapore is 200 km north of the equator.

Hence, the correct option is (B).

**13.** Kyushu Island (Japan) is not a Coral Reef Island.

- A coral island is a type of island formed from coral detritus and associated organic material. It occurs in tropical and sub-tropical areas, typically as part of coral reefs which have grown to cover a far larger area under the sea.

- The Great Barrier Reef is the world's largest Coral Reef System composed of over 2900 individual reefs and 900 islands stretching for over 2,300 km over an area of approximately 344,400 km². The reef is located in the Coral Sea, off the coast of Queensland, Australia.

- The Rainbow Reef is a reef in the Somosomo Strait between the Fijian islands of Taveuni and Vanua Levu.

It is one of the most famous dive sites in the South Pacific.

- Swaraj Island is part of Ritchie's Archipelago, in India's Andaman Islands. It's known for its dive sites and beaches, like Elephant Beach, with its coral reefs.

Hence, the correct option is (D).

**14.** The sea of Azov is connected to Black Sea.

The Sea of Azov is an internal sea with passage to the Atlantic Ocean going through the Black, Marmara, Aegean, and Mediterranean seas. It is connected to the Black Sea by the Strait of Kerch, which at its narrowest has a width of 4 kilometers (2.5 mi) and a maximum depth of 15 meters (49 ft).

- The Black Sea is a marginal sea of the Atlantic Ocean lying between Europe and Asia; east of the Balkans, south of the East European Plain in Eastern Europe, west of the Caucasus, and north of Anatolia in Western Asia. It is supplied by major rivers, principally the Danube, Dnieper, and Don.

- The Baltic Sea: It is an arm of the Atlantic Ocean, enclosed by Denmark, Estonia, Finland, Germany, Latvia, Lithuania, Sweden, Poland, Russia, and the North and Central European Plain. The sea stretches from 53°N to 66°N latitude and from 10°E to 30°E longitude.

- The Mediterranean Sea is a sea connected to the Atlantic Ocean, surrounded by the Mediterranean Basin and almost completely enclosed by land: on the north by Western and Southern Europe and Anatolia, on the south by North Africa, and the east by the Levant.

- The North Sea is a sea of the Atlantic Ocean between Great Britain, Jutland, Norway, two States of Germany, the Netherlands, Belgium, and Hauts-de-France. An epeiric sea on the European continental shelf connects to the ocean through the English Channel in the south and the Norwegian Sea in the north.

Hence, the correct option is (A).

**15.** Climax Mine, the largest producer of molybdenum, is located in USA.

- The Climax mine, historically the world's largest source of molybdenum, is north of Leadville, Colorado.

- Climax first produced molybdenum in 1915 and was worked continuously from 1924 until it was shut down in 1995.

- Colorado, a western U.S. state, has a diverse landscape of arid desert, river canyons, and the snow-covered Rocky Mountains, which are partly protected by Rocky Mountain National Park.

- Elsewhere, Mesa Verde National Park features Ancestral Puebloan cliff dwellings. Perched a mile above sea level, Denver, Colorado's capital and largest city, features a vibrant downtown area.

Hence, the correct option is (B).

**16.** Lakshadweep is the Union Territories of India which is the smallest in the geographical area. Lakshadweep is India's smallest Union Territory. Our country, Indian consists of 28 states and 8 union territories.

About Lakshadweep:

- The Kavaratti is the capital of the Union Territory Lakshadweep in India.

- India's smallest Union Territory Lakshadweep is an archipelago consisting of 36 islands with an area of 36 sq km² only.

- The population on this island is approximately 65,000.

Hence, the correct option is (D).

**17.** The Palk Strait is a strait between India(Tamil Nadu) and Sri Lanka(Jaffna). The Gulf of Mannar is situated near Mannar Island, Sri Lanka. The Palk Strait and The Gulf of Mannar are connected via Adam's Bridge(Rama Setu), which is 50 Km long.

The Gulf of Mannar is a large shallow bay forming part of the Laccadive Sea in the Indian Ocean. It lies between the southeastern tip of India and the west coast of Sri Lanka, in the Coromandel Coast region.

Hence, the correct option is (C).

**18.** The largest mica producer in the world in 2021 was China, producing an estimated 95,000 metric tons of mica.

Mica is a silicate mineral, known as sheet silicates because they form in distinct layers. Mica is heat-resistant and does not conduct electricity. There are 37 different mica minerals.

Example purple lepidolite, black biotite, brown phlogopite, and clear muscovite.

Hence, the correct option is (D).

**19.** The Atlantic Ocean is the world's second-largest ocean, with an area of about 106,460,000 km² (41,100,000 square miles).

It covers roughly 20 percent of Earth's surface and about 29 percent of its water surface area. It is known to isolate the "Old World" from the "New World" in the European cognition of the World. The biggest sea of Atlantic Ocean is Sargasso Sea.

Hence, the correct option is (A).

**20.** Western disturbance is an extra-tropical storm that originates in the Mediterranean region causing sudden winter rain in the northern parts of the Indian subcontinent.

The moisture in these storms usually originates over the Mediterranean Sea, the Caspian Sea, and the Black Sea.

Western disturbance (WD) as the name suggests is an extra-tropical storm with its origin in the Mediterranean i.e. the disturbance travels from the "west" to the "east" direction.

The disturbance causes an area of "disturbed" or decreased air pressure.

Hence, the correct option is (D).

**21.** The mesosphere is the coldest atmospheric layer.

The Mesosphere is located between 50 and 80 kilometers (approx.) above Earth's surface. The average temperature of the mesosphere is about minus 85 degrees Celsius.

Hence, the correct option is (D).

**22.** Most of the country's mangrove vegetation is found along the eastern and western coasts.

The Indian Sundarbans forest region is the third-largest enclosed mangrove ecological zone in the world. Mangrove forest is found mainly in the warm and subtropical regions between 25° north and 25° south latitudes.

Hence, the correct option is (C).

**23.** The four planets closest to the sun - Mercury, Venus, Earth, and Mars are called terrestrial planets.

These planets are solid and rocky like Earth. The Jovian Planets or Outer Planets are Jupiter, Saturn, Uranus, and Neptune because they are all gigantic compared to Earth, and they have gaseous nature.

Hence, the correct option is (A).

**24.** Greenland, the world's largest island, lying in the North Atlantic Ocean. It covers an area of 2,130,800 km² (970 sq mi).

Greenland is noted for its vast tundra and immense glaciers.

Although Greenland remains a part of the Kingdom of Denmark, the island's home-rule government is responsible for most domestic affairs. The Greenlandic people are primarily Inuit (Eskimo).

Hence, the correct option is (A).

**25.** The Pampas is a mid-latitude grassland in South America.

The Pampas are fertile South American lowlands that cover more than 1,200,000 square kilometers (460,000 sq mi) and include the Argentine provinces of Buenos Aires, La Pampa, Santa Fe, Entre Ríos and Córdoba; all of Uruguay; and the southernmost state of Brazil, Rio Grande do Sul.

Hence, The correct option is (B).

**26.** Myanmar shares a total border of 1643 km with India.

The Indian states that share international borders with Myanmar are Arunachal Pradesh, Nagaland, Mizoram and Manipur.

Myanmar is bordered by Bangladesh and India to its northwest, China to its northeast, Laos and Thailand to its east and southeast, and the Andaman Sea and Bay of Bengal to its south and southwest. It is the 10th largest country in Asia.

Hence, the correct option is (A).

**27.** Chilika Lake is a brackish water lake and a shallow lagoon with estuarine character spread across the districts of Puri, Khurda and Ganjam in the state of Odisha in eastern India.

Chilika is Asia's largest and world's second-largest lagoon. It lies on the east coast of India in the state of Odisha, separated from the mighty Bay of Bengal by a small strip of sand.

Hence, the correct option is (A).

**28.** Mumbai high is famous for the oil fields of the Petroleum and the natural gas. About 63% per cent of India's petroleum production is from Mumbai High. This has give an impetus to the Indian Gas Production.

Hence, the correct option is (B).

**29.** The Rihand River Valley Project is in Uttar Pradesh.

It is on the Rihand River which is the tributary of the Son River. It is also known as the Govind Ballabh Pant Sagar which the largest dam in India by the amount of water stored by Volume.

The catchment area of this dam is spread out in Uttar Pradesh, Madhya Pradesh and Chhattisgarh.

Hence, the correct option is (C).

**30.** Rajiv Gandhi International Airport is an international airport that serves Hyderabad, the capital of the Indian state of Telangana. It is located in Shamshabad, about 24 kilometres (15 mi) south of Hyderabad.

Hence, the correct option is (A).

**Q.1** The Centre has announced a public holiday on which day on account of the birth anniversary of Dr. BR Ambedkar?
**A.** 11 April     **B.** 12 April     **C.** 13 April     **D.** 14 April

**Q.2** When is World Humanitarian Day observed?
**A.** 17 August          **B.** 18 August
**C.** 19 August          **D.** 20 August

**Q.3** August 12 is celebrated as:
*[Indian Military Academy (IMA), 2020], [Officers Training Academy (OTA), 2020]*
**A.** The World Environment Day
**B.** The World No-Tobacco Day
**C.** The International Day against Drug Abuse and Illicit Trafficking
**D.** The International Youth Day

**Q.4** World No Tabacco Day is observed on:
**A.** May 31          **B.** June 11
**C.** September 28          **D.** October 10

**Q.5** When is Navy Day celebrated every year?
**A.** 1 December          **B.** 2 December
**C.** 3 December          **D.** 4 December

**Q.6** World Wetland Day is observed on-
**A.** 2nd February          **B.** 4th February
**C.** 2nd March          **D.** 23rd March

**Q.7** When is the International Workers' Day?
**A.** 15 April          **B.** 12 December
**C.** 1 May          **D.** 1 August

**Q.8** 20 August is celebrated as -
**A.** Earth Day          **B.** Sadbhavana Diwas
**C.** No Tobacco Day          **D.** None of these

**Q.9** 15 January is celebrated as the -
**A.** Republic Day          **B.** Ugadhi
**C.** Teachers' Day          **D.** Army Day

**Q.10** 'Teachers' Day' is observed on which of the date?
**A.** 5 September          **B.** 11 January
**C.** 14 November          **D.** 2 October

**Q.11** Which day is observed as Parakram Diwas, birth anniversary of Netaji Subhas Chandra Bose?
**A.** January 24          **B.** January 23
**C.** January 19          **D.** February 22

**Q.12** Which day is observed as World Food Day?
**A.** 10 September          **B.** 16 August
**C.** 4 November          **D.** 16 October

**Q.13** 14 September is celebrated as -
**A.** Engineer's Day

**B.** National Hindi Diwas
**C.** National Voters Day
**D.** World Cancer Day

**Q.14** 15 September is celebrated in India -
**A.** National Army Day          **B.** Wetlands Day
**C.** World Cancer Day          **D.** Engineer's Day

**Q.15** 5 October is celebrated as -
**A.** World Radio Day
**B.** International Teachers' Day
**C.** Thinking Day
**D.** World Consumer Rights Day

**Q.16** 12 January is celebrated as -
**A.** National Youth Day
**B.** International Sculpture Day
**C.** World Malaria Day
**D.** World Yoga Day

**Q.17** Which day is observed as Martyrs' Day or Mahatma Gandhi Death Anniversary?
**A.** January 31          **B.** January 29
**C.** January 28          **D.** January 30

**Q.18** 4 February is celebrated as -
**A.** Thinking Day
**B.** World Radio Day
**C.** World Cancer Day
**D.** World Wild Life Day

**Q.19** International Women's Day is celebrated on:
**A.** March 8          **B.** March 11
**C.** March 18          **D.** March 21

**Q.20** The following day is observed as 'International Family Day'?
**A.** 5th May          **B.** 15th May
**C.** 20th May          **D.** 25th May

**Q.21** The following Day is celebrated as 'World Heritage Day'.
**A.** 8th March          **B.** 18 th March
**C.** 8th April          **D.** 18th April

**Q.22** Which day is celebrated on January 1 every year?
**A.** International Literacy Day
**B.** World Peace Day
**C.** World Egg Day
**D.** International Volunteer Day for Economic and Social Development

**Q.23** World Milk Day is celebrated on:
**A.** 1 June          **B.** 3 June
**C.** 5 June          **D.** None of the above

**Q.24** World Music Day is celebrated on:

**A.** 19 June  **B.** 20 June

**C.** 21 June  **D.** None of the above

**Q.25** 23 rd June is celebrated as:

**A.** A international Refugee Day

**B.** International Picnic Day

**C.** International Day of Innocent Children Victims of Aggression

**D.** International Olympic Day

**Q.26** Which day is celebrated as National Unity Day?

**A.** May 31  **B.** October 31

**C.** February 27  **D.** October 26

**Q.27** Which day is celebrated as National Police Day?

**A.** May 25  **B.** October 21

**C.** February 23  **D.** October 25

**Q.28** Which one of the following days is observed as the Father's Day?

**A.** 1st Sunday of June  **B.** 2nd Sunday of June

**C.** 3rd Sunday of June  **D.** 4th Sunday of June

**Q.29** World AIDS Day is observed on which of the following days?

**A.** January 1  **B.** March 1

**C.** May 1  **D.** December 1

**Q.30** 23 rd January is celebrated as the birthday of:

**A.** Guru Govind Singh

**B.** Subhash Chandra Bose

**C.** Devendra Nath Tagore

**D.** Chandra Shekhar Azad

# // Smart Answer Sheet //

**Correct** — Indicates percentage of students who answered questions correctly.

**Skipped** — Indicates percentage of students who skipped questions.

| Q. | Ans. | Correct / Skipped |
|---|---|---|
| 1 | D | 84.63 % / 11.95 % |
| 2 | C | 76.22 % / 13.99 % |
| 3 | D | 78.89 % / 13.78 % |
| 4 | A | 78.41 % / 10.49 % |
| 5 | D | 86.13 % / 11.87 % |
| 6 | A | 82.6 % / 11.9 % |

| Q. | Ans. | Correct / Skipped |
|---|---|---|
| 7 | C | 80.89 % / 11.14 % |
| 8 | B | 87.7 % / 11.83 % |
| 9 | D | 77.1 % / 14.73 % |
| 10 | A | 81.3 % / 13.9 % |
| 11 | B | 82.05 % / 12.34 % |
| 12 | D | 83.24 % / 15.88 % |

| Q. | Ans. | Correct / Skipped |
|---|---|---|
| 13 | B | 88.05 % / 11.74 % |
| 14 | D | 88.07 % / 10.62 % |
| 15 | B | 82.82 % / 15.68 % |
| 16 | A | 77.72 % / 10.74 % |
| 17 | D | 83.46 % / 14.52 % |
| 18 | C | 83.72 % / 12.11 % |

| Q. | Ans. | Correct / Skipped |
|---|---|---|
| 19 | A | 78.46 % / 18.42 % |
| 20 | B | 88.62 % / 11.34 % |
| 21 | D | 78.46 % / 12.6 % |
| 22 | B | 86.18 % / 11.29 % |
| 23 | A | 83.4 % / 14.35 % |
| 24 | C | 78.11 % / 20.23 % |

| Q. | Ans. | Correct / Skipped |
|---|---|---|
| 25 | D | 88.42 % / 10.25 % |
| 26 | B | 84.21 % / 14.18 % |
| 27 | B | 86.79 % / 10.33 % |
| 28 | C | 89.06 % / 10.62 % |
| 29 | D | 88.69 % / 10.43 % |
| 30 | B | 86.41 % / 13.37 % |

## Performance Analysis

| | |
|---|---|
| Avg. Score (%) | 46.67% |
| Toppers Score (%) | 60.0% |
| Your Score | |

# //Hints and Solutions//

**1.** The Centre has announced a public holiday on April 14, 2021, on account of the birth anniversary of Dr. BR Ambedkar.

The Ministry of Personnel, Public Grievances and Pensions has declared in a notification that April 14 will be a public holiday for all central government offices including industrial establishments.

Hence, the correct option is (D).

**2.** 19 August is World Humanitarian Day observed.

World Humanitarian Day is observed across the world on August 19 to pay tribute to workers who risk their lives in humanitarian services and to gather support for people affected by crises around the world. The day was designated by the UN General Assembly to commemorate the 19 August 2003 bombing of the United Nations headquarters in Baghdad, Iraq.

Hence, the correct option is (C).

**3.** August 12 is celebrated as 'International Youth Day.'

The International Youth Day

- International Youth Day is observed globally on 12th August every year.
- The day is celebrated to recognize the efforts put in by the youth for the betterment of society.
- The Day aims to promote the ways to engage the youth and make them more actively involved in their communities through positive contributions.

Theme

- The theme of International Youth Day 2020, "Youth Engagement for Global Action".
- The theme highlights the ways in which the engagement of young people at the local, national and global levels is enriching national and multilateral institutions and processes, as well as drawing lessons on how their representation and engagement in formal institutional politics can be significantly enhanced.

History of International Youth Day

- In 1999, the General Assembly endorsed the recommendation made by the World Conference of Ministers Responsible for Youth (Lisbon, 8-12 August 1998) that 12 August be declared International Youth Day.
- This day is the first time observed on August 12, 2000, the day marks an awareness day and draws attention to a given set of cultural and legal issues surrounding youth.

Hence, the correct option is (D).

**4.** World No Tabacco Day is observed on May 31.

Every year, on 31 May, WHO and partners mark World No Tobacco Day (WNTD), highlighting the health and additional risks associated with tobacco use, and advocating for effective policies to reduce tobacco consumption.

Hence, the correct option is (A).

**5.** Navy Day is celebrated every year on 4 December.

The day is celebrated in honor of the Indian Navy's role during the war with Pakistan in 1971 when Indian warships attacked Karachi port.

The day is also celebrated to highlight the role the Navy plays in securing the country's marine borders during peacetime and carrying out humanitarian missions.

Hence, the correct option is (D).

**6.** World Wetlands Day is celebrated each year internationally on 2 February.

It denotes the anniversary of the signing of the Convention on Wetlands of International Importance in Ramsar, Iran, on 2 February 1971.

World Wetlands Day was first celebrated in 1997.

Several agencies, non-government organizations celebrated World Wetlands Day to raise public awareness of wetland values and benefits and promote the conservation and wise use of wetlands.

These activities include seminars, nature walks, festivals, the announcement of new Ramsar sites, newspaper articles, radio interviews, and wetland rehabilitation.

Hence, the correct option is (A).

**7.** 1 May is the International Workers' Day.

International Workers' Day, also known as labour day in most countries and often referred to as May Day, is a celebration of labourers and the working classes that is promoted by the international labour movement and occurs every year on 1 May.

Hence, the correct option is (C).

**8.** Rajiv Gandhi's birthday is celebrated as Sadbhavana Diwas on 20 August.

Every year India observes Sadbhavana Diwas on August 20 to commemorate the birth anniversary of late erstwhile Prime Minister, Rajiv Gandhi. This year on 20th August 2021, we are going to celebrate the 77th birth anniversary of former Prime Minister Rajiv Gandhi. The Indian National Congress instituted Rajiv Gandhi Sadbhavana Award in 1992, a year after his death.

Hence, the correct option is (B).

**9.** Army Day is celebrated on 15 January every year in India as it is on this historic day that General K. M. Cariappa became the first Indian to take charge of the Indian Army in 1949.

Hence, the correct option is (D).

**10.** Teachers day is observed on 5 September.

September 5th is the birth anniversary of a great teacher Dr Sarvepalli Radhakrishnan, who was a staunch believer of education and was a well-known diplomat, scholar, the President of India and above all, a teacher.

Hence, the correct option is (A).

**11.** Parakram Diwas is celebrated annually on 23 January. It is a national event celebrated in India to mark the birthday of the prominent Indian freedom fighter Netaji Subhas Chandra Bose. He played a pivotal role in Indian independence movement. He was the head of Indian National Army (Azad Hind Fouj). He was the founder-head of the Azad Hind Government.

Hence, the correct option is (B).

**12.** 16 October is observed as World Food day.

World Food Day was first launched in 1945. The reason World Food Day was created was to celebrate the launch of the United Nation's Food and Agriculture Organisation.

The main principle which World Food Day celebrates is the furtherance of food security all over the world, especially in times of crisis. The launch of the Food and Agriculture Organisation by the UN has played a huge role in taking this worthy goal forward. Its annual celebration serves as a marker of the importance of this organisation and helps to raise awareness of the crucial need for successful agriculture policies to be implemented by governments across the world to ensure there is ample food available for everyone.

Hence, the correct option is (D).

**13.** 14 September is celebrated as National Hindi Diwas.

The Constituent Assembly of India adopted Hindi as the official language of the Republic of India on 14 September 1949. However, the idea of using it as the official language was accepted by the country's constitution on 26 January 1950. According to Article 434 of the Indian constitution, Hindi written in Devanagari script was adopted as the official language of India.

Hence, the correct option is (B).

**14.** 15 September is celebrated in India as Engineer's Day.

India chose 15 September to celebrate National Engineer's Day in order to pay tribute to one of the most visionary and eminent civil engineers the country has had, Sir M. Visvesvaraya.

Hence, the correct option is (D).

**15.** 5 October is celebrated as International Teachers' Day.

World Teachers' Day is celebrated on 5 October every year in the whole world to commemorate the anniversary of the adoption of the ILO/UNESCO recommendation concerning the status of Teachers in 1966.

Hence, the correct option is (B).

**16.** 12 January is celebrated as National Youth Day.

National Youth Day, also known as Vivekananda Jayanti, is celebrated on 12 January, being the birthday of Swami Vivekananda.

Hence, the correct option is (A).

**17.** 30 January each year mark the death anniversary of the father of nation, Mahatma Gandhi. The day is also celebrated as Martyrs' Day to commemorate freedom fighters who sacrificed their lives to get us freedom. On January 30th, 1948, Mahatma Gandhi was assassinated by Nathuram Godse in the Birla House.

Hence, the correct option is (D).

**18.** 4 February is celebrated as World Cancer Day.

World Cancer Day is observed every year on 4 February by the Union for International Cancer Control (UICC). The day is celebrated to raise awareness and education about cancer, and pressing governments and individuals across the world to take action against the disease.

Hence, the correct option is (C).

**19.** International Women's Day is celebrated on 8 March.

International Women's Day (IWD) is a global holiday celebrated annually on March 8 to commemorate the cultural, political, and socioeconomic achievements of women.[3] It is also a focal point in the women's rights movement, bringing attention to issues such as gender equality, reproductive rights, and violence and abuse against women.

Hence, the correct option is (A).

**20.** 15th May is observed as 'International Family Day'.

On International Day of Families, celebrate all the eccentric traditions that you and your family share. Every family is unique, and there are countless stories, memories, and adventures we all have shared with our families that are significant only to us. Just like Festivus was a tradition at George Costanza's home in "Seinfeld," the traditions carried on within families are all relived today.

Hence, the correct option is (B).

**21.** 18th April is celebrated as 'World Heritage Day'.

The day was first observed first in 1983 by United Nations Educational, Scientific and Cultural Organization (UNESCO). It gained recognition as a world event during the 22nd General Conference of UNESCO.

The aim in celebrating this day is to spread awareness about the cultural heritage and diversity on the planet.

Hence, the correct option is (D).

**22.** World Day of Peace, celebrated on January 1 every year, is primarily a Catholic feast day dedicated to universal peace on the Solemnity of Mary, the Mother of God.

Hence, the correct option is (B).

**23.** World Milk Day is celebrated on 1 June.

In 2001, World Milk Day was established by the Food and Agriculture Organisation of the United Nations to recognize the importance of milk as a global food, and to celebrate the dairy sector. Each year since, the benefits of milk and dairy products have been actively promoted around the world, including how dairy supports the livelihoods of one billion people.

Hence, the correct option is (A).

**24.** World Music Day is an annual celebration observed on 21 June around the world.

It is a day to encourage young and amateur musicians to perform. On this day, also known as Music Day or Make Music

Day, anyone can play their favourite instruments for enjoyment and relaxation.

Hence, the correct option is (C).

**25.** On 23 June, Olympic Day is celebrated all around the world.

Hundreds of thousands of people – young and old – participate in sports activities, such as runs, exhibitions, music and educational seminars.

Hence, the correct option is (D).

**26.** National Unity Day is celebrated in India on 31 October. It was introduced by the Government of India in 2014. The day is celebrated to mark the birth anniversary of Sardar Patel who had a major role in the political integration of India.

Hence, the correct option is (B).

**27.** The National Police Day is honoured on 21st October every year. It remembers the sacrifices of the ten policemen who have martyred their lives defending the country at the borders of China in 1959. October 21 every year is observed as 'Commemoration Day' by the Police forces all over India.

Hence, the correct option is (B).

**28.** 3rd Sunday of June is observed as the Father's Day.

Father's Day is a celebration of fathers, honouring fatherhood, paternal bonds and the role fathers play in society. It is celebrated on the third Sunday of June. Father's Day is commemorated in most parts of the world on the third Sunday of June.

Hence, the correct option is (C).

**29.** World AIDS Day, observed each year on December 1, is an opportunity for people worldwide to unite in the fight against HIV, show their support for people living with HIV, and remember those who have died from an HIV-related illness.

Hence, the correct option is (D).

**30.** 23 rd January is celebrated as the birthday of Subhash Chandra Bose.

Subhas Chandra Bose, byname Netaji (Hindi: "Respected Leader"), (born c. January 23, 1897, Cuttack, Orissa [now Odisha], India— died August 18, 1945, Taipei, Taiwan?)

Hence, the correct option is (B).

**Q.1** Who built the Brihadishwara temple in Thanjavur, Tamil Nadu?

**A.** Rajaraja Chola I
**B.** Vijayalaya
**C.** Sundara Chola
**D.** Rajendra Chola I

**Q.2** The Kailasanathar temple at Kanchipuram was built during the rule of:

*[RRB (NTPC), 2017]*

**A.** Pandyas     **B.** Cholas     **C.** Pallavas     **D.** Cheras

**Q.3** Which of the following is not a correct statement about Indus Valley Civilization?

**A.** Mohenjodero was located on the banks of the river Indus.
**B.** Lothal site was located on the bank of the Narmada river.
**C.** Chanhudaro was located within the boundaries of Pakistan.
**D.** Lothal was on the mouth of the Gulf of Cambay.

**Q.4** Which of the following places, the remains of horse bones have been found?

**A.** Surkotada
**B.** Dholavira
**C.** Lothal
**D.** Mohenjodaro

**Q.5** The famous king Pulakeshin II, belonged to which of the following dynasty?

**A.** Chola
**B.** Chera
**C.** Rashtrakuta
**D.** Chalukya

**Q.6** Which one of the following was not a part of the dhamma of King Ashoka?

*[UPSC NDA, 2021]*

**A.** Honouring the king
**B.** Tolerance of religions other than one's own
**C.** Respecting Brahmanas
**D.** Promoting the welfare of his subjects

**Q.7** Out of the following remains excavated in Indus Valley, which one indicates the commercial and economic development?

**A.** Pottery     **B.** Seals     **C.** Boats     **D.** Houses

**Q.8** Which of the following is the oldest surviving rock-cut caves in India?

**A.** Ajanta Cave
**B.** Ellora Cave
**C.** Udayagiri and Khandagiri Cave
**D.** Barabar Hill Caves

**Q.9** Who were the Nayanars?

*[Indian Military Academy (IMA), 2019], [Officers Training Academy (OTA), 2019]*

**A.** Those who were immersed in devotion to Vishnu
**B.** Those who were devotees of Buddha
**C.** Leaders who were devotees of Shiva
**D.** Leaders who were devotees of Basveshwara

**Q.10** Who were Alvars?

*[Indian Military Academy (IMA), 2019], [Officers Training Academy (OTA), 2019]*

**A.** Those who immersed in devotion to Vishnu
**B.** Devotees of Shiva
**C.** Those who worshipped abstract form of God
**D.** Devotees of Shakti

**Q.11** Where did the first freedom struggle begin in 1857?

*[UPSESSB PGT History, 2015]*

**A.** Lucknow
**B.** Jhansi
**C.** Meerut
**D.** Kanpur

**Q.12** Hindustan Socialist Republican Association was formed-

*[UPSESSB PGT History, 2015]*

**A.** By Subhash Chandra Bose
**B.** By Rash Behari Bose
**C.** By Chandrashekhar Azad
**D.** By Sardar Bhagat Singh

**Q.13** Who were the first among the Europeans to come for trade?

*[UPSESSB PGT History, 2015]*

**A.** Dutch
**B.** British
**C.** French
**D.** Portuguese

**Q.14** The first Satyagraha launched in India by Mahatma Gandhi was-

*[UPSESSB PGT History, 2015]*

**A.** Champaran Satyagraha
**B.** Kheda Satyagraha
**C.** Rowlatt Satyagraha
**D.** None of these

**Q.15** Who was the eldest son of Mahatma Gandhi?

*[UPSESSB PGT History, 2011]*

**A.** Manilal Gandhi
**B.** Harilal Gandhi
**C.** Devdas Gandhi
**D.** Firoz Gandhi

**Q.16** 'Who first used the word 'Pakistan'?

*[UPSESSB PGT History, 2011]*

**A.** Sir Syed Ahmed
**B.** Mohammad Iqbal
**C.** Mohammad Ali Jinnah
**D.** Chaudhary Rahmat Ali

**Q.17** How many Indian women participated in the 1889 AD Bombay session of the All India Congress?

*[UPSESSB PGT History, 2011]*

**A.** Ten     **B.** Eight     **C.** Five     **D.** Seven

**Q.18** In the first battle of Tarain, who was defeated by Prithviraj Chauhan?

**A.** Ahmed Shah Abdali  **B.** Muhammad Ghazni
**C.** Sher Shah Suri  **D.** Muhammad Ghori

**Q.19** The official language of the Mughal period was:

**A.** Urdu  **B.** Persian  **C.** Turkish  **D.** Arabic

**Q.20** In which year was Razia Sultan removed from the throne?
*[Rajasthan Police Constable, 2020]*

**A.** In 1236  **B.** In 1238  **C.** In 1240  **D.** In 1242

**Q.21** The Mosque of Moth was constructed during whose reign?
*[Rajasthan Police Constable, 2020]*

**A.** Sikandar Lodhi
**B.** Muhammad Tughlaq
**C.** Alauddin Khilji
**D.** Qutbuddin Aibak

**Q.22** In which year was the first battle of Panipat fought?
*[Rajasthan Police Constable, 2020]*

**A.** In 1226  **B.** In 1530  **C.** In 1526  **D.** In 1556

**Q.23** During the rule of Firoz Shah Tughlaq, Kharaj was a tax on __________.

**A.** Land  **B.** Nonmuslim people
**C.** Property  **D.** War

**Q.24** Which of the following statements about Saguna bhakti traditions is/are correct?

1. Saguna bhakti traditions focus on the worship of specific deities such as Vishnu or his avatars.

2. In Saguna bhakti traditions, Gods and Goddesses are conceptualised in anthropomorphic forms.

Select the correct answer using the code given below:
*[UPSC NDA, 2021]*

**A.** 1 only  **B.** 2 only
**C.** Both 1 and 2  **D.** Neither 1 nor 2

**Q.25** Who among the following was considered to be the preceptor of Mirabai?
*[UPSC NDA, 2021]*

**A.** Dadu  **B.** Raidas
**C.** Ramanand  **D.** Surdas

**Q.26** Which one of the following statements about the Ain-i-Akbari is not correct?
*[UPSC NDA, 2021]*

**A.** It was written by Abu'l Fazl.
**B.** It is a part of a larger work called Akbar Nama.
**C.** It describes the Mughal Empire as having a diverse population and a composite culture.
**D.** It was later revised by Sadullah Khan on the orders of Shah Jahan.

**Q.27** The year of the foundation of the Women's Indian Association (WIA) is:

**A.** 1947  **B.** 1937  **C.** 1927  **D.** 1917

**Q.28** Mohandas Karamchand Gandhi was born on 2nd October:

**A.** 1869  **B.** 1859  **C.** 1888  **D.** 1900

**Q.29** Which empire lasted the longest among the following?

**A.** The Palas  **B.** The Pratiharas
**C.** The Rashtrakutas  **D.** The Senas

**Q.30** Who was the founder of the Sena dynasty?

**A.** Ballal Sena  **B.** Hemanta Sen
**C.** Lakshman Sen  **D.** Vijay Sen

# // Smart Answer Sheet //

| Correct | Indicates percentage of students who answered questions correctly. |

| Skipped | Indicates percentage of students who skipped questions. |

| Q. | Ans. | Correct / Skipped |
|---|---|---|
| 1 | A | 88.49 % / 10.84 % |
| 2 | C | 86.57 % / 10.55 % |
| 3 | B | 76.86 % / 14.59 % |
| 4 | A | 87.69 % / 11.78 % |
| 5 | D | 83.23 % / 16.49 % |
| 6 | A | 87.55 % / 10.86 % |

| Q. | Ans. | Correct / Skipped |
|---|---|---|
| 7 | B | 78.45 % / 17.76 % |
| 8 | D | 87.49 % / 10.92 % |
| 9 | C | 89.3 % / 10.38 % |
| 10 | A | 84.85 % / 10.12 % |
| 11 | C | 89.91 % / 10.05 % |
| 12 | C | 83.18 % / 15.91 % |

| Q. | Ans. | Correct / Skipped |
|---|---|---|
| 13 | D | 76.39 % / 21.06 % |
| 14 | A | 89.58 % / 10.09 % |
| 15 | B | 88.13 % / 10.85 % |
| 16 | D | 79.54 % / 18.51 % |
| 17 | A | 77.32 % / 17.93 % |
| 18 | D | 78.55 % / 16.55 % |

| Q. | Ans. | Correct / Skipped |
|---|---|---|
| 19 | B | 89.58 % / 10.27 % |
| 20 | C | 83.36 % / 13.38 % |
| 21 | A | 82.27 % / 12.31 % |
| 22 | C | 85.58 % / 14.28 % |
| 23 | A | 88.73 % / 10.74 % |
| 24 | C | 82.03 % / 17.14 % |

| Q. | Ans. | Correct / Skipped |
|---|---|---|
| 25 | B | 87.54 % / 10.96 % |
| 26 | D | 83.28 % / 13.17 % |
| 27 | D | 89.95 % / 10.03 % |
| 28 | A | 84.54 % / 10.37 % |
| 29 | C | 88.1 % / 10.78 % |
| 30 | B | 83.91 % / 13.66 % |

| Performance Analysis | |
|---|---|
| Avg. Score (%) | 33.33% |
| Toppers Score (%) | 66.67% |
| Your Score | |

# //Hints and Solutions//

**1.** Rajaraja Chola I built the Brihadishwara temple in Thanjavur, Tamil Nadu.

He was one of the greatest emperors of the Chola empire. In his reign, the Cholas expanded beyond South India stretching from Kalinga in the north to Sri Lanka in the south. He fought many battles with the Chalukyas in the north and the Pandyas in the south. He built the Brihadishwara temple in Thanjavur dedicated to Lord Shiva.

Hence, the correct option is (A).

**2.** The Kailasanathar temple at Kanchipuram was built during the rule of Pallavas.

The Kanchi Kailasanathar temple is the oldest structure in Kanchipuram located in Tamil Nadu, India. The temple was built from 685-705 AD by a Rajasimha ruler of the Pallava Dynasty. It is a Hindu temple (dedicated to Lord Shiva) in the Dravidian architectural style.

Hence, the correct option is (C).

**3.** The archaeological remains of the Harappan port-town of Lothal are located along the Bhogava river, a tributary of Sabarmati, in the Gulf of Khambat.

Hence, the correct option is (B).

**4.** The remains of Horse bones were found at Surkotda.

The evidence of the horse comes from a superficial level of Mohenjo-Daro and from a doubtful terracotta figurine from Lothal. The remains of the horse are reported from Surkotada, situated in western Gujarat and belong to around 2000 B.C. But the identity is doubtful. In any case, the Harappan culture was not horse-centered.

It is an Indus valley site currently present in Gujarat.

Hence, the correct option is (A).

**5.** The famous king Pulakeshin II belonged to the Chalukya dynasty.

Pulakesi II reigned over the Chalukyas of Badami, an Indian royal dynasty that ruled large parts of southern and central India between the sixth and the twelfth centuries.

Pulakeshin II reigned from 610 to 642 CE.

Hence, the correct option is (D).

**6.** Ashoka's dhamma was neither a new religion nor a new political philosophy, it was a way of life. Ashoka denounced all useless ceremonies and sacrifices held under the influence of superstition. One of the striking features of Asoka's edicts is that he regards himself as a father figure for the people. So, honoring the king was not dhamma.

Ashoka's major dhamma is inscribed in 14 rock edicts. Some of the important dhamma are:

- Prohibition of animal sacrifices in festive and public gatherings.

- It pleads for toleration amongst all religions.

- Respect for others and regard even for slaves and servants and donations to sramanas and Brahmans.

- Emphatic plea for toleration amongst the various religions.

- Plantation of medicinal herbs and trees and digging of wells along the roads, which describes the promotion of welfare of the people.

Hence, the correct option is (A).

**7.** Seals indicate commercial and economic development.

They were used in trade. They would be made on ceramics or the clay tags used to seal the rope around bundles of goods.

Hence, the correct option is (B).

**8.**

- The Barabar Hill Caves is the oldest surviving rock-cut cave in India.

- It is located in the Jehanabad district of Makhdumpur province, Bihar.

- Such caves are found in the Barabar (four caves) and Nagarjuna (three caves) Twin Hills.

- The Ajanta caves are rock-cut Buddhist cave monuments.

- This is one of the world's largest rock-cut monastic-temple cave complexes.

- Udayagiri and Khandagiri Cave are archaeological caves, partly natural and partly artificial.

Hence, the correct option is (D).

**9.** Nayanars were the leaders devotees of Shiva.

- Alvars were the devotees of Vishnu.

- Followers of Basveshwara were called Lingayats.

- Both Nayanars and Alvars were influenced by the Bhakti Movement 7th-8th Century CE.

- Lingayats are the 12th-century followers of Basveshwara, a social reformer from the 12th century who used to say his Vachanas.

- He along with Sharanas launched a strong religious and spiritual rebel against Brahminical Hegemony propagating Equality of all.

- Buddha propagated the middle path between self-indulgence and self-mortification.

Hence, the correct option is (C).

**10.** The seventh to ninth centuries saw the emergence of new religious movements, led by the Nayanars (saints devoted to Shiva) and Alvars (saints devoted to Vishnu)

- They came from all castes including those considered "untouchable" like the Pulaiyar and the Panars.

- They were sharply critical of the Buddhists and Jainas and preached ardent love of Shiva or Vishnu as the path to salvation.

- They drew upon the ideals of love and heroism as found in the Sangam literature (the earliest example of Tamil literature, composed during the early centuries of the Common Era) and blended them with the values of bhakti.

- The Nayanars and Alvars went from place to place composing exquisite poems in praise of the deities enshrined in the villages they visited and set them to music.

- There were 63 Nayanars, who belonged to different caste backgrounds such as potters, "untouchable" workers, peasants, hunters, soldiers, Brahmanas, and chiefs.

- The best known among them were Appar, Sambandar, Sundarar and Manikkavasagar. There are two sets of compilations of their songs – Tevaram and Tiruvacakam.

- There were 12 Alvars, who came from equally divergent backgrounds, the best known being Periyalvar, his daughter Andal, Tondaradippodi Alvar and Nammalvar. Their songs were compiled in the Divya Prabandham.

Hence, the correct option is (A).

**11.** The first freedom struggle started from Meerut in 1857. Later, this revolution spread like fire all over the country. This created the role of uprooting the British from India and finally India got independence in 1947.

Hence, the correct option is (C).

**12.** Hindustan Socialist Republican Association was formed in Kanpur in October 1924 by the revolutionary Ramprasad Bismil, Yogesh Chandra Chatterjee, Chandrashekhar Azad and Shachindranath Sanyal etc. of Indian freedom struggle.

Hence, the correct option is (C).

**13.** Portuguese were among the first Europeans to come for trade. After them, Dutch Englishmen came to Danish and French. The new sea route to India was discovered by Portuguese merchant Vasco da Gama on 17 May 1948, reaching Calicut, a port on the west coast of India.

Hence, the correct option is (D).

**14.** A Satyagraha took place in Champaran district of Bihar in 1917 under the leadership of Gandhiji. It is known as Champaran Satyagraha. This was the first Satyagraha done in India under the leadership of Gandhiji.

Hence, the correct option is (A).

**15.** Harilal Gandhi (23 August 1888 - 18 June 1948) was the eldest son of Mohandas Karamchand Gandhi. He had three younger brothers Manila Gandhi, Ramdas Gandhi, and Devdas Gandhi. Harilal was born on 23 August 1888 when his father went to England for higher education.

Hence, the correct option is (B).

**16.** Chaudhary Rahmat Ali was one of the first supporters to demand Pakistan. On 28 January 1933, the word Pakistan came to the world and the word was given by Chaudhary Rahmat Ali.

Hence, the correct option is (D).

**17.** Ten Indian women participated in the 1889 AD Bombay session of the All India Congress. This session was held in Pune but due to famine there Gokuldas Tejpal held in Sanskrit school in Bombay.

Hence, the correct option is (A).

**18.** In the first battle of Tarain, Muhammad Ghori was defeated by Prithviraj Chauhan.

The real name of Muhammad Ghori was Shahabuddin alias Muizuddin Muhammad Ghori. He began his journey with Multan in 1175 A.D, against a Muslim ruler and got victorious. He fought two important battles, i.e. the first battle of Tarain in 1191 A.D, where he was defeated by Prithviraj Chauhan. The second battle of Tarain in 1192 A.D where Prithviraj Chauhan defeated and killed by him.

Hence, the correct option is (D).

**19.**

- The official language of the Mughal Empire was Persian because the first Mughal emperor Babur came from Afghanistan.

- Persian is a native language of Iran and was also used in Afghanistan.

- So when the Mughals came to India, they bought over the Persian language with them.

Hence, the correct option is (B).

**20.** Razia Sultan was removed from the throne in 1240.

Razia Sultan (1236 AD-1240 AD) belonged to the Slave Dynasty. She was the first and last Muslim woman ruler of Medieval India. She appointed Jamaluddin Yakoot as the highest officer of cavalry. Razia Sultan abandoned Pardah and appeared before the public in male dress. She saved the empire from Mongol invasion. She died in the year 1240 AD.

Hence, the correct option is (C).

**21.** The Mosque of Moth was constructed during the reign of Sikandar Lodi.

Moth Ki Masjid was built in 1505 by Wazir Miya Bhoiya who was a Prime Minister at the Royal Courts of Sultan Sikandar Lodhi.

Sikandar Lodhi (1489 AD-1517 AD) was the son of Bahlol Lodhi who conquered Bihar and western Bengal. Noblest of the three Lodhi rulers, real name was Nizam Khan (son of Bahalul Lodhi). He conquered Bihar and Bengal in 1504 AD. He built a new city named Agra and made it his capital. He shifted his capital from Delhi to Agra, a city founded by him. He broke the sacred images of the Jwalamukhi Temple at Nagarkot and ordered the temples of Mathura to be destroyed. He introduced the Gaz-i-Sikandari (Sikandar's yard) of 32 digits for measuring cultivated fields. He was a poet and wrote verses in Persian under the pet name Gularukh. He repaired Qutub Minar.

Hence, the correct option is (A).

**22.** The First Battle of Panipat (21 April 1526) fought near a small village of Panipat Haryana.

The battle was fought between the invading forces of Zahir-ud-din Babur and Lodi Empire during the rule of Ibrahim Lodi. The Mughal forces of Babur, the ruler of Kabulistan, defeated the ruling army of Ibrahim Lodi, Sultan of Delhi. Babur's tactics of Tulughma and Araba led him to victory.

Hence, the correct option is (C).

**23.** During the rule of Firoz Shah Tughlaq, Kharaj was a tax on land. The land tax was equal to one-tenth of the produce of the land. Firoz Shah Tughlaq was the third ruler of the Tughlaq dynasty that ruled over Delhi from 1320 to 1412 AD.

Hence, the correct option is (A).

**24.** At a different level, historians of religion classified bhakti traditions into two broad categories:

- Saguna (with attributes): The Saguna included traditions focused on the worship of specific deities such as Shiva, Vishnu, and his avatars (incarnations). So, statement 1 is correct.

- Forms of the goddess or Devi, all often conceptualized in anthropomorphic forms. So, statement 2 is correct.

- Nirguna (without attributes): Nirguna bhakti on the other hand was the worship of an abstract form of god.

Hence, the correct option is (C).

**25.** Raidas was considered to be the preceptor of Mirabai.

Born in Mandur near Kashi, bhakta–poet Raidas was the son of a cobbler. It is a general consensus that he was born in Samvat 1433 (1377 CE), on Magh sud 15 (Purnima). Since the day was a Sunday, he was named Ravidas, which later became Raidas in Hindi and Rohidas in Gujarati.

Hence, the correct option is (B).

**26.** "It was later revised by Sadullah Khan on the orders of Shah Jahan." statement about the Ain-i-Akbari is not correct.

Ain-i-Akbari was written by Abu'l Fazl in the Persian language in the 16th century.

The Akbar Nama is divided into three books: The third is the Ain-i Akbari.

- It deals with Akbar's administration, army, revenues, household, and geography of his empire.

- It provides rich details about the traditions and culture of the people living in India.

- It also got statistical details about crops, yields, prices, wages, and revenues.

Hence, the correct option is (D).

**27.** The year of the foundation of the Women's Indian Association (WIA) is 1917

On 8 May 1917 in Adyar, Madras, a multiethnic group of women established the Women's Indian Association (WIA). The WIA was one of the first organizations to boldly connect Indian women's social and sexual subjugation with patriarchy, poverty, and political disenfranchisement.

Hence, the correct option is (D).

**28.** Mohandas Karamchand Gandhi was born on 2nd October 1969.

To celebrate his contribution to the nation, 2nd October is celebrated every year as a national holiday. The day is also celebrated as the International Day of Non-Violence by the United Nations. Born on 2nd October 1869, Mohandas Karamchand Gandhi was India's tallest leader of the independence movement.

Hence, the correct option is (A).

**29.** Rashtrakutas empire lasted the longest.

The Rashtrakutas (755 - 975 AD) were of Kannada origin and Kannada language was their mother tongue.

Hence, the correct option is (C).

**30.** Hemantasena was the founder of the dynasty.

This was originally a tributary of the Pala dynasty. In the mid-11th century he declared his independence and set himself up as king.

Hence, the correct option is (B).

**Q.1** Which of the following UN agencies promotes International Labour Rights?

*[RRB (NTPC), 2021]*

**A.** IMO **B.** ICAO **C.** ILO **D.** IMF

**Q.2** _______ in Hyderabad is responsible for remote sensing satellite data acquisition and processing, data dissemination, aerial remote sensing and decision support for disaster management.

*[RRB (NTPC), 2021]*

**A.** National Remote Sensing Centre (NRSC)
**B.** National Informatics Centre (NIC)
**C.** Indian Space Research Organization (ISRO)
**D.** Indian Institutes of Science Education and Research (IISER)

**Q.3** Where is the headquarter of Sahitya Akedmi?
**A.** Bengaluru **B.** Uttar Pradesh
**C.** Punjab **D.** New Delhi

**Q.4** North Atlantic Treaty Organization (NATO) was established in:
**A.** 1949 **B.** 1948 **C.** 1947 **D.** 1946

**Q.5** In which of the following cities is the 'Central Arid Zone Research Institute (ICAR)' of Rajasthan located?

*[Rajasthan Police Constable, 2020]*

**A.** Bikaner **B.** Jaisalmer
**C.** Jodhpur **D.** Jaipur

**Q.6** Where are the headquarters of the OECD is located?

*[RRB (NTPC), 2020]*

**A.** Rome **B.** Paris
**C.** New York **D.** Geneva

**Q.7** Which is correctly matched?
*[Rajasthan Teachers Eligibility Test - Level 1 Primary Level (RTET), 2017]*

**A.** Bombay Natural History Society – New Delhi
**B.** Botanical Survey of India - Kolkata
**C.** Wildlife Institute of India - Coimbatore
**D.** National Botanical Research Institute - Jodhpur

**Q.8** Who established the Atomic Energy Commission (AEC) of India in 1948?
**A.** P.K. Iyengar **B.** M.R. Srinivasan
**C.** Vikram Sarabhai **D.** Homi Bhabha

**Q.9** In which city is Indian Railway-Rail Coach Factory (RCF) located?
**A.** Bengaluru **B.** Kapurthala
**C.** Chennai **D.** Chittaranjan

**Q.10** Where is the headquarter of Kumaon Regiment located in Uttarakhand?
**A.** Ranikhet **B.** Rishikesh

**C.** Pithoragarh **D.** None of the above

**Q.11** The organization which publishes the 'Red Data Book' of species is:
*[Rajasthan Teachers Eligibility Test - Level 1 Primary Level (RTET), 2021]*

**A.** ICFRE **B.** WWF **C.** IUCN **D.** UNEP

**Q.12** The headquarter of National Bank of Agriculture and Rural Development (NABARD) is situated at:
**A.** Delhi **B.** Kolkata
**C.** Mumbai **D.** Bengaluru

**Q.13** The Headquarter of Asian Infrastructure Investment Bank is located at:
**A.** Beijing **B.** Kuala Lumpur
**C.** Singapore **D.** Manila

**Q.14** Where is the headquarter of the World Bank located?
**A.** San Francisco **B.** Boston
**C.** Philadelphia **D.** Washington, D.C

**Q.15** Where is the headquarters of Securities and Exchange Board of India (SEBI)?
**A.** Mumbai **B.** Lucknow
**C.** Vadodara **D.** Hyderabad

**Q.16** Where is the headquarters of Small Industries Development Bank of India(SIDBI)?
**A.** Lucknow **B.** New Delhi
**C.** Mumbai **D.** Kolkata

**Q.17** Where is the headquarters of National Housing Bank (NHB)?
**A.** Kolkata **B.** Bengaluru
**C.** Mumbai **D.** New Delhi

**Q.18** How many organisations are a part of the United Nations in India ?
**A.** 28 **B.** 22 **C.** 12 **D.** 26

**Q.19** The World Food Programme is headquartered in:
**A.** Washington DC **B.** Nairobi
**C.** Rome **D.** New Delhi

**Q.20** Who is the Head of the World Health Organisation (WHO) and where is its headquarters located?
**A.** Tedros Adhanom, The Hague
**B.** Pascal Lamy, Geneva
**C.** Pascal Lamy, The Hague
**D.** Tedros Adhanon, Geneva

**Q.21** What is the full form of SAARC -
**A.** The South Atlantic Association for Regional Corporation
**B.** The South Asian Association for Regional Cooperation
**C.** The South African Association for Regional Corporation
**D.** The Southern Asia Association for Regional Cooperation

**Q.22** Where is the Amnesty International headquarter situated?

**A.** London, United Kingdom

**B.** Australia

**C.** Switzerland

**D.** None of the above

**Q.23** 'BIMSTEC' is a sub-regional group comprising of seven countries of South Asia and South East Asia headquartered at:

**A.** Kathmandu      **B.** New Delhi

**C.** Colombo      **D.** Dhaka

**Q.24** What does UNHCR stand for?

*[RRB (NTPC), 2017]*

**A.** United Nations Human Capital Research

**B.** United Nations Humanity Committee for Rufugees

**C.** United Nations High Commissioner for Refugees

**D.** United Nations Humanity Commission for Refugees

**Q.25** The headquarters of International Monetary Fund (IMF) is located at _____.

*[Delhi Forest Guard, 2021]*

**A.** Geneva      **B.** London

**C.** Paris      **D.** Washington D. C.

**Q.26** The headquarters of the World Trade Organization is located at:

*[SSC Sub Inspector (CPO), 2020]*

**A.** Bonn    **B.** Geneva    **C.** Dubai    **D.** Paris

**Q.27** How many countries are members of 'SAARC'?

**A.** 6      **B.** 3      **C.** 8      **D.** 5

**Q.28** Which of the following countries is NOT a member of BIMSTEC?

**A.** Maldives      **B.** India

**C.** Bhutan      **D.** Nepal

**Q.29** Who among the following is a current non-permanent member of UN Security Council?

**A.** Pakistan      **B.** Australia

**C.** India      **D.** All of these

**Q.30** Where is the headquarters of NATO?

**A.** Saudi Arab      **B.** China

**C.** Kathmandu      **D.** Belgium

# // Smart Answer Sheet //

**Correct** — Indicates percentage of students who answered questions correctly.

**Skipped** — Indicates percentage of students who skipped questions.

| Q. | Ans. | Correct / Skipped |
|---|---|---|
| 1 | C | 85.82 % / 11.84 % |
| 2 | A | 76.89 % / 17.35 % |
| 3 | D | 84.98 % / 11.98 % |
| 4 | A | 80.73 % / 10.04 % |
| 5 | C | 76.71 % / 17.14 % |
| 6 | B | 84.29 % / 11.93 % |
| 7 | B | 80.66 % / 17.13 % |
| 8 | D | 84.58 % / 12.39 % |
| 9 | B | 86.13 % / 12.89 % |
| 10 | A | 76.07 % / 22.59 % |
| 11 | C | 79.48 % / 15.64 % |
| 12 | C | 77.76 % / 15.48 % |
| 13 | A | 85.55 % / 11.52 % |
| 14 | D | 88.1 % / 10.41 % |
| 15 | A | 79.38 % / 13.44 % |
| 16 | A | 84.84 % / 14.71 % |
| 17 | D | 81.36 % / 14.53 % |
| 18 | D | 83.35 % / 12.6 % |
| 19 | C | 85.13 % / 11.7 % |
| 20 | D | 88.08 % / 11.52 % |
| 21 | B | 87.17 % / 12.43 % |
| 22 | A | 79.59 % / 15.24 % |
| 23 | D | 88.84 % / 11.12 % |
| 24 | C | 79.55 % / 10.14 % |
| 25 | D | 79.41 % / 14.21 % |
| 26 | B | 76.05 % / 13.05 % |
| 27 | C | 87.39 % / 12.48 % |
| 28 | A | 86.2 % / 12.9 % |
| 29 | C | 87.79 % / 11.39 % |
| 30 | D | 79.31 % / 13.21 % |

## Performance Analysis

| | |
|---|---|
| Avg. Score (%) | 53.33% |
| Toppers Score (%) | 70.0% |
| Your Score | |

# //Hints and Solutions//

**1.** ILO promotes International Labour Rights.

The International Labor Organization (ILO) is devoted to promoting social justice and internationally recognized human and labour rights, pursuing its founding mission that labour peace is essential to prosperity.

Hence, the correct option is (C).

**2.** In Hyderabad, the National Remote Sensing Center is responsible for remote sensing satellite data acquisition and processing. It is also responsible for data dissemination, aerial remote sensing, and decision support for disaster management.

- National Remote Sensing Centre (NRSC) at Hyderabad has been converted into a full-fledged centre of ISRO since September 1, 2008.

- Earlier, NRSC was an autonomous body called the National Remote Sensing Agency (NRSA) under the Department of Space (DOS).

- NRSC has a data reception station at Shadnagar near Hyderabad for acquiring data from Indian remote sensing satellites as well as others.

- NRSC Ground station at Shadnagar acquires Earth Observation data from Indian remote-sensing satellites as well as from different foreign satellites.

- NRSC is also engaged in executing remote sensing application projects in collaboration with the users.

Hence, the correct option is (A).

**3.** The Sahitya Akademi, India's National Academy of Letters, is an organization dedicated to the promotion of literature in the languages of India. Founded on 12 March 1954, it is supported by, though independent of, the Indian government. It is in Rabindra Bhavan near Mandi House in Delhi.

Hence, the correct option is (D).

**4.** The North Atlantic Treaty Organization was established in 1949 by the United States, Canada, and several Western European nations to provide collective security against the Soviet Union. NATO was the first peacetime military alliance the United States entered into outside of the Western Hemisphere.

Hence, the correct option is (A).

**5.** The 'Central Arid Zone Research Institute (ICAR)' of Rajasthan is located in Jodhpur.

- It was established by the Government of India in 1959. Its current director is Dr. O.P. Yadav.

- This institute does arid zone research and development. It comes under the Indian Council of Agricultural Research.

- ICAR comes under the aegis of the Ministry of Agriculture and Farmers Welfare.

Hence, the correct option is (C).

**6.** The headquarters of the OECD is located in Paris.

- OECD is the acronym of Organisation for Economic Co-operation and Development.

- OECD is an international organisation that works to build better policies for better lives.

- OECD is an intergovernmental economic organisation with 38 member countries.

- It was founded in 1961 to stimulate economic progress and world trade.

- The headquarters of the OECD is located in Paris in France.

- India is not a member of OECD but a key economic partner.

- Colombia in 2020 and Costa Rica in 2021 were the most recent countries to join the OECD.

Hence, the correct option is (B).

**7.** Botanical Survey of India: Botanical Survey of India (BSI) located in Kolkata, West Bengal, India.

- It was founded on 13 February 1890, by the Government of India Ministry of Environment, Forest and Climate Change.

- It is an organization for the survey, research and conservation of plant wealth of India, flora and endangered species of India.

- It also includes collecting and maintaining germplasm and gene bank of endangered, patent and vulnerable plant species.

Hence, the correct option is (B).

**8.** Homi Bhabha established the Atomic Energy Commission (AEC) of India in 1948.

The Indian Atomic Energy Commission (AEC) was formed in the Department of Atomic Energy in accordance with a Government Resolution dated 1st March 1958.

Homi Bhabha was the First Chairman of the Atomic Energy Commission of India. He was known as the Father of Nuclear Physics in India. Homi Bhabha was awarded the Padma Bhushan (1954), and Adams Prize (1942).

Hence, the correct option is (D).

**9.** Indian Railway-Rail Coach Factory (RCF) is located in Kapurthala.

Kapurthala Rail Coach Factory is a coach manufacturing unit for the Indian Railways, located in the state of Punjab. It is located on the Jalandhar-Firozpur railway line.

Established in 1986, RCF has manufactured more than 30,000 passenger coaches of various types, including self-propelled passenger vehicles, making up more than 50% of the total Indian Railway coach population.

Hence, the correct option is (B).

**10.** The headquarters of Kumaon Regiment is located in Ranikhet, Uttarakhand.

- Ranikhet (Kumaoni: Rānikhèt) is a hill station and cantonment town in Almora district in the Indian state of Uttarakhand. It is the home for the Military Hospital, Kumaon Regiment (KRC) and Naga Regiment and is maintained by the Indian Army.

- The Kumaon Regiment is stationed in the world's highest battlefield, Siachen Glacier. The Kumaon Regiment has received several awards including 2 Param Vir Chakra, 4 Ashoka Chakra, 10 Mahavir Chakra, 6 Kirti Chakra. They are the most dangerous regiment of the Indian Army.

Hence, the correct option is (A).

**11.** The organization which publishes the 'Red Data Book' of species is IUCN.

It also deals with fungi as well as some local subspecies that exist within the territory of the state or country. This book provides central information for studies and monitoring programs on rare and endangered species and their habits. The International Union for Conservation of Nature (IUCN) Red List was founded in 1964.

Hence, the correct option is (C).

**12.** The headquarters of National Bank of Agriculture and Rural Development (NABARD) is situated at Mumbai. Dr. G.R. Chintala is the Chairman of NABARD. NABARD was established on the recommendations of B.Sivaramman Committee on 12 July 1982 to implement the National Bank for Agriculture and Rural Development Act 1981.

Hence, the correct option is (C).

**13.** The Asian Infrastructure Investment Bank (AIIB) is a multilateral development bank and the aim of AIIB is to improve economic and social outcomes in Asia. The Headquarters of Asian Infrastructure Investment Bank is located at Beijing. The bank has 104 members including 17 prospective members from around the world.

Hence, the correct option is (A).

**14.** The headquarters of the World Bank is in Washington D.C, USA. It has a total membership of 189 countries. The World Bank is an international financial institution that provides loans and grants to the governments of low- and middle-income countries for the purpose of pursuing capital projects. David Malpass is the 13th President of the World Bank. The World Bank was established in the year 1944.

Hence, the correct option is (D).

**15.** The Securities and Exchange Board of India (SEBI) is the regulatory body for securities and commodity market in India under the ownership of Ministry of Finance, Government of India. It was established on 12 April 1988 and given Statutory Powers on 30 January 1992 through the SEBI Act, 1992. Its Headquarter is in Mumbai, Maharashtra. Mr. Ajay Tyagi is the Chairman of SEBI.

Hence, the correct option is (A).

**16.** Small Industries Development Bank of India (SIDBI) is the apex regulatory body for overall licensing and regulation of micro, small and medium enterprise finance companies in India. It is under the jurisdiction of Ministry of Finance , Government of India headquartered at Lucknow. Mr. Sivasubramanian Ramann is the Chairman and Managing Director of Small Industries Development Bank of India (SIDBI).

Hence, the correct option is (A).

**17.** National Housing Bank (NHB), is the apex regulatory body for overall regulation and licensing of housing finance companies in India. It is under the jurisdiction of Ministry of Finance, Government of India. Its headquarter is in New Delhi, India. Mr. Sarada Kumar Hota is managing director of National Housing Bank.

Hence, the correct option is (D).

**18.** The United Nations and the Government of India have a long history of close cooperation, and the United Nations system in India now includes 26 organisations having the honour of serving in the country.

- The United Nations is an intergovernmental organisation whose mission is to keep the world safe and secure.

- The United Nations Organization was formed on 24th October 1945, after World War II.

Hence, the correct option is (D).

**19.** The World Food Programme is the world's largest humanitarian Organisation. It is headquartered in Rome, Italy.

It is addressing the issue of hunger and promoting food security. It is a food assistance branch of the United Nations.

Hence, the correct option is (C).

**20.** The headquarters of World Health Organisation (WHO) is located in Geneva, Switzerland. Tedros Adhanon is the Director-General of the World Health Organization.

- He is the first non-physician and first African in the role of Director-General of the World Health Organization.

- The World Health Organization is a specialized agency of the United Nations responsible for international public health.

- The WHO was established by constitution on 7 April 1948, which is commemorated as World Health Day.

Hence, the correct option is (D).

**21.** South Asian Association for Regional Cooperation (SAARC):

- It was established with the signing of the SAARC Charter in Dhaka on 8 December 1985.

- Afghanistan became the newest member of SAARC at the 13th annual summit in 2007.

- The Headquarters and Secretariat of the Association are in Kathmandu, Nepal.

Hence, the correct option is (B).

**22.** Amnesty International is a non-governmental organization with its headquarters in London, the United Kingdom focused on human rights.

- It was founded by Peter Benenson.

- It was founded in July 1961.

Hence, the correct option is (A).

**23.** 'BIMSTEC' is a sub-regional organisation came into being on June 6, 1997, on account of the Bangkok Declaration. It is headquartered in Dhaka, Bangladesh.

It comprises of seven member countries: Bangladesh, Bhutan, India, Nepal, Sri Lanka, Myanmar and Thailand.

Hence, the correct option is (D).

**24.** The United Nations High Commissioner for Refugees (UNHCR) is a United Nations agency mandated to support and protect refugees, displaced populations, and stateless people and to assist in their voluntary repatriation, local integration, or relocation to a third country.

UNHCR was set up in 1950 to resolve the refugee crisis that occurred as a result of World War II.

Hence, the correct option is (C).

**25.** International Monetary Fund headquarters is located at Washington D. C in the United States. It was founded in 1944.

International Monetary Fund is an Organization of 190 countries. It is working to secure financial stability, facilitate international trade, promote high employment and economic growth and reduce poverty around the world.

Hence, the correct option is (D).

**26.** World Trade Organization(WTO) is an intergovernmental organization that is concerned with the regulation of international trade between nations founded in 1995. Its headquarter is in Geneva, Switzerland. It has 164 member countries.

Hence, the correct option is (B).

**27.** SAARC comprises eight member states:

- Afghanistan
- Bangladesh
- Bhutan
- India
- Maldives
- Nepal
- Pakistan
- Sri Lanka

Hence, the correct option is (C).

**28.** Seven countries are members of BIMSTEC:

1. Bangladesh
2. Bhutan
3. India
4. Nepal
5. Sri Lanka
6. Myanmar
7. Thailand

Hence, the correct option is (A).

**29.** India is a current non-permanent member of the UN Security Council.

- The United Nations Security Council is one of the six main organs of the UN, and it is primarily responsible for maintaining international peace and security.
- It consists of 15 members -five permanent members and 10 non-permanent members.
- The five permanent members are the US, UK, Russia, China, and France.
- Every year, five non-permanent members are elected for a tenure of two years.
- To be elected as a non-permanent member of the council, each member-country requires a two-thirds majority of the entire assembly.

Hence, the correct option is (C).

**30.** NATO is headquartered in Brussels, Belgium.

The North Atlantic Treaty Organization (NATO) is headquartered in a complex in Haren, part of the City of Brussels municipality of Belgium. The staff at the headquarters is composed of national delegations of NATO member states and includes civilian and military liaison offices and officers or diplomatic missions and diplomats of partner countries, as well as the International Staff (IS) and International Military Staff (IMS) filled from serving members of the armed forces of member states.

Hence, the correct option is (D).

**Q.1** Which one of the following articles were called the 'heart and soul of the Constitution' by Dr B.R. Ambedkar?
**A.** Article 32
**B.** Article 19
**C.** Article 350
**D.** Article 363

**Q.2** Which of the following constitutional amendments provided for the Right to Education?
**A.** 88th Amendment
**B.** 89th Amendment
**C.** 87th Amendment
**D.** 86th Amendment

**Q.3** Who from among the following appoints the Secretary of Gram Panchayat?
**A.** Panchayat Samiti
**B.** Zila Parishad
**C.** Panchayat President
**D.** State Government

**Q.4** After how many years the Gram Panchayat elections are held in India?
**A.** 4
**B.** 3
**C.** 5
**D.** 6

**Q.5** Which one of the following is the chief source of political power in India?
**A.** Constitution
**B.** Supreme Court
**C.** People
**D.** Parliament

**Q.6** The concept of five-year plans in the Constitution of India is borrowed from ______.

*[SSC Constable (GD), 2019]*

**A.** Russia
**B.** England
**C.** The United States
**D.** Germany

**Q.7** Which among the following is the first state in India to have the Panchayati Raj system?
**A.** Madhya Pradesh
**B.** Rajasthan
**C.** West Bengal
**D.** Uttar Pradesh

**Q.8** Which of the following Amendments to the Constitution of India grants Constitutional status to the 'Panchayati Raj System'?
**A.** 71$^{st}$ Amendment
**B.** 72$^{nd}$ Amendment
**C.** 73$^{rd}$ Amendment
**D.** 75$^{th}$ Amendment

**Q.9** Which of the following Articles includes a provision for Election commission?
**A.** Article 324
**B.** Article 143
**C.** Article 243
**D.** Article 233

**Q.10** In which year, Bihar Panchayati Raj Act was passed?
**A.** 2006
**B.** 2003
**C.** 1997
**D.** 2011

**Q.11** By whom is the joint meeting of Lok Sabha and State Council convened?
**A.** President
**B.** Speaker of Lok Sabha
**C.** Parliament
**D.** Chairman of Rajya Sabha

**Q.12** Which of the following is appointed by the Governor of a state?
**A.** Finance Commission
**B.** UPSC
**C.** State Election Commission
**D.** Inter State Council

**Q.13** According to the Indian Constitution, which of the following has been given Residuary Powers?

*[UPTET Social Studies, 2019]*

**A.** Centre
**B.** States and Centre
**C.** Local Bodies
**D.** States

**Q.14** In which year was the first amendment to the Constitution of India made?
**A.** 1951
**B.** 1952
**C.** 1950
**D.** 1953

**Q.15** Which one of the following Schedules of the Constitution of India contains provisions regarding anti-defection?
**A.** Second Schedule
**B.** Fifth Schedule
**C.** Eighth Schedule
**D.** Tenth Schedule

**Q.16** The Indian National Congress made demand for the first time for a Constituent Assembly in ________.
**A.** 1934
**B.** 1938
**C.** 1946
**D.** 1949

**Q.17** What are middle-level Panchayats generally known as?
**A.** Gram Sabha
**B.** Panchayat Samiti
**C.** Gram Panchayat
**D.** Zila Parishad

**Q.18** A proclamation of emergency issued under Article 352 must be approved by the Parliament within _________.
**A.** 1 month
**B.** 6 weeks
**C.** 2 month
**D.** 3 month

**Q.19** The Annual Financial Statement is caused to be laid before both Houses of Parliament by the ___________.
**A.** President
**B.** Speaker
**C.** Vice-President
**D.** Finance Minister

**Q.20** Where is the word "Federal" used in the constitution of India?
**A.** Preamble
**B.** Part 3
**C.** Article 368
**D.** Nowhere in constitution

**Q.21** By which Constitutional Amendment OBCs have been given 27 percent reservation in the admission to educational institutions?

*[Uttarakhand Public Service Commission (UKPSC), 2014]*

**A.** 92nd
**B.** 93rd
**C.** 94th
**D.** 96th

**Q.22** Which article was referred to as the 'the heart and soul' of the constitution by Dr. B. R. Ambedkar?
**A.** Article 4
**B.** Article 32

**C.** Article 28        **D.** Article 30

**Q.23** Which of the following authority is the principal channel of communication between the President and the council of ministers?

**A.** Vice President
**B.** Speaker of Lok Sabha
**C.** Prime Minister
**D.** None of these

**Q.24** The 'Right to move out of the country and right to come back to the country' is enshrined in which Article of the constitution?

**A.** Article  19      **B.** Article  14
**C.** Article  25      **D.** Article  21

**Q.25** The ideal of Justice - social, economic and political in the Preamble are borrowed from which country?

**A.** USA     **B.** Britain     **C.** Russia     **D.** Canada

**Q.26** Which among the following States does not come under the Sixth Schedule of Indian Constitution?

**A.** Tripura     **B.** Mizoram     **C.** Assam     **D.** Sikkim

**Q.27** How many tiers are in the Panchayati Raj system of India?

**A.** One-tier      **B.** Two-tier
**C.** Three-tier      **D.** Four-tier

**Q.28** Which schedule was added to the constitution by the 73rd Constitutional Amendment?

**A.** 6th     **B.** 7th     **C.** 9th     **D.** 11th

**Q.29** India has been described in the constitution as?

**A.** A Union of State
**B.** Semi-Federal
**C.** Federation of States and Territories
**D.** Partly Unitary and Partly Federal

**Q.30** How many years is the tenure of Gram Panchayats in Madhya Pradesh?

**A.** 4 years     **B.** 5 years     **C.** 6 years     **D.** 3 years

# // Smart Answer Sheet //

**Correct**  Indicates percentage of students who answered questions correctly.

**Skipped**  Indicates percentage of students who skipped questions.

| Q. | Ans. | Correct / Skipped |
|---|---|---|
| 1 | A | 81.68 % / 11.78 % |
| 2 | D | 86.09 % / 12.29 % |
| 3 | D | 88.35 % / 10.32 % |
| 4 | C | 89.98 % / 10.01 % |
| 5 | C | 83.9 % / 15.02 % |
| 6 | A | 76.59 % / 18.81 % |

| Q. | Ans. | Correct / Skipped |
|---|---|---|
| 7 | B | 81.82 % / 12.53 % |
| 8 | C | 80.73 % / 15.73 % |
| 9 | A | 80.92 % / 16.24 % |
| 10 | A | 85.67 % / 12.2 % |
| 11 | A | 81.21 % / 18.25 % |
| 12 | C | 83.63 % / 13.85 % |

| Q. | Ans. | Correct / Skipped |
|---|---|---|
| 13 | A | 81.69 % / 12.68 % |
| 14 | A | 88.61 % / 10.96 % |
| 15 | D | 89.55 % / 10.05 % |
| 16 | A | 76.18 % / 17.8 % |
| 17 | B | 79.54 % / 18.08 % |
| 18 | A | 88.55 % / 10.2 % |

| Q. | Ans. | Correct / Skipped |
|---|---|---|
| 19 | A | 87.8 % / 10.7 % |
| 20 | D | 85.44 % / 13.96 % |
| 21 | B | 77.92 % / 19.25 % |
| 22 | B | 80.01 % / 18.28 % |
| 23 | C | 86.89 % / 11.59 % |
| 24 | D | 86.13 % / 13.76 % |

| Q. | Ans. | Correct / Skipped |
|---|---|---|
| 25 | C | 79.28 % / 11.17 % |
| 26 | D | 88.06 % / 10.93 % |
| 27 | C | 79.02 % / 15.05 % |
| 28 | D | 88.64 % / 10.84 % |
| 29 | A | 81.39 % / 15.72 % |
| 30 | B | 81.94 % / 13.08 % |

| Performance Analysis | |
|---|---|
| Avg. Score (%) | 43.33% |
| Toppers Score (%) | 60.0% |
| Your Score | |

# //Hints and Solutions//

**1.** Dr. B. R. Ambedkar called Article $32$ of the Indian Constitution i.e. Right to Constitutional remedies as ' the heart and soul of the Constitution'.

It was made so because the mere declaration of the fundamental right without a piece of effective machinery for enforcement of the fundamental rights would have been meaningless.

Also, a right that does not have a remedy is a worthless declaration.

Thus, the framers of our constitution adopted the special provisions in article $32$ which provided remedies to the violated fundamental rights of citizens.

Hence, the correct option is (A).

**2.** The $86$th amendment to the Constitution of India in $2002$, provided the Right to Education as a Fundamental Right in Part-III of the Constitution.

The amendment inserted Article $21$A which made the Right to Education a fundamental right for children between $6 - 14$ years.

The $86$th amendment provided for follow-up legislation for the Right to Education Bill $2008$ and finally the Right to Education Act, $2009$.

Hence, the correct option is (D).

**3.** The Gram Panchayat has a Secretary who is also the Secretary of the Gram Sabha. This person is not an elected person but is appointed by the government. The Secretary is responsible for calling the meeting of the Gram Sabha and Gram Panchayat and keeping a record of the proceedings. The Secretary of Gram Panchayat is nominated by State Government.

Hence, the correct option is (D).

**4.** A Gram panchyat's term of office is five years. Every five years elections take place in the village. All people over the age of $18$ who are residents of the territory of that village's Gram panchayat can vote.

Hence, the correct option is (C).

**5.** Democracy is defined as the government of the people, by the people and for the people. The People are the chief source of political power in India.

The preamble makes it very clear when it says that "We, the people of India, having solemnly resolved to constitute India into a SOVEREIGN SOCIALIST SECULAR DEMOCRATIC REPUBLIC and to secure to all its citizens." The enacting words "We, the people of India in our constituent assembly do hereby adopt, enact and give to ourselves this constitution", signifies the democratic principle that power ultimately rests in the hands of the people. It also emphasizes that the constitution is made by and for the Indian people and is not given to them by any outside power (such as the British Parliament.

Hence, the correct option is (C).

**6.** The concept of five-year plans in the Constitution of India is borrowed from Russia.

The constitution of India has borrowed most of its provisions from the constitution of different countries in the world. According to Dr. B R Ambedkar, the constitution of India has been framed after ransacking all the known constitutions of the world.

The important provisions borrowed from Russia are:

- Five-year plan.
- Fundamental duties.

Hence, the correct option is (A).

**7.** The Panchayati Raj System is described in Part IX of the Indian Constitution. Rajasthan is the first state where this system was first implemented in $1959$ in the Nagaur district. Later, it also became the first state to have this system placed in all the districts of the state. The $73^{rd}$ Amendment $1992$ is associated with this system in India.

Hence, the correct option is (B).

**8.** The Parliament passed the $73^{rd}$ Constitutional Amendment Act to grant the Panchayati Raj Institutions in India a legislative status by adding Article $243$ and Part IX of the Indian Constitution. Pursuant to Article $243$, the Act was imposed on all state governments to amend their Panchayat Laws in compliance with the Constitutional Provisions.

Hence, the correct option is (C).

**9.** Article $324$ includes provision for Election commission.

- Articles $324(1)$ states that "The superintendence, direction, and control of the preparation of the electoral rolls for, and the conduct of, all elections to Parliament and to the Legislature of every State and of elections to the offices of President and Vice-President held under this Constitution shall be vested in a Commission".
- Article $324(2)$ states that "The Election Commission shall consist of the Chief Election Commissioner and a number of other Election Commissioners".

Hence, the correct option is (A).

**10.** In $2006$ Bihar Panchayati Raj Act was passed. In pursuance of the provisions made in the $73$rd Constitution (Amendment) Act, $1992$, the Bihar Panchayat Raj Act, $2006$ has been enacted, which provides for the establishment of Gram Panchayat at village level, Panchayat Samiti at Block level and Zila Parishad at the district level.

Hence, the correct option is (A).

**11.** The joint sitting of the House of People and the Council of States is summoned by The President. The Speaker presides over a joint sitting. The quorum to constitute a joint sitting is $\frac{1}{10}^{th}$ of the total number of members of the House.

Article $108$ of the Indian Constitution deals with the Joint sitting of both Houses in certain cases.

- If after a Bill has been passed by one House and transmitted to the other House.

- The Bill is rejected by the other House.

- The Houses have finally disagreed as to the amendments to be made in the Bill.

- More than six months elapse from the date of the reception of the Bill by the other House without the Bill being passed by it.

Hence, the correct option is (A).

**12.** State Election Commission is appointed by the Governor of a state.

The State Election Commission has been tasked with holding free, equal, and impartial elections for local government bodies in the state.

Article $324$ of the Constitution provides that the power of superintendence, direction, and control of elections to parliament, state legislatures, the office of the president of India, and the office of vice-president of India shall be vested in the election commission.

Hence, the correct option is (C).

**13.** According to Article $248$ in the constitution of India the residuary powers of legislation, in respect to any matter not mentioned in the concurrent list or state list, parliament has exclusive authority to make any law.

The supreme law-making body of India, headed by the President of India holds the residuary powers. It means that the parliament is powered to legislate on the matters that are excluded in the list of state and union and also the concurrent ones.

Hence, the correct option is (A).

**14.** The first amendment to the Constitution of India was made in $1951$.

It was amended for the welfare of scheduled castes, tribes and backward classes.

It provided a $10$ per cent quota for economically weaker sections in educational/academic institutions.

It amended Articles $15, 19, 85, 87, 174, 176, 341, 342, 372$ and $376$. It also inserted Ninth Schedule to the Indian Constitution. Articles $31\,A$ and $31\,B$ were also inserted.

Hence, the correct option is (A).

**15.** The Tenth Schedule was inserted into the Constitution in $1985$ by the $52^{nd}$ Amendment Act.

It deals with the Anti defection law i.e, provisions as to disqualification on the ground of defection.

Decision on questions as to disqualification on the ground of defection:

- If any question arises as to whether a member of a House has become subject to disqualification under this Schedule, the question shall be referred for the decision of the Chairman or, as the case may be, the Speaker of such House and his decision shall be final.

- Provided that where the question which has arisen is as to whether the Chairman or the Speaker of a House has become subject to such disqualification, the question shall be referred for the decision of such member of the House as the House may elect on this behalf and his decision shall be final.

Hence, the correct option is (D).

**16.** In $1934$, for the first time, the Indian National Congress made demanded a Constituent Assembly. The Constituent Assembly of India was elected to frame the Constitution of India. It was elected by the 'Provincial Assembly'. Following India's independence from the British Government in $1950$, its members served as the nation's first Parliament.

An idea for a Constituent Assembly was proposed in $1934$ by M. N. Roy, a pioneer of the Communist movement in India and an advocate of radical democracy.

Hence, the correct option is (A).

**17.** Panchayat Samiti (also called Taluka Panchayats or Block Panchayats.) is the intermediate level in Panchayati Raj Institutions. The Panchayat Samiti acts as the link between Gram Panchayat (Village) and District Panchayat (Zilla). These blocks do not hold elections for the Panchayat Samiti council seats.

Hence, the correct option is (B).

**18.** The emergency is imposed by the President on request by the Prime Minister's cabinet of ministers. Article 352 of the Indian Constitution states that an emergency can be called in the event of imminent danger to the national security due to armed rebellion, war, or external aggression. Every proclamation is required to be laid before each House of Parliament, it will cease to operate after one month from the date of its issue unless in the meantime it is approved by the parliament, the proclamation may continue for a period of 6 months unless revoked by the president.

Hence, the correct option is (A).

**19.** The Annual Financial Statement is caused to be laid before both Houses of Parliament by the President. Article 112 of the Indian Constitution says that every year "the President of India shall cause to be laid before both the houses of the parliament" the "Annual Financial Statement". This is popularly known as Budget. The Budget gives the complete picture of the estimated receipts and expenditures of the Government of India for that year. This picture is actually based on the budget figures of the previous years.

Hence, the correct option is (A).

**20.** Though India has a federal system of governance, the word 'Federal' is nowhere mentioned in the constitution. Instead, Article-1 defines India as a "Union of states".

Hence, the correct option is (D).

**21.** 93rd Constitutional Amendment, 2005, provides for reservation related to admission in educational institutions of socially and educationally weaker people (OBCs).

**Extension of 27% reservation:**

The 93rd Constitutional Amendment allows the government to make special provisions for the "advancement of any socially and educationally backward classes of citizens", including their admission in aided or unaided private educational institutions.

Hence, the correct option is (B).

**22.** Dr. B R Ambedkar, the chairman of the Drafting committee called the fundamental right to constitutional remedies as the heart and soul of the Indian constitution. According to this right, a person can move the Supreme Court in case of violation of their fundamental rights. The enforcing of fundamental rights since then happened. In the Indian constitution, there are 5 writs according to Article 32 that empower the Supreme court to enforce the Fundamental right of an individual. Without these fundamental rights would be useless.

Hence, the correct option is (B).

**23.** Prime Minister is the principal channel of communication between the President and the council of ministers.

The Prime Minister enjoys the following powers in relation to the President:

- To communicate to the President all decisions of the council of ministers relating to the administration of the affairs of the Union and proposals for legislation.

- To furnish such information relating to the administration of the affairs of the Union and proposals for legislation as the President may call for.

- If the President so requires, to submit for the consideration of the council of ministers any matter on which a decision has been taken by a minister but which has not been considered by the council.

- He advises the president with regard to the appointment of important officials like the attorney general of India, Comptroller and Auditor General of India, chairman and members of the UPSC, election commissioners, chairman, and members of the Finance commission.

Hence, the correct option is (C).

**24.** The freedom of movement has two dimensions, viz, internal (right to move inside the country) and external (right to move out of the country and right to come back to the country). Article $19$ protects only the first dimension. The second dimension is dealt with by Article $21$ (right to life and personal liberty).

Article $21$ declares that no person shall be deprived of his life or personal liberty except according to the procedure established by law. Supreme Court declared many other rights to be the part of 'Right to Life'.

Hence, the correct option is (D).

**25.** The ideal of Justice - social, economic and political in the Preamble are borrowed from Russia. It was enacted after the enactment of the entire Constitution of India.

**Important facts about the Preamble of the Indian Constitution:**

- Socialist, Secular, and Integrity were added to the Preamble of the Indian Constitution by the $42$nd Constitutional Amendment Act of $1976$.

- The Preamble secures all citizens of India liberty of belief, faith and worship.

- It gives us fundamental values and highlights of the Constitution.

Hence, the correct option is (C).

**26.** The Sixth Schedule of the Indian Constitution consists of provisions for the administration of Tribal Area in Assam, Meghalaya, Tripura, and Mizoram. It seeks to safeguard the rights of the tribal population through the formation of Autonomous District Councils (ADC).

Hence, the correct option is (D).

**27.** There are three-tier in the Panchayati Raj system of India. Panchayati Raj system has three levels: Gram Panchayat (village level), Mandal Parishad or Block Samiti or Panchayat Samiti (block level), and Zila Parishad (district level).

Hence, the correct option is (C).

**28.** The Constitution ( $73$rd Amendment) Act, $1992$ has added a new part IX consisting of $16$ Articles and the $11$th Schedule to the Constitution. The $73$rd amendment thus envisages the Gram Sabha as the foundation of Panchayat Raj System.

Hence, the correct option is (D).

**29.** Article $1$ in the Constitution states that India, that is Bharat, shall be a Union of States. The territory of India shall consist. The territories of the states, The Union territories and Any territory that may be acquired. The names of the States and the Unions have been described in the First Schedule.

Hence, the correct option is (A).

**30.** The tenure of Gram Panchayats in Madhya Pradesh is of $5$ years. Panchayat is an institution of self-government constituted under article $243$B, for the rural areas. All the seats in a Panchayat shall be elected directly from territorial constituencies in the Panchayat area. The Panchayat is elected for $5$ years from the date of the first meeting. It can be dissolved earlier in accordance with the procedure prescribed by state law. If Panchayat dissolved before its tenure then the elections must take place within 6 months of its dissolution.

Hence, the correct option is (B).

**Q.1** Which is the first private space company to send astronauts into space?

**A.** Blue Origin      **B.** Tesla

**C.** SpaceX      **D.** Orbital

**Q.2** Which technology company has introduced the health monitoring device 'Halo Band'?

**A.** Microsoft      **B.** Apple

**C.** Google      **D.** Amazon

**Q.3** Bluetooth technology allows:

**A.** Wireless communication between equipments

**B.** Signal transmission on mobile phones only

**C.** Landline to mobile phone communication

**D.** Satellite television communication

**Q.4** Crescograph was invented by:

**A.** S.N. Bose      **B.** P.C. Roy

**C.** J.C. Bose      **D.** P.C. Mahalanobis

**Q.5** India's first COVID-19 vaccine to get approval for children above 12 Years was ________.

**A.** Covaxin      **B.** Sputnik

**C.** ZyCoV-D      **D.** Covishield

**Q.6** In December 2021, SpaceX has launched 52 Starlink internet satellites into orbit from California base. Which rocket has been used to launch these sattellites?

**A.** Voyger Cassini      **B.** Falcon-9

**C.** Falcon-7      **D.** Rover-4

**Q.7** The term Log4Shell related to _________.

**A.** Cybersecurity      **B.** Nanotechnology

**C.** Robotics      **D.** Biotechnology

**Q.8** GSLV stands for:

**A.** Global Stationary Launching Vehicle

**B.** Geosynchronous Satellite Launching Vehicle

**C.** Global Satellite Launch Vehicle

**D.** Geosynchronous Satellite Launch Vehicle

**Q.9** Satellite Mission - TRISHNA is for:

**A.** Eco-system stress and water use monitoring

**B.** Pesticide monitoring

**C.** Ecological balance monitoring

**D.** None of the above

**Q.10** Homeopathy was invented by?

**A.** Sushrutha      **B.** Charaka

**C.** Hippocrates      **D.** Samuel Hahnemann

**Q.11** Plasmodium was discovered by:

**A.** Charles Laeveron      **B.** Ronald Ross

**C.** Robert Koch      **D.** Robert Hook

**Q.12** The World Health Organization (WHO) has recommended Baricitinib and Sotrovimab drugs for the treatment of __________.

**A.** Diabetes Mellitus      **B.** H5N1

**C.** HIV/AIDS      **D.** Covid-19

**Q.13** Who among the following discovered the Microwave?

**A.** Percy Spencer      **B.** Henri Becquerel

**C.** Dmitri Mendeleev      **D.** Wilson Greatbatch

**Q.14** In which state, India's first liquid mirror telescope has been commissioned in June 2022?

**A.** Himachal Pradesh      **B.** Tamil Nadu

**C.** Uttarakhand      **D.** Arunachal Pradesh

**Q.15** India's first super computer PARAM 8000 was launched in year _____.

**A.** 1990    **B.** 1991    **C.** 1989    **D.** 1992

**Q.16** Which Indian institution developed an intensive care unit (ICU) grade ventilator under the name of 'Project Praana'?

**A.** Indian Institute of Science (IISc)

**B.** AIIMS

**C.** IIT- Delhi

**D.** IIT- Patna

**Q.17** Which of the following country's doctors have successfully transplanted the world's first genetically-modified pig heart into the human body?

**A.** United Kingdom

**B.** India

**C.** China

**D.** United States of America

**Q.18** Which organization developed Indian robot named "Vyommitra" ?mmitra" ?

**A.** C-DAC, Pune      **B.** ISRO

**C.** TIFR      **D.** DRDO

**Q.19** The Indian Space Research Organisation (ISRO) has launched the Polar Satellite Launch Vehicle __________ carrying three satellites on 14 February  2022.

**A.** PSLV-C52      **B.** PSLV-C51

**C.** PSLV-C49      **D.** PSLV-C45

**Q.20** NASA launched world's largest and most powerful space telescope in December 2021. What is the name of the telescope?

**A.** Spitzer Space Telescope

**B.** James Webb Space Telescope

**C.** Hubble Space Telescope

**D.** Extremely Large Telescope

**Q.21** Which country launched the second satellite, Noor-2, into space in March 2022?

**A.** Israel  **B.** UAE
**C.** Saudi Arabia  **D.** Iran

**Q.22** Which of the following IITs has developed a catalytic technology for the sustainable and economical synthesis of chiral molecules?

**A.** IIT Delhi  **B.** IIT Bombay
**C.** IIT Madras  **D.** IIT Kanpur

**Q.23** In June 2021, which of the following institutes developed a new technique called "SWASTIIK" for disinfecting water by using natural oils?

**A.** Agharkar Research Institute
**B.** Tata Institute of Fundamental Research
**C.** National Chemical Laboratory
**D.** National Institute of Oceanography

**Q.24** Chandrayaan - 2 was launched from which of the following states by ISRO?

**A.** Maharashtra  **B.** Rajasthan
**C.** Kerala  **D.** Andhra Pradesh

**Q.25** Genetic screening is ________.

**A.** the analysis of DNA to check the presence of a particular gene in a person
**B.** analysis of gene in a population
**C.** pedigree analysis
**D.** screening of infertility in parents

**Q.26** Which type of waves used by an artificial satellite for communication purpose?

**A.** Microwaves
**B.** Radiowaves
**C.** A.M.
**D.** Frequency of $10^{16}$ series

**Q.27** Compounds of which of the following metals are used in black and white photography?

**A.** Ag  **B.** Cu  **C.** Au  **D.** Al

**Q.28** Starlink satellites operated by which one of the following private space firms?

**A.** Blue Origin  **B.** SpaceX
**C.** Virgin Galactic  **D.** Boeing

**Q.29** Which among the following is the name of the rover landed by NASA on Mars' surface?

**A.** Perseverance  **B.** Explore
**C.** Outer Space  **D.** Progress

**Q.30** In October 2021, which country launched its first homegrown space rocket?

**A.** Japan  **B.** China
**C.** South Korea  **D.** Russia

# // Smart Answer Sheet //

**Correct**   Indicates percentage of students who answered questions correctly.

**Skipped**   Indicates percentage of students who skipped questions.

| Q. | Ans. | Correct / Skipped | Q. | Ans. | Correct / Skipped | Q. | Ans. | Correct / Skipped | Q. | Ans. | Correct / Skipped | Q. | Ans. | Correct / Skipped |
|---|---|---|---|---|---|---|---|---|---|---|---|---|---|---|
| 1 | C | 42.5 % / 47.17 % | 7 | A | 43.5 % / 32.04 % | 13 | A | 50.71 % / 33.89 % | 19 | A | 47.0 % / 42.39 % | 25 | B | 66.39 % / 31.25 % |
| 2 | D | 63.51 % / 34.08 % | 8 | D | 49.41 % / 46.63 % | 14 | C | 59.21 % / 39.69 % | 20 | B | 41.74 % / 49.12 % | 26 | A | 65.02 % / 33.7 % |
| 3 | A | 63.72 % / 32.96 % | 9 | A | 40.43 % / 48.76 % | 15 | B | 48.69 % / 48.29 % | 21 | D | 59.22 % / 31.25 % | 27 | A | 66.01 % / 31.42 % |
| 4 | C | 59.67 % / 32.52 % | 10 | D | 50.27 % / 33.13 % | 16 | A | 48.92 % / 35.87 % | 22 | A | 46.36 % / 38.81 % | 28 | B | 63.79 % / 31.21 % |
| 5 | C | 66.96 % / 32.4 % | 11 | A | 67.44 % / 30.82 % | 17 | D | 44.94 % / 50.86 % | 23 | C | 12.02 % / 76.69 % | 29 | A | 60.04 % / 32.71 % |
| 6 | B | 67.0 % / 32.51 % | 12 | D | 46.43 % / 47.26 % | 18 | B | 50.48 % / 37.42 % | 24 | D | 66.97 % / 30.68 % | 30 | C | 64.88 % / 32.98 % |

| Performance Analysis | |
|---|---|
| **Avg. Score (%)** | **53.33%** |
| **Toppers Score (%)** | **53.33%** |
| **Your Score** | |

# //Hints and Solutions//

**1.** California-based American aerospace manufacturing and space transportation services firm SpaceX has become the first private company to send astronauts into space.

- The firm is owned by the tech-billionaire Elon Musk.
- The Crew Dragon spacecraft of SpaceX carried two astronauts of NASA Doug Hurley and Bob Behnken to the International Space Station (ISS).

Hence, the correct option is (C).

**2.** E-commerce and technology Major Amazon has launched 'Halo Band. Thus, officially venturing into the health monitoring segment.

The wrist band uses AI software to monitor personal wellness parameters. The device is said to have a three-dimensional scan feature for measuring body fat and voice detection to evaluate the user's emotion.

Hence, the correct option is (D).

**3.** Bluetooth is a wireless technology standard for exchanging data over short distances (using short-wavelength UHF radio waves in the ISM band from 2.4 to 2.485 GHz) from fixed and mobile devices and building personal area networks (PANs).

Hence, the correct option is (A).

**4.** A Crescograph is a device for measuring the growth in plants. It was invented in the early 20th century by Sir Jagadish Chandra Bose.

Hence, the correct option is (C).

**5.** India's first COVID-19 vaccine to get approval for children above 12 Years was ZyCoV-D.

India's drug regulator recently approved Zydus Cadila's three-dose COVID-19 DNA vaccine for emergency use in adults and children aged 12 years and above, bringing in the sixth vaccine authorised for use in the country.

Hence, the correct option is (C).

**6.** A SpaceX rocket carried 52 Starlink internet satellites into orbit from California on 18 December 2021. The two-stage Falcon 9 rocket lifted off from coastal Vandenberg Space Force Base.

The Falcon's first stage returned and landed on a SpaceX drone ship in the ocean. The mission was the 34th launch for Starlink, a constellation of nearly 2,000 satellites in low Earth orbit.

Hence, the correct option is (B).

**7.** The term Log4Shell related to Cybersecurity.

A new vulnerability named Log4Shell is being touted as one of the worst cybersecurity flaws to have been discovered. The vulnerability is based on an open-source logging library used in most applications by enterprises and even government agencies.

Hence, the correct option is (A).

**8.** GSLV stands for Geosynchronous Satellite Launch Vehicle.

Geosynchronous Satellite Launch Vehicle is an expendable launch system operated by the Indian Space Research Organization.

- The first stage comprises a solid booster with a propellant and four liquid strap-on motors.
- The second stage is a liquid engine carrying liquid propellant.
- The third stage is the indigenously built Cryogenic Upper Stage.

Hence, the correct option is (D).

**9.** Satellite Mission - TRISHNA is for Eco-system stress and water use monitoring. It stands for Thermal infraRed Imaging Satellite for High-resolution Natural resource Assessment. ISRO and CNES have completed the feasibility study to realize the earth observation satellite mission with a thermal infrared imager.

Hence, the correct option is (A).

**10.** Homeopathy was invented by Samuel Hahnemann. Homeopathy is a system of alternative medicine that originated in 1796.

Homeopathy achieved its greatest popularity in the 19th century. It was introduced in the United States in 1825 with the first homeopathic school opening in 1835.

Hence, the correct option is (D).

**11.** Plasmodium was discovered by Charles Laeveron.

Plasmodium is a protozoan that causes the disease malaria. There are different plasmodium varieties like P. vivax, P. malaria, and P. falciparum P. falciparum is the most fatal one.

Hence, the correct option is (A).

**12.** The World Health Organization (WHO) has recommended two drugs, Baricitinib and Sotrovimab, for treatment of Covid-19.

Baricitinib is also used to treat rheumatoid arthritis. It is an oral drug. It has now been "strongly recommended" for patients with severe or critical Covid-19 in combination with corticosteroids.

Sotrovimab is an investigational monoclonal antibody for use in treating conditions caused by a coronavirus. The WHO has conditionally recommended its use for treating mild or moderate Covid-19 in patients who are at high risk of hospitalisation.

Hence, the correct option is (D).

**13.** American engineer Percy Spencer credited with inventing the modern microwave oven from radar technology. Electromagnetic waves of wavelength range $10^{-3}$ m to $10^{-2}$ m are called microwaves.

Hence, the correct option is (A).

**14.** India's first liquid mirror telescope has been commissioned atop Devasthal, a hill in Uttarakhand. The telescope, which is the largest in Asia, will help survey the sky and make it possible to observe several galaxies and other astronomical objects.

Hence, the correct option is (C).

**15.** India's first super computer PARAM 8000 was launched in year 1991.

The PARAM 8000 was the first machine in the series and was built from scratch. Vijay P. Bhatkar is best known as the architect of India's national initiative in supercomputing where he led the development of Param supercomputers.

Hence, the correct option is (B).

**16.** Indian Institute of Science (IISc) developed an intensive care unit (ICU) grade ventilator under the name of 'Project Praana'.

A team of engineers at the Indian Institute of Science (IISc) had developed an intensive care unit (ICU) grade ventilator under the name of 'Project Praana'. Recently, the team has successfully completed the prototyping of the ventilator, which is now in the process of being commercialised.

Hence, the correct option is (A).

**17.** The United States of America's doctors have successfully transplanted the world's first genetically-modified pig heart into the human body.

A US man has become the first person in the world to get a heart transplant from a genetically-modified pig. David Bennett is doing well three days after the experimental seven-hour procedure in Baltimore.

Hence, the correct option is (D).

**18.** ISRO developed Indian robot named "Vyommitra" .

The word 'Vyommitra' is made up of two words of the Sanskrit language 'Vyom' and 'Mitra' which means space and friend respectively. This is the prototype of the Half-Humanoid female robot developed by ISRO.

Hence, the correct option is (B).

**19.** The Indian Space Research Organisation (ISRO) launched the Polar Satellite Launch Vehicle, PSLV-C52, carrying three satellites on 14 Feb 2022 from the Satish Dhawan Space Centre in Sriharikota. It was carrying EOS-04, a radar imaging satellite.

The other two satellites include one student satellite (INSPIREsat-1) from IIST, and a technology demonstrator satellite (INS-2TD) from ISRO.

Hence, the correct option is (A).

**20.** The world's largest and most powerful space telescope rocketed away on 25 Dec 2021 to behold light from the first stars and galaxies.

NASA's James Webb Space Telescope soared from French Guiana on South America's northeastern coast, on a European Ariane rocket.

Hence, the correct option is (B).

**21.** Iran's paramilitary Revolutionary Guard launched a second satellite into space in March 2022. The Noor-2 satellite reached a low orbit on the Ghased satellite carrier. Ghased is a three-phase, mixed fuel satellite carrier.

Hence, the correct option is (D).

**22.** Researchers at the Indian Institute of Technology (IIT) Delhi have developed a catalytic technology for the sustainable and economical synthesis of chiral molecules. Chiral molecules are

essential building blocks to produce pharmaceuticals, agrochemicals, and biologically active compounds.

Hence, the correct option is (A).

**23.** The CSIR-National Chemical Laboratory (CSIR-NCL) at Pune has developed the novel hybrid technology called SWASTIIK for disinfecting water by using natural oils.

Disinfection of water is essential for removing pathogenic microorganisms that are responsible for causing a number of water-borne diseases. The technology was developed by CSIR-NCL with support from the Water Technology Initiative of the department of science and technology (DST).

Hence, the correct option is (C).

**24.** Chandrayaan-2 was launched from Andhra Pradesh by ISRO.

Chandrayaan-2 was launched from the Satish Dhawan Space Centre in Andhra Pradesh. The mission of Chandrayaan-2 was lunar exploration. The launch vehicle used was GSLV Mark III-M1.

Hence, the correct option is (D).

**25.** Genetic screening is analysis of gene in a population.

It is a process to analyze blood or skin for the systematic search for persons with a particular genotype in a defined population. It also serves as an important tool of modern preventive medicine.

Hence, the correct option is (B).

**26.** In artificial satellites, mostly microwaves are used for communication.

It is an electromagnetic wave with frequency ranges between 300MHz (0.3 GHz) and 300 GHz in the electromagnetic spectrum. It is specially used in spacecraft communication, TV and long-distance telephone lines.

Hence, the correct option is (A).

**27.** Compounds of Ag are used in black and white photography.

The compounds of Silver(Ag), silver bromide and silver chloride are used in black and white photography. These two are photosensitive compounds. They get easily decomposed on exposure to light. So, they are used in black and white photography and films.

Hence, the correct option is (A).

**28.** The Starlink satellite is operated by SpaceX.

Starlink is a satellite Internet conglomerate operated by SpaceX that provides satellite Internet access coverage across much of Earth. It aims to provide low-cost and reliable space-based Internet services to the world.

Hence option (B) is correct.

**29.** Perseverance is the name of the rover landed by NASA on Mars' surface.

NASA's Mars mission aims to conduct research in many fields such as astronomy, including the discovery of signs of ancient microorganisms. This is the first mission in which Martian rock and sediment will be collected and brought to Earth.

Hence, the correct option is (A).

**30.** South Korea launched its first homegrown rocket on 21 October 2021.

The rocket is called Nuri. It was launched from the country's Naro Space Center. Nuri is the country's first space launch vehicle developed and built completely with South Korean technology. The rocket is designed to carry a payload of up to 1.5 tons to an orbit 600 to 800 kilometers above Earth.

Hence, the correct option is (C).

**Q.1** The player who was awarded with Arjuna Award, Dronacharya Award, Rajiv Gandhi Khel Ratna and Padma Shri is:

*[Madhya Pradesh Public Service Commission (MPPSC), 2018]*

**A.** Abhinav Bindra      **B.** Sachin Tendulkar
**C.** Prakash Padukone      **D.** Pullela Gopichand

**Q.2** In which of the following sports, the words 'crawl', 'breaststroke', and 'butterfly' are used?
**A.** Swimming      **B.** Shooting
**C.** Tennis      **D.** Badminton

**Q.3** Smriti Mandhana is a _____.

*[SSC Sub Inspector (CPO), 2020]*

**A.** left arm batsman, left arm bowler
**B.** right arm batsman, left arm bowler
**C.** right arm batsman, right arm bowler
**D.** left arm batsman, right arm bowler

**Q.4** The Vishvamitra honour of Madhya Pradesh given for excellent performance in which Field?
**A.** Excellent performance in sports
**B.** Social work-related activities
**C.** Excellent performance in sports training
**D.** Out-standing award for literature

**Q.5** Benson Hedges Cup is related to which of the following sports?
**A.** Hockey      **B.** Cricket
**C.** Football      **D.** Basket Ball

**Q.6** When was the World Chess Federation founded?
**A.** 1935    **B.** 1924    **C.** 1905    **D.** 1896

**Q.7** What is the motto of Olympic Council of Asia?
**A.** Ever Onward      **B.** Ever Freedom
**C.** Ever Unity      **D.** All Together

**Q.8** When was the Women's Hockey World Cup first held?
**A.** 1974    **B.** 1971    **C.** 1985    **D.** 1990

**Q.9** In which world cup, India won its second "Cricket World Cup Champion" title?
**A.** 2003 Cricket World Cup
**B.** 2007 Cricket World Cup
**C.** 2011 Cricket World Cup
**D.** 2015 Cricket World Cup

**Q.10** Which three cricket world cups are consecutively won by Australia?
**A.** 1992, 1996, 1999      **B.** 1991, 1995, 1998
**C.** 1999, 2003, 2007      **D.** 1998, 2002, 2006

**Q.11** Which countries participated in the final match of the first FIFA Football World Cup held in 1930?
**A.** Yugoslavia Vs United States of America
**B.** Uruguay Vs Argentina
**C.** France Vs Mexico
**D.** Uruguay Vs United States of America

**Q.12** Which of the following are the all-time record holders for the most number of Olympic medals in tennis?
**A.** Kathleen McKane Godfree and Venus Williams
**B.** Kathleen McKane Godfree and Serena Williams
**C.** Venus Williams and Serena Williams
**D.** Gigi Fernandez and Mary Joe Fernandes

**Q.13** Which sport's code of rules is known as the "Marquess of Queensberry Rules"?
**A.** Boxing      **B.** Wrestling
**C.** Fencing      **D.** Basketball

**Q.14** What is Pankration?
**A.** An ancient sport which is a mix of tennis and table tennis
**B.** An ancient sport which is a mix of baseball and basketball
**C.** An ancient sport which is a mix of karatte and taekwondo
**D.** An ancient sport which is a mix of boxing and wrestling

**Q.15** Who is the all-time leader for the most Olympic medals in badminton?
**A.** Lin Dan      **B.** Fu Haifeng
**C.** Gao Ling      **D.** Zhao Yunlei

**Q.16** What is "Augusta National Club" famous for?
**A.** As a golf club
**B.** As a tennis club
**C.** As a badminton club
**D.** As a football club

**Q.17**
Indian GM who posted his second win over world champion Magnus Carlsen?
**A.** Praggnanandhaa      **B.** Gukesh D
**C.** Girish Koushik      **D.** Prithu Gupta

**Q.18** Which Indian Cricketer was appointed as an ambassador for Karnataka Brain Health Initiative?
**A.** Robin Uthappa      **B.** Ravindra Jadeja
**C.** Shikhar Dhawan      **D.** Dinesh Karthik

**Q.19** Which medal has been won by Indian shuttler Mithun Manjunath at the Orleans Masters 2022?
**A.** Silver    **B.** Bronze    **C.** Gold    **D.** All these

**Q.20**
Which player is named ICC Men's Player of the Month for March 2022?
**A.** Babar Azam      **B.** David Warner
**C.** Keegan Petersen      **D.** Shreyas Iyer

**Q.21**

Name the Indian duo who paired to win the gold medal in the mixed double event of the 2022 WSF World Doubles Squash championship?

- **A.** Dipika Pallikal and Mahesh Mangaonkar
- **B.** Joshna Chinappa and Harinder Pal Sandhu
- **C.** Dipika Pallikal and Saurav Ghosal
- **D.** Joshna Chinappa and Ramit Tandon

**Q.22** The venue selected for Common wealth Games to be held in the year 2022 is:

- **A.** Birmingham
- **B.** Gold Coast
- **C.** Incheon
- **D.** Durban

**Q.23** Who among the followings has been appointed as the brand ambasssador of online gaming company Games $24 \times 7$ in January 2022?

- **A.** Rishabh Pant
- **B.** Ranveer Singh
- **C.** Mithali Raj
- **D.** Hrithik Roshan

**Q.24** India won how many medals at the Singapore Weightlifting International in February 2022?

- **A.** 4
- **B.** 6
- **C.** 8
- **D.** 10

**Q.25** Who is the captain of the Indian team which won the ICC U-19 World Cup in 2022?

- **A.** Yash Dhull
- **B.** Raj Bara
- **C.** Nishant Sindhu
- **D.** Shaik Rasheed

**Q.26** Who was the first Indian to become the Junior Wimbledon Champion?

- **A.** Ramanathan Krishnan
- **B.** Premjit Lal
- **C.** Vijay Amritraj
- **D.** Leander Paes

**Q.27** Who founded the International Tennis Hall of Fame, the largest tennis museum in the world?

- **A.** Walter Clopton Wingfield
- **B.** Jimmy Van Alen
- **C.** Arthur Ashe
- **D.** Harry Hopman

**Q.28** Which state has won the 12th Hockey India Sub-Junior Women's National Championship 2022?

- **A.** Kerala
- **B.** Punjab
- **C.** Tamil Nadu
- **D.** Haryana

**Q.29** In May 2022, JAIN (Deemed-to-be University) became the winner of the Khelo India University Games 2021 with _______ gold medals.

- **A.** 12
- **B.** 15
- **C.** 18
- **D.** 20

**Q.30** Who has won a bronze medal in 57 kg category at the IBA Women's World Boxing Championships?

- **A.** Riya Jadon
- **B.** Sift Kaur Samra
- **C.** Jyothi Yarraji
- **D.** Manisha Moun

# // Smart Answer Sheet //

**Correct** — Indicates percentage of students who answered questions correctly.

**Skipped** — Indicates percentage of students who skipped questions.

| Q. | Ans. | Correct / Skipped |
|----|------|-------------------|
| 1 | D | 51.58 % / 38.07 % |
| 2 | A | 41.52 % / 38.29 % |
| 3 | D | 63.04 % / 32.5 % |
| 4 | C | 56.77 % / 30.53 % |
| 5 | B | 55.43 % / 44.44 % |
| 6 | B | 59.97 % / 30.04 % |
| 7 | A | 50.97 % / 33.36 % |
| 8 | A | 46.19 % / 40.9 % |
| 9 | C | 58.78 % / 36.73 % |
| 10 | C | 14.43 % / 76.02 % |
| 11 | B | 30.01 % / 67.63 % |
| 12 | A | 14.22 % / 79.5 % |
| 13 | A | 23.4 % / 75.26 % |
| 14 | D | 17.32 % / 70.29 % |
| 15 | C | 29.91 % / 67.17 % |
| 16 | A | 16.78 % / 75.9 % |
| 17 | A | 27.46 % / 69.51 % |
| 18 | A | 20.69 % / 79.12 % |
| 19 | A | 20.15 % / 71.13 % |
| 20 | A | 21.53 % / 75.7 % |
| 21 | C | 27.69 % / 70.25 % |
| 22 | A | 42.53 % / 40.9 % |
| 23 | D | 44.07 % / 31.65 % |
| 24 | C | 47.98 % / 38.42 % |
| 25 | A | 82.71 % / 14.91 % |
| 26 | A | 22.87 % / 72.46 % |
| 27 | B | 28.59 % / 70.85 % |
| 28 | D | 57.45 % / 36.1 % |
| 29 | D | 41.29 % / 57.52 % |
| 30 | D | 58.68 % / 35.34 % |

| Performance Analysis | |
|----------------------|--------|
| Avg. Score (%) | 46.67% |
| Toppers Score (%) | 53.33% |
| Your Score | |

# //Hints and Solutions//

**1.**

- Pullela Gopichand is a former Indian badminton player.

- Presently, he is the Chief National Coach for the Indian Badminton team.

- He received the Arjuna Award in 1999, Rajiv Gandhi Khel Ratna in 2001, the Dronacharya Award in 2009, Padma Bhushan in 2014 and Padma Shri in 2005.

Hence, the correct option is (D).

**2.** The words crawl, breaststroke, and butterfly are associated with the game of swimming.

In this game, the entire body of the person is moved through the water. In pools or open water, the sports take place. The events butterfly, breaststroke, freestyle, and individual medley are associated with swimming. A set of specific techniques is required by swimming. There are distinct regulations in competition.

Hence, the correct option is (A).

**3.** Smriti Mandhana is a left arm batsman, right arm bowler.

Smriti Mandhana won ICC's woman cricketer of the Year and women's ODI player of the Year in 2018. Smriti Shriniwas Mandhana is an Indian cricketer who plays for the Indian women's national team. In June 2018, the Board of Control for Cricket in India (BCCI) named her as the Best Women's International Cricketer. In December 2018 , the International Cricket Council (ICC) awarded her with the Rachael Heyhoe-Flint Award for the best female cricketer of the year.

Hence, the correct option is (D).

**4.** Vishvamitra honour of Madhya Pradesh has given for excellent performance in sports training.

- Vishwamitra honour was started in the year 1996.

- As of 2018, a total of 72 trainers have been awarded the Vishwamitra Award.

- Kabir Samman award was established by the Government of Madhya Pradesh in 1986.

- It is conferred annually for distinguished works in Literature (Poetry).

Hence, the correct option is (C).

**5.** The Benson & Hedges Cup was a one-day cricket competition for first-class counties in England and Wales that was held from 1972 to 2002, one of cricket's longest sponsorship deals

Hence, the correct option is (B).

**6.** The Federation Internationale des Echecs (FIDE), or World Chess Federation, was formed on Sunday, July 20, 1924.

Hence, the correct option is (B).

**7.** "Ever Onward" is the motto of the Asian Games. The Asian Games, also known as Asiad, is a continental multi-sport event held every four years among athletes from all over Asia.

Hence, the correct option is (A).

**8.** The first edition of the Women's Hockey World Cup was held in 1974, three years after the first men's World Cup. In that year Netherlands Women's Hockey team defeated Argentina women's team in the final and they are the first champion of women's hockey world cup.

Hence, the correct option is (A).

**9.** Mahendra Singh Dhoni was the "Man of the Match in the final" in the 2011 Cricket World Cup, in which India won its second "Cricket World Cup Champion" title.

Hence, the correct option is (C).

**10.** The Australian cricket team is the most successful team in the Cricket World Cup winning the 1987, 1999, 2003, 2007 and 2015 editions. This also makes them the only team to have won the world cup in all the regions (group of countries) that have hosted the world cup till now.

Hence, the correct option is (C).

**11.** In the final, hosts and pre-tournament favourites Uruguay defeated Argentina 4–2 in front of a crowd of 68,346 people to become the first nation to win the World Cup. The final was played at the Estadio Centenario in Montevideo, Uruguay, on 30 July, a Wednesday.

Hence, the correct option is (B).

**12.** Venus Williams (four gold, one silver) and Kathleen McKane Godfree (one gold, two silvers, and two bronzes) are the all-time record holders for the most Olympic tennis medals, with five each. Serena Williams and Venus Williams won a record four gold medals.

Hence, the correct option is (A).

**13.** Marquess of Queensberry rules, code of rules that most directly influenced modern boxing. Written by John Graham Chambers, a member of the British Amateur Athletic Club, the rules were first published in 1867 under the sponsorship of John Sholto Douglas, ninth marquess of Queensberry, from whom they take their name.

Hence, the correct option is (A).

**14.** pankration, ancient Greek sports event that combined boxing and wrestling, introduced at the XXXIII Olympiad (648 bce). As with all sports, the Greeks believed a god or a hero to be responsible for inventing the rules, and in the case of pankration it was believed that, Theseus is responsible.

Hence, the correct option is (D).

**15.** Gao Ling is the all-time leader for the most Olympic medals in badminton, with two gold, one silver, and one bronze. Gao has not earned an Olympic gold medal in women's double but earned a bronze medal in 2000 with Qin Yiyuan, and a silver medal with Huang Sui in 2004. From 2001 through 2006 she and Huang captured a record six consecutive women's doubles titles at the venerable.

Hence, the correct option is (C).

**16.** Augusta National Golf Club sometimes referred to as Augusta or the National, is a golf club in Augusta. Unlike most private clubs which operate as non-profits, Augusta National is a for-profit corporation, and it does not disclose its income, holdings, membership list, or ticket sales

Hence, the correct option is (A).

**17.** Indian GM Praggnanandhaa posted his second win over world champion Magnus Carlsen. Indian GM Praggnanandhaa posted his second win over world champion Magnus Carlsen in 3 months, he stunned the Norwegian at the Chessable Masters online rapid chess tournament.

Hence, the correct option is (A).

**18.** The Karnataka Health Department has appointed Indian Cricket Player Robin Uthappa as the brand ambassador for Karnataka Brain Health Initiative (KA-BHI) (Launched in January 2022). Training of doctors and preparations to start Brain Health Clinics in the three pilot hospitals has also commenced.

Hence, the correct option is (A).

**19.** Indian shuttler Mithun Manjunath has won the silver medal in men's singles at the badminton tournament Orleans Masters 2022. a badminton tournament held from 29th March to 3rd April 2022 in Orleans, France. Playing in his maiden BWF final, the 79th ranked Indian shuttler lost 11-21, 19-21 to world number 32 Frenchman Toma Junior Popov at the Palais des Sports Arena.

Hence, the correct option is (A).

**20.** Pakistan captain Babar Azam has been named as the ICC Men's Player of the Month for March 2022. The ICC Men's Player of the Month Nominees for March 2022 include Australian Skipper Pat Cummins, Pakistan Skipper Babar Azam and West Indies Skipper Kraigg Brathwaite.

Hence, the correct option is (A).

**21.** The second-seeded Indian duo Dipika Pallikal Karthik and Saurav Ghosal won the mixed double title at the 2022 WSF World Doubles Squash championship at Glasglow. The Indian duo thrashed the fourth-seeded pair of Adrian Waller and Alison Waters of England in the mixed doubles finals in straight sets 11-6, 11-8.

Hence, the correct option is (C).

**22.** The commonwealth games for 2022 are scheduled to be held in Birmingham, England.

This is the third time England is hosting the game after 1934 (London) and 2002 (Manchester). The city was announced as the host by the Commonwealth Games Federation.It was decided at a press conference at the Arena Academy in Birmingham on 21 December 2017. The 2018 Commonwealth Games were held in Gold Coast, Queensland, Australia. This was the fifth time Australia hosted the game.

Hence, the correct option is (A).

**23.** Mumbai-headquartered online gaming company Games $24 \times 7$ has roped in Hrithik Roshan as brand ambassador for its online skill gaming platform, Rummy Circle. The association is for one year. The company wants to promote Rummy as a highly engaging game of skill in northern India, where the game is yet to gain popularity. The rummy industry's $60 - 65\%$ of revenues come from southern India.

Hence, the correct option is (D).

**24.** India won 8 medals at the Singapore Weightlifting International in February $2022.$

Indian weightlifters Vikas Thakur and Venkat Rahul Ragala qualified for the Commonwealth Games by winning gold and bronze medals respectively at the Singapore Weightlifting International on 27 February 2022. India thus ended its campaign in the competition with 8 medals, including 6 gold, 1 silver, and 1 bronze.

Hence, the correct option is (C).

**25.** Yash Dhull is the captain of the Indian team which won the ICC U 19 World Cup in $2022.$

Yash Dhull captained India to a ICC U-19 World Cup glory this year, defeating England in the final. The Indian U-19 team led by Yash Dhull won the 2022 ICC U-19 World Cup in Antigua, after beating England by 4 wickets.

Hence, the correct option is (A).

**26.** In 1954, Young Ramanathan Krishnan became the first Junior Wimbledon Champion. He was also the first Asian to do so.

- Winner of the Wimbledon Junior Championship in 1979 and French Open Junior title in 1979. Ranked World number 1 among juniors in 1979.
- Won the Grand Prix Tournament in 1984 at France.
- Received the Arjuna award in 1978-79 and Padma Shri in 1998

Hence, the correct option is (A).

**27.** Jimmy Van Alen founded the International Tennis Hall of Fame, the largest tennis museum in the world. James Van Alen was an American tennis official. In 1954, the late tennis innovator Jimmy Van Alen founded the Hall of Fame in Newport, Rhode Island as a "shrine to the ideals of the game."

Hence, the correct option is (B).

**28.** Haryana emerged winners of the 12th Hockey India sub-junior women's national championship 2022 after defeating Hockey Jharkhand (2-0) in the final in Imphal on 22nd May.

Uttar Pradesh Hockey defeated Madhya Pradesh Hockey (3-0) to secure third place in the tournament.

A total of 25 teams participated in the tournament which was held in Imphal, Manipur from 11 to 22 May 2022.

Hence, the correct option is (D).

**29.** JAIN (Deemed-to-be University) became the winner of the Khelo India University Games 2021 on 3 May 2022. The University team topped the chart with 20 gold, 7 silver and 5 bronze medals.

It was followed by Lovely Professional University (LPU) with 17 golds and Punjab University with 15 gold medals.

A total of 20 games were played and saw participation of 3900 students from 210 Universities.

Hence, the correct option is (D).

**30.** Two Indian boxers Manisha Moun in 57 kg and Parveen Hooda in 63 kg category won bronze medals at the IBA Women's World Boxing Championships.

With this, the Indian contingent concluded its campaign with three medals.

India's overall medal tally in World Women's Boxing Championships has gone up to 39, including 10 gold, eight silver, and 21 bronze in the 12 editions of the prestigious event.

Hence, the correct option is (D).

# // Notes //

# // Notes //